MON   FEB 1 4 2003

Islands of Silence

Islands of Silence

Martin Booth

THOMAS DUNNE BOOKS

ST. MARTIN'S PRESS

NEW YORK

for Brooks

*In human intimacy there is a secret barrier: neither
the experience of being in love, nor that of passion,
can traverse it, even if lips are joined together in
terrible silence and the heart breaks to pieces with love.*

ANNA AKHMATOVA

*This is my letter to the World
That never wrote to Me—*

EMILY DICKINSON

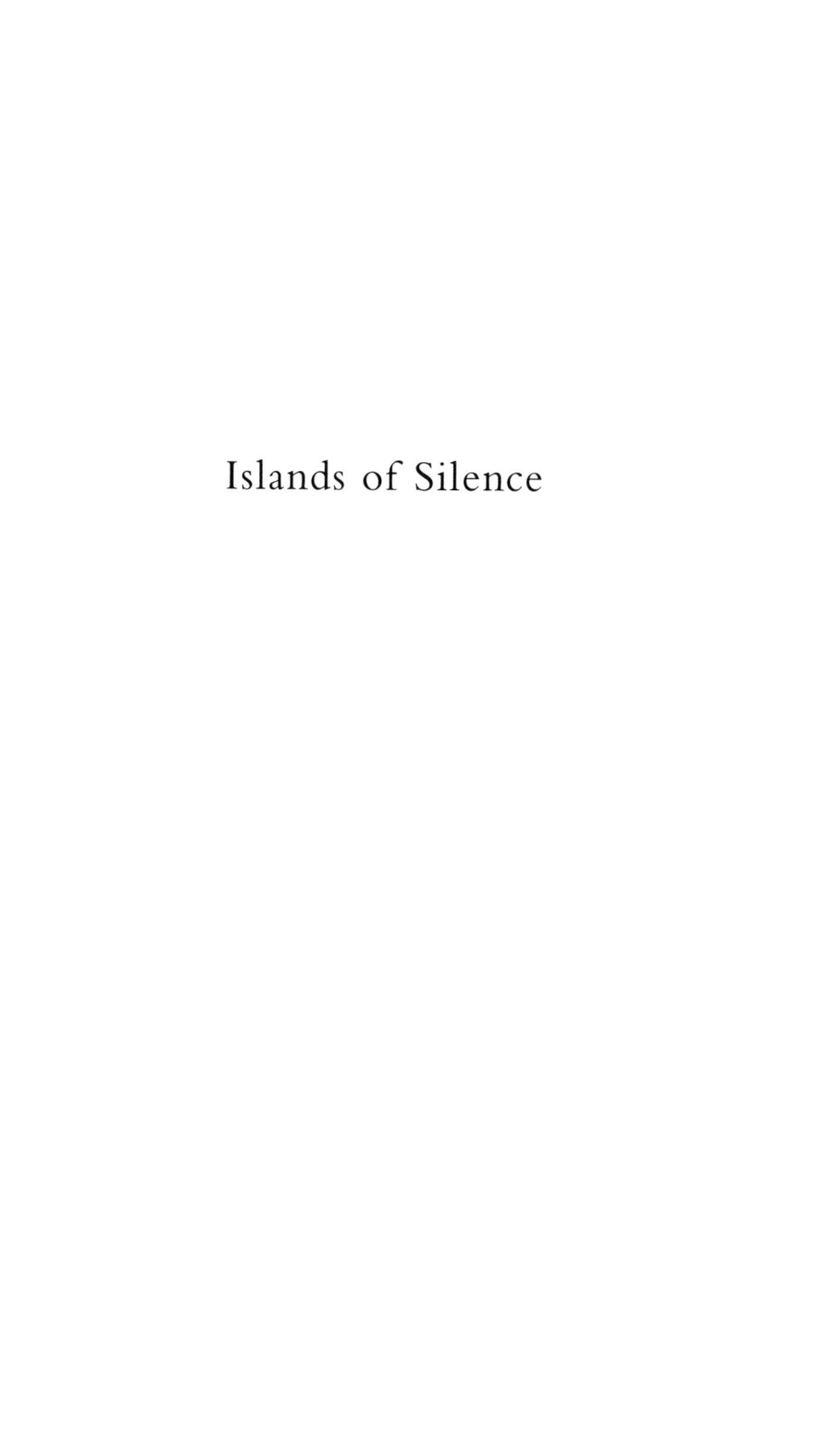

Islands of Silence

1

Over the last few weeks, the young doctor with responsibility for my case has been studiously examining me. He has meticulously collected blood samples and urine specimens, X-rayed and probed me, attached me to several pieces of complex electronic equipment and, from time to time, had one of the orderlies sit with me in the evening, as I fell asleep.

Or so I led them to believe. Once I was breathing gently, the orderly departed and I spent the remainder of my waking hours in my precious solitude.

This morning, armed with a black plastic clipboard, the doctor came to visit me as I sat at my window. Announcing his presence with a gentle knock on the door, he entered slowly. I sensed a certain tentativeness in his step.

'Good morning, Alec,' he said, pulling over the chair from my desk and sitting to my right.

He shuffled briefly through the papers on the clipboard and I could tell this was not so much to retrieve information as to delay his next sentence.

'I have received back the results of some of our tests.'

I, of course, showed no sign of having heard him and have to admit to admiring his perseverance. For months now, since he took on my case, he has spoken to me as if he expected a reply, yet in the full and certain knowledge that the chances of my uttering a single syllable in response were as great as the stars in the hemisphere of the southern sky.

Again, he fumbled with his papers.

'I'm afraid I have some unsettling news.'

Were I not a man of silence, I should have laughed.

'In general terms, you are in remarkably good health for your age. . . . '

The farcicality of it! Here was I, old beyond my luck, being told by a man of the white cloth with a fresh demeanour unsullied by time, and possessing but a microscopic fragment of my experience of the vagaries of existence, that my days were numbered.

'Your chest X rays are clear. No sign of any ominous lingering shadows . . . '

He gave me a quick half-smile of partial encouragement.

My urge to laugh passed away, to be replaced by sympathy for this young man with his cheap watch and his concerned, earnest face. He does not realise, from his twenty-eight or so years, that all our days are counting down. It is just that he has a greater store of them left than I do. Possibly.

He thumbed some more paper, unable to find my birth date. I have long since forgotten it and my now somewhat tattered medical records have seemingly shed some pages over the voyage of my life across the institutional universe.

'Your liver is functioning adequately for the time being, your circulation likewise. There are a few minor conditions, a touch of eczema on your right leg, some synovitis in the joint of your right knee, but these are to be expected in advancing years. The blister you suffered from last month may be the onset of pemphigus, but we have addressed this with corticosteroids.'

This all meant nothing to me, nor was it so intended. He was sparring, a few little taps and touches before the punch to the solar plexus.

'However,' he carried on, 'we have discovered you are suffering from atrial fibrillation. This is the irregular beating of the heart. In rare cases, of which you are one, the symptoms of shortness of breath and palpitations do not exhibit themselves. The cause of this condition is unknown and, in itself, it is not life-threatening. But that said, it can cause complications of which a pulmonary embolism, in layman's terms a blood clot, is a frequent consequence. This can be fatal or bring about permanent disability.'

He was telling me to prepare for death and cannot know that I have overcome any concern whatsoever for that condition, medical, pathological or spiritual.

'There is no treatment except anticoagulant drugs. I shall be prescribing a course of Coumadin.'

For a few moments, he noted down his recommended treatment on a buff-coloured card, scribbled instructions to the pharmacist upon a prescription pad, tore the page off and fastened it to the clipboard. This done, he placed the clipboard on the floor and leaned towards me.

'Is there nothing you want to say, Alec? Nothing you want to tell me?' His voice was as low and cajoling as a priest's to a sinner trapped in the confessional by the limp, black silk curtain and his guilt. 'Whatever you tell me will go no further. It's called doctor-patient privilege. I cannot disclose what you tell me to anyone. I cannot even note it down on your file. The only exception to this rule is if you tell me information of a crime committed. If that were the case, I am legally bound to go to the police, but, even then, I need not reveal the source of that information.'

I had been looking steadfastly out of the window throughout his prognosticatory speech. Now, I slowly turned my head to gaze upon him. He sat up slightly. There was in his face that sudden, expectant hope of the man who thought he was at last getting somewhere. It was the look that must have shone in the eyes of Christ as he conducted his first miracle and waited to see if it worked.

'Yes, Alec?' he encouraged me.

For a moment, I felt guilty that I was leading him on, teasing him.

I had so much to say to him and yet I had nothing. There is no point in repeating a lesson when the class either has not grasped it already or is too moribund to understand the problem.

As for a crime, I could tell him of the greatest crimes on earth, yet he could not go to the authorities with the knowledge. They would not be interested, for they already possess it and are aware that no solution for it exists.

Nor ever will.

2

It was a Saturday in spring, in a century that was still young, in a world that had heard neither cry of pain nor plea for mercy for a long time. The pastures were turning from winter's dull jade into the expectant green of the first weeks after the new equinox. Early calves and new-dropped lambs were staggering in the fields as if intoxicated by a life they did not know would end with the butcher's knife, in a room of cracked glazed tiles where the floor was slick with blood and bile, in the walls of which were fossilised the squeals and screeches of a decade's dead meat.

We were moving fast along a country road in a bright yellow two-seater Model T Ford Roadster. As we passed by blurred hedgerows or field gates, its gaudy coachwork stood out against the background of twigs, bursting buds and freshly ploughed sods. It matched the profusion of primroses growing on the banks, the occasional daffodil nodding in the breeze of its passage. In the temperature gauge mounted into the radiator cap, the needle was far over to the right. A thin line of steam leaked from an ill-fitting seal. The engine had been running at speed for a while. The two headlamps were huge, reminiscent of the eyes of a prehistoric marine creature used to living in the dark night of the ocean and now startled by the brilliance of an English sky washed by an overnight shower, festooned with the soft boulders of fair weather cumuli drifting east on an indolent westerly.

Like the vehicle, we were created for excitement, our skin young and taut, our faces eager to take life on. Every turn of the wheel, every bend in the road over the downland was designed not to avoid a ditch, obey a long-forgotten tort or create a boundary between one farmer's orchard and another's pasture, but to put us to the test. Travelling through this bright morning in the spring of our lives, with the unwholesome aroma of hawthorn flowers tainting the breeze like the odour of a broken corpse hidden in the undergrowth and the woods hazy with the first blossoming of bluebells, we were not merely seeking simple pleasures but looking for ordeals against which we could pit ourselves, yet in the sure and certain knowledge that we would surpass them all.

The streets of Abingdon were almost empty as we drove through them in the fresh first hour of sunlight. Only one person was about in Ock Street as we headed west out of the town. It was a Catholic priest in a black soutane carrying a small mahogany case rather like those in which freemasons carried their regalia to their secretive lodge meetings in their redbrick halls tucked away in the back streets of provincial cities and middle-class suburbs.

'Looks like a bat that hasn't made it back to its roost by sun-up,' Rupert remarked, then added, 'He's been giving extreme unction. Or . . .' he pursed his lips into a lascivious kiss '. . . sucking fresh blood from a virgin's jugular.'

'Rupert! How can you possibly know that?' I replied. I was scandalised then, an innocent in a world that knew nothing of corruption.

'The extreme unction or the vampirism?'

'The extreme unction.'

'Walking about at this hour of the day? It's not Sunday. And that little briefcase. It contains his portable folding cross, stole, a little bottle of blessed cheap claret and a few wafers.' He steered the car around a puddle in the cobbles. 'A little wooden box of celestial clemency, a holy doctor's bag of divine absolution.' The rear wheel splashed muddy water against the wall of a house, but the mudguard protected the pristine paintwork of the Roadster. 'And you can tell by the serene, self-satisfied smirk on his face. He's just saved another poor bugger from Satan, snatching him back to salvation at the last breath.'

I laughed at Rupert's irreverence, secure in the knowledge that I, armed with optimism and shielded by the years to come, was more powerful than any god.

We motored down a wide valley, the road twisting in parallel with a chalk stream along the banks of which were growing a few stands of pollarded willows. Sloping fields rose on either side of us. On the skyline was a lone copse of beech trees, the verdant foliage the light emerald of newly unfolded leaves.

Both of us were dressed in white: white shirts, white trousers, white socks, white pullovers with a blue line edging the collar—white shoes, even. From the trunk behind the seats, the half-open lid of which was held down by two leather straps, protruded the handle of a cricket bat and the top of a set of batsman's pads. Only Rupert broke our conformity of uniform, for he was wearing a tweed cap with the peak bent into an arch over a pair of soft leather driving goggles. My own eyes streamed from the breeze.

After a mile or so, a large village appeared at the end of the valley, the buildings preceded by a farm from the yard of which a herd of cows was sauntering onto the road. Rupert slowed and parped the rubber bulb of the brass hooter, curled like a French horn, mounted by his side. A few of the cows turned their heads in mild curiosity; the remainder continued to amble diagonally across the road towards a gate into a meadow. The herdsman walking behind them, tapping any malingerers on their rumps with a switch, gave a cursory wave.

By the village green, along the edge of which the lower reaches of the chalk stream ran, separating the common land from the gardens of the cottages, was a barn and one time farrier's forge now converted into a garage. The doors were open, the sound of hammering echoing within. To one side was a newly installed petrol pump, painted scarlet like a Royal Mail letterbox, with a scallop shell made of frosted glass mounted on the top.

Rupert pulled up by the pump. The rear wheels of the Roadster skidded slightly as we halted. The hammering ceased and a man in greasy brown overalls came out, walking with a stoop and licking at an oily thumb. Like the petrol pump, he, too, wore the shell of a scallop embroidered on his breast pocket.

'Morning!' he greeted us. 'Jus' skinned meself, I 'ave.' He surveyed the vehicle. 'A Ford. Now that's what I call a motor car!' he exclaimed with the enthusiasm of a dedicated admirer. 'I ain't seen one of they before.' He wiped his hand on his overalls and stroked the mudguard as if tenderly caressing a docile animal which might still just bite if he were to overstep the boundary of bestial decorum. 'You'll be wantin' petroleum,' he continued, stating the obvious, then called out over his shoulder, 'Timothy!'

A boy of six or so scampered into sight. He was also besmirched with grease and oil.

While the lad held the nozzle in the fuel tank and the man swung the pump handle to and fro, Rupert positioned his goggles over the peak of his cap and walked round the Roadster, flicking off any blemishes of mud and dust with a damp chamois leather he kept under the seat cushion for just this purpose. I crossed the road and sat upon a milestone, watching him and easing my muscles. The suspension in the Roadster was hard and Rupert a fast driver. The milestone gave distances to London, Oxford, Newbury and Winchester.

Across the other side of the stream, in one of the cottage gardens, an elderly woman was hanging out her laundry. Her neighbour was turning the soil in his vegetable patch, his back arched to the spade. He dug with an easy, slow motion born of years of manual labour.

I glanced back at the car. The refuelling was completed. Rupert advanced the fuel lever. The garage owner obligingly turned the crank handle. The Roadster sputtered once, then fired. Rupert retarded the lever.

'We're ready!' he called out over the din of the engine, lowering his goggles and adjusting them over his eyes. I took my place in the passenger seat once more.

As he let off the hand brake, the Roadster rolled forwards, the engine pitch rising. He advanced the throttle lever farther and the clutch bit with a jerk. Over my shoulder, I saw the garage mechanic and the boy watching us set off much as two saved disciples might have observed the departure of their deliverer.

Once it left the valley, the road narrowed, entering a flatter landscape of water meadows, stands of beech, ash or hazel, and pasture bisected by channels. We were driving faster now, the wheels kicking aside gravel on the bends. It showered into the grass. On the edge of a wood, the road dipped, sunken between two banks, worn down into the ground by a millennium of feet, hooves and wheels.

At the point where the road came out into the open once more, a narrow lane joined it from the left, at an angle just past a corner. The engine revved as Rupert put the Roadster into the corner, not slowing, not caring, not thinking of the future that is always only a second away.

The horse was already out of the lane. The brassware of its bridle glittered in the sun piercing the canopy of a hornbeam overhanging the junction. It had blinkers on, could not see the speeding vehicle, yet its ears turned to register the approaching, unfamiliar noise. The carter, seated on the bench in front of a load of potatoes newly taken from the winter store, also heard the gathering din, but he understood it. He started to tug hard on the reins, force the horse to begin to reverse. The horse was confused by the noise and its master's command. It stood and turned its head.

For a moment, I registered the scene as if it were a tableau—the horse not quite side on to the Roadster, the carter not quite in sight behind a holly bush, the glint of the brass, the sweat-sleek hide of the animal's flank, its ear inclined in my direction, the scatter of white wood anemones on the bank behind.

Rupert saw it, too. He wrenched on the brake lever, the brake bands whining as they tried to grip, acrid smoke drifting back from the axles. He twisted the steering wheel. The Roadster rose momentarily onto two wheels as it veered. Rupert sensed the vehicle was toppling and corrected the steering, the Roadster falling heavily back onto all four wheels and hitting the horse a glancing blow. The front near mudguard bent back, slicing through the animal's chest. An artery burst. We were sprayed with warm equine blood. The glass of Rupert's goggles misted with a pink film. He could not see through them and ripped them down from his face to hang at his throat like a bizarre necklace.

The Roadster finally came to a stop fifty yards down the road. The yellow paintwork was spotted with blood which was running down the metal. The mudguard was wrenched round and doubled under the chassis, the running board twisted out of shape. From a jagged edge hung a strip of horsehide, one side slick and brown, the other fibrous and red. The front wheel was buckled on its hub. One wooden spoke had split.

I touched a gob of blood on my white shirt. It was deep red, dense and sticky, with the consistency of half-set gelatine. When I lifted my finger from it, the blood trailed out as if eager not to let go of me. On my trousers, the bloodstains were already soaking into the material, spreading out and darkening. I was aware of a wetness on my cheek and a dampness halfway down my left shin. Afraid I had been struck by a piece of metal, I quickly felt my face and leg. I was not injured, but my hands were smeared with blood.

Together, Rupert and I ran back to the junction. The horse was lying on its side, still in the traces of the cart, one of which had splintered and penetrated the animal's rib cage. Frothy, pink-tinged bubbles were gathering and bursting around the wound. The carter removed the blinkers, his fingers fumbling with the small brass buckles. The horse's eyes were wide, staring and afraid. Its mouth opened and it whinnied softly.

'Jesus!'

It was all Rupert could find to say.

The horse's hooves shone as if polished, varnished like good-quality furniture. Its mane had been combed.

There was nothing anyone could do. We stood awkwardly with our hands by our sides, as loose and as helpless as a cripple's. The carter knelt by the horse's head, whispering soft words to it and stroking its velvet nostrils. Suddenly, the beast had a spasm. The froth stopped bubbling and its eyes glazed over. One ear continued to flick in death, as if trying to drive away the flies that had yet to gather to feed upon its wounds and plant their eggs in its ripped tissue.

The carter got up. He was a man in his early twenties, not much older than we were, yet he was already somewhat grizzled by years of working the land, his hands grimy and his hair matted by the wind, as coarse as the horse's tail. He wore stiff moleskin trousers and an old jacket. His shirt had no collar and his heavy workman's shoes, with binding twine for laces, were dusty and scuffed.

Turning, he looked at us, saying nothing. Tears rolled down his cheeks, moved through the stubble on his chin and dripped onto his shirt. He wiped his nose on the sleeve of his jacket, as a child might, leaving a smear of glutinous mucus.

I made to console him, but he put his hand up, signalling me away. Nothing could address or ease his desolation. Rupert fumbled in his pocket for his wallet. He could think of nothing else but to recompense the carter for his loss. I glanced at Rupert, as if to tell him to leave his money where it was. Perhaps he did not understand; perhaps he was too busy wondering how much he should offer, how much a cart horse was worth. He removed three white ten-pound notes from his wallet and held them out, unable to say anything, able only to make this gesture.

The carter looked at the money, then at Rupert. 'Shove your money up your arse,' he said.

It was, although we were not to know it, the first real lesson for all three of us in the subterfuge of sorrow.

3

Simple. Perhaps some of them think of me as simple, an imbecile yet to be tutored in the arts of drooling, a steadily advancing case of senile dementia, albeit one that can still feed itself, dress itself and reach round to wipe its own backside.

This is not to say they lack compassion. I am never treated with other than respect and kindness, although the latter can often be quite clinical. My every need is catered to: bedsheets are changed on the third day, the room cleaned thoroughly twice a week. Meals arrive with a military punctuality and are always edible and nutritious and even sometimes quite tasty. The medication I am obliged to take is provided on time every morning just before nine o'clock and at four in the afternoon, give or take a quarter of an hour. Members of the staff are gentle, giving assistance when required but otherwise keeping their distance. The young doctor is considerate, soft-spoken and blessed with a refined bedside manner. All of the nurses are efficient in the way of their profession; one or two of them are actually quite pretty, although their aesthetic qualities are of little consequence to me. No one is ever rude or curt, takes advantage or is dismissive behind one's back; their patience seems inexhaustible, at least where I am concerned. I am ignorant of how the other inmates, patients, residents, clients—call us what you will—are treated, for I rarely have anything to do with them.

I think what confuses the staff, sets me apart from the others in their minds, is my silence. They are puzzled by it, cannot understand how, for as long as I have been in their charge, I have uttered not one single word. My dossier, apart from the usual medical notes, must make light reading. They know all about the condition of my body in detail, my touch of osteoporosis, my blood pressure (usually atypically low) and the scars on my chest and arms, yet they are in complete ignorance of the man that occupies this imperfect flesh.

Nor, much to their consternation, do I call out if in pain, moan if my muscles are stiff or mutter a brief, incomprehensible expletive when I bark my shin or bang my elbow. It is beyond their comprehension that I make no sounds other than those of my breathing and a light, involuntary snore when I sleep.

Their worlds are full of noise, voices and orders and conversation, the calls and grunts and groans of my fellow inmates and the din of common human activity. Mine has a Zen-like tranquillity that they will never be able to achieve. Perhaps they envy me my exquisite solitude. But there again, had they experienced my life in order to achieve this state, they might prefer the inanities of common banter and the sheer liberation of uttering a therapeutic curse whenever they catch their finger in a drawer.

My room is spartan but most comfortable. Quite unlike those usually found in institutions of this sort, with metal heads like the bars of a cage, the bed has a polished oak frame which has been lowered a few inches to make it more easily accessible. There is a chest of drawers, a dressing table–cum–writing desk with an upright chair before it, an armchair with a sprung, padded footrest operated by a small lever in the side and a bedside table over which, mounted on the wall, is a small lamp containing a forty-watt bulb inside a cream shade decorated with a frieze of daisies. In a corner stands a small porcelain basin with two brass taps. Upon one wall hangs a colourful print of an archetypal English village street of thatched houses, a church, a few shops, a shallow stream crossed by a ford and a wooden footbridge and, as if to remind one that no idyll is all it seems, a set of public stocks against a wall by the village pump. It is the work of one Mervyn Stanwood and dated 1898. The artist clearly owes a debt to Constable's *The Haywain* in that, in the middle of the ford, there stands a farm cart laden with apples. The curtains match the lampshade and hang on either side of a pair of french windows giving onto a terrace beyond which is a lawn of about two acres surrounded by well-tended flower beds and shrubberies. To one side of the lawn is an ancient oak tree. It being summer, the bushes in full leaf, one cannot quite see the high walls that surround this garden, nor the tight entanglement of barbed wire running along the top.

This establishment, which I only know of as St. Justin's, a fragment of information picked up from eavesdropping upon one of the orderlies' conversations, is secure. No one may get in or out save through the front gate. Whilst this may inconvenience some of my fellow internees, it suits me fine. What can't get out can't get in, either.

I have few personal possessions other than my clothing. What I do have has been closely vetted. For example, although I am allowed to keep my medals, these have had the pins removed from the tops of the ribbons. I am permitted writing and drawing materials, should I want them, but no pens; pencils and watercolours must suffice. If a pencil were to break or go blunt, an orderly would shave it to a point for me with his pocket knife. As he would with the pencil, he also shaves me every second day: I am forbidden a razor. In the tiny bathroom beside my room, the mirror is made of highly polished sheet steel, the tooth mug moulded out of pliable plastic, and there are no hooks anywhere from which clothing—or anything else—may be hung. The central light fitting is hung close to the ceiling and there is no piece of electrical flex more than eight inches in length.

This attention to the thwarting of self-mutilation and felo-de-se I find quite touching, yet equally lacking in imagination. A man can just as readily kill himself with a Winsor and Newton size 7 watercolour brush or a Rexel HB pencil, ramming it down his throat, as he can open a vein in his wrist with the sharp edge of a piece of paper.

In my time, I have considered both these, and many other, options.

It appears as if, despite the aforementioned precautions being applied to me, I am not regarded to be of risk to myself. I am given a degree of freedom, within the confines of the brick wall, refused to most of the others. When the weather is kind, I am permitted unsupervised access to the garden. Even in winter, if rain is not forecast, I am allowed out. The french windows are often closed yet never locked, and I do not need permission to open them. If I happen to be outside when a meal arrives, or it is time for my medication, a nurse comes out and leads me back in by the hand. Once or twice, in years past, I have even had my meals served to me on the terrace outside my room.

How long I have been an inpatient of St. Justin's I do not know. Time has no meaning for me now, other than to count the hours from waking to sleeping, and the staff do not inform me of the passage of days, months, years. I only know I am old. Very old. Appreciably older than the other inmates, and Nestor by comparison to the staff.

Nor can I clearly remember or date my coming here. Yet I can recall memories of much earlier times, and it is these I want the brick wall to keep at bay.

4

It was winter. The windowsills of Rupert's rooms were piled with snow, drifted up against the leading between the panes. A mean draught intermittently blew through a crack in the ill-fitting wooden frame. In the courtyard outside, a college servant was shovelling the pathway clear, another scattering rock salt upon it to melt that which the spade could not collect. Every now and then, we could hear the gentle rushing sound of a miniature avalanche sliding down the slated roof, followed by a soft thud as it hit the ground. Despite the fact that a coal fire burned in the tiny grate and Rupert having lit two of the lamps, one on his desk and the other on the low table scattered with the loose pages of his thesis, the air was touched by the heavy greyness of the last vestiges of feeble daylight filtering through the dismal, glowering sky.

We sat, glasses in our hands, opposite each other across the table upon which stood a silver bowl of demerara sugar. On the hot plates on either side of the grate were a small copper pan of simmering melted butter and a kettle of water, the steam eking from the spout to be whisked up the chimney. Our tumblers were filled with hot buttered rum.

For some minutes, we did not bother to speak, content to be in each other's company. It had been like this during our final year at school when, as senior prefects, we had shared a study at the top of a flight of spiral stairs in the tower over the main gate. Up there, we were cut off from the hubbub of the class- and common-rooms below, the noisy dormitories of the junior boys and the house prefects' cubicles. Self-contained, Rupert and I studied and dreamed together, plotting the paths of our futures as accurately as any cartographer. I, the archaeologist, was going to discover a lost city in the deserts of the Sudan, or an unknown monastery on a mountain summit in Tibet. Perhaps, with luck, I would find a new civilisation in the upper reaches of the Amazon, where the men wore jackets made out of the plumage of macaws and the women adorned themselves with polished uncut emeralds. Rupert, ever practical and consumed by a love of numbers, was going to develop a new system of accounting based upon binary mathematics, which would be called the Ellis Accounting Method, Ellis being not only his surname but also an acronym for *Ellis Lateral Long Integer System*.

'Have you ever wondered what it would be like to hold power in your hands?' Rupert asked at last.

I shrugged. It was the sort of question Rupert often posed. As a mathematician, he lived in a remote world of numbers, theories and logic; I existed in one of solid artefacts.

'If someone were to give me Henry the Eighth's Great Seal,' I replied, 'I suppose I would think of the concept of power.'

'But that's not to hold actual power,' Rupert said, 'just a manifestation of it. You can't exercise power with it. Only Henry the Eighth can. Or could. Now the seal would be nothing more than an antique. What I mean is, what if someone handed to you something that gave you immense power. Power over other men. Immediate power, over life and death.'

I sipped the last dregs in my glass and put it down on the table. Rupert passed me the bottle of Captain Morgan's rum standing on the floorboards by his chair. I poured out a measure and added hot water and melted butter, slowly stirring in sugar from the bowl. The drink and warmth of the room were making me pleasantly lethargic.

'Only gods have power like that.'

'There aren't any gods,' Rupert announced.

I made no reply. In those days, I was irrationally afraid of Rupert's agnosticism. Merely saying there was no god sent a frisson of fear up my spine. It was not that I was a Christian, yet I was afraid that by denying the existence of a god I might somehow be damning myself in my ignorance to eternity dragging my heels through purgatory.

'Do you remember my brother Desmond?' Rupert asked.

I nodded. Rupert's older brother was ten years our senior. He had left the school before we entered it, but his reputation lingered. The masters had described him, charitably, as an errant individualist, and the opinion was frequently voiced that his sibling would not follow in his miscreant footsteps.

'When he was eighteen,' Rupert continued, 'he decided he didn't want to go up to Oxford and, much to my grandfather's annoyance, he declined a position at Strutt and Harper—that's the merchant bank founded by my great-grandfather. Instead, he went to America.'

'To make his fortune,' I suggested.

'And, according to my grandfather, to lose it,' said Rupert. 'He lives now in a small town called Uvalde. In Texas. In his last letter, he said the place was summed up by the fact that its most famous citizen was an outlaw who became town sheriff, who was indicted six times for murder but got off each time, was ambidextrous with a six-gun, and was killed in a shoot-out with an infamous bandit called Ben Thompson in a vaudeville theatre in San Antonio.'

'What does your brother do there?' I enquired.

'He writes for the town newspaper, part-owns a general store and factors in corn and pecan nuts. Apparently the nuts, which grow wild along a nearby river, are much sought after in New York and Boston. He sells them for a dollar a peck.' Rupert got to his feet and removed a package wrapped in brown paper from a shelf on a bookcase by the door. 'He's sent me a gift.'

As he placed it on the table, I could tell it was heavy. Tied around with coarse string, it had been secured at each knot with gold wax into which an official seal had been pressed. On the front, above the address, were stuck a number of U.S. Mail stamps of high denominations.

'What is it?' I enquired.

'Desmond calls it a piece of the real America.'

Rupert slid the string off, spreading the wrapping paper out. It contained what I took to be a worn leather pouch, closed with a rusty buckle, wrapped in oilcloth and greasy tissue paper. Unfastening the buckle, he put his hand into the pouch, withdrawing from it a pistol with a wooden butt stained dark by use.

'It's a Colt .45 revolver, as used by the U.S. Army until 1875,' Rupert said, holding the gun in two hands as if about to offer it at an altar. 'This model has the longer, seven-and-a-half-inch barrel. It takes the .45 Long Colt cartridge, which fires a two-hundred-and-fifty gram lead-and-tin amalgam bullet with a flattened nose, projected by a forty-gram black powder charge.'

It was clear to me that he revelled in all this esoteric information: to him, the data consisted of exactitudes, which fascinated the existentialist, the dispassionate mathematician, in him. For Rupert, the world was not made of passion and possibility but only of the stark truth of fact. The chaos or disorder that was the main component of everyone else's life was something he neither acknowledged nor was prepared to accept. His parents had been responsible for his detached view of reality: his father was a doctor and his mother a chemist. Tried procedures and proven formulæ, not emotion, controlled the family.

His ambivalence to emotion had been what had first attracted me to him when he had joined my class in the Remove. One winter's evening, I was sitting at a table in the library, struggling with the algebra syllabus, when he leaned over my shoulder.

'Factoring,' I said glumly without looking up.

'ax^2+bx+c,' he began aloud, 'equals $-20x^2$ . . . Use 1 and minus 3 as the factors for c.'

I was still at a loss. With three or four deft flicks of his pencil, he completed the equation I was unable to resolve. He then quite impassively showed me how he had arrived at the solution.

'Thank you,' I said, surprised by his unsolicited help.

'It's a pleasure,' he replied, then smiled and walked to his table. I saw he was working with Kennedy's *Latin Primer.*

'I'm not too bad at conjugating,' I offered.

'I'm all right,' he replied. 'It's just a matter of the application of logic.' He bent to his exercise book.

I was grateful not just for the answer to the algebraic conundrum but also for his having helped me without expecting reparation.

As if it were fragile, Rupert placed the gun on the table and slid it towards me.

'Pick it up,' he offered.

I did so. The butt fitted neatly into my hand and, despite the length of the barrel, seemed perfectly balanced, as if there were an invisible fulcrum beneath my index finger which naturally rested upon the trigger.

'Just think,' Rupert said. 'You have in your hands the latent ability to control destiny. Yours or another's. The choice rests with you.'

'I trust it's not loaded,' I replied, feeling the weight of the weapon dragging my forearm down.

Rupert tipped up the leather pouch. A dozen brass-cased cartridges slid out to rattle across the veneer of the table. One of them chinked against my glass.

'No, it's not loaded,' he assured me, 'but you have only to reach out. Slip a few shells into the cylinder. Lean out the window. Wait for the next undergraduate to appear from a door. Aim. Hold it firmly, for it has a sharp upwards recoil. It is quite accurate up to about fifty feet. The trajectory will only lose about three inches at that range. Aim for the base of the neck'—he touched the hollow beneath his Adam's apple—'and you'll hit the heart.'

Just the thought sent a shiver of loathing through me. I wanted to put the weapon down, rub the pungent gun oil off my hands with all the fervour of Pontius Pilate ridding himself of his guilt. Yet I did not.

'You feel it, don't you?' Rupert said quietly.

I made no response, but I knew what he meant. There was a dreadful fascination about the revolver, an exquisite yet terrible beauty. Looking at it, turning it in my hands, I could not help but admire the skill of its engineering.

'Pull the trigger,' Rupert demanded.

Very slowly, I tightened my index finger, taking up the slack in the pivotal hinge. The mechanism was stiff but smooth, the hammer pulling back and the cylinder revolving with symmetrical precision. When the hammer reached its fullest extent and snapped forward, the click of the firing pin against the register plate was filled with a macabre menace.

'That is what I mean by power,' Rupert said quietly, adding somewhat grandiloquently, 'the ultimate power, the giddy gift of death.'

As if it were made of brittle crystal, I placed the gun back on the table. It was no longer an object of fascination but one of fear, its potential declared as if, in its own mute fashion, it had spoken to me of its capabilities and dared me to put it to the test.

From outside the window came the sound of voices muted by the snow. Rupert picked the gun up and, taking one of the bullets, loaded it into one of the chambers. Coolly closing the cylinder, he spun it hard and, going to the window as the rattle of the ratchet died out, opened the casement. A blast of frigid air swept into the room. Leaning slightly over the sill, he raised the revolver and, pointing it down into the courtyard, took aim along the barrel at the foresight.

'What the hell are you doing?' I said, alarmed as much by his composure as his bizarre actions.

'I'm introducing an undergraduate called Offerton to life's great lottery,' he replied, looking at me over his shoulder. There was a faint, almost taunting, smile on his lips.

For a brief moment, I wondered what he meant.

Without taking his eyes from mine, Rupert pulled the trigger. I heard every movement of the weapon's mechanism as a succession of distinct, individual sounds—the retardation of the hammer, the turning of the cylinder, the crack of the trigger. There was a deafening report which set my ears ringing. A cloud of acrid cordite smoke blew into the room, stinging my nostrils and eyes.

'For fuck's sake, Rupert!' I shouted.

Jumping to my feet, I ran to the window, pushing him aside. From below issued a torrent of belligerent shouting. I looked down. In a circle of lamplight under an archway, one of the college servants was leaning on the shaft of a broad snow shovel, scanning the windows to see from which one the shot had come. Standing in the snow were two men wearing short undergraduate gowns over their jackets, staring up at me. One of them had dropped some books in the snow. Neither, it appeared, had been hit.

Rupert lowered the gun.

'What?' he replied, nonchalantly.

'You could have killed someone.'

'From your remark,' he said, 'I assume that I missed.'

'You're bloody mad,' I came back at him, growing angry at his indifference and still only just able to hear my own voice through the numbness of my ears. 'And what if the fucking thing had hit one of them?'

'If,' he said, 'my aim had been fortuitously on the mark and the "fucking thing," as you so eloquently put it, had hit one of them, I could indeed have at least wounded, possibly killed, Offerton or Gravesbury, who was walking with him. And if that had happened, I should have had to own up to my actions, plead them in front of a judge and either hang for what I did in Oxford prison or spend the rest of my life in a Northampton asylum like poor, insane John Clare, writing pastoral verse based upon events and places I had not seen for years. As it is, I shall just have to explain myself to the Dean in the morning.'

'And what the hell do you think you've proved by that?' I retorted, further exasperated by this logical, mathematical progression.

'I did not intend to prove anything,' he said. 'One only seeks to prove a possible known quantity, justify an anticipated result. When the outcome of an action has a multitude of probabilities, one does not try to prove it. One merely experiments to see what numerical loading the chances of one probability might be over another.'

'So you did it for some sort of vicarious enjoyment,' I declared.

'No,' Rupert replied, 'not for the thrill of it, although I concede there was an element of excitement involved in my actions. I did it to remind myself—and to illustrate to you, Alec—the risk of exercising the ultimate power. For one millisecond, as the hammer moved forwards towards the cylinder, I was the master of not just my own fate but of another's. Where mine was concerned, I was willing to accept whatever consequences arose from my actions. One has to admit one's liabilities in life. Yet Offerton? What right had I to kill him? What reason, even? He's an affable dolt, but that confers on me no privileges. I have no more right to shoot him than I have to slap him in the face or kick him in the balls.'

Rupert seemed to realise he was still holding the gun and put it down on the table.

'For just one moment,' Rupert continued, 'I disregarded the only factor that differentiates us from the beasts of the fields and the fowls of the air. It is not self-determination or the ability to reason. It is not even the fear of death which I think is particularly human. It is morality.' He sat down again and raised his glass of hot buttered rum as if to propose a toast. 'May Offerton, amiable buffoon that he is, live in peace and remain in ignorance of how close he came today to a long trip through eternity.'

Putting down his glass, he picked up the revolver and, opening the cylinder, showed it to me.

Thinking aloud, Rupert said, 'To toy with another's life, rather than one's own, is, perhaps, the greatest immorality of all.'

At that moment, I came to the realisation that nothing more substantial than a set of self-imposed guidelines for civilised behaviour kept order in our lives, breath in our lungs, a pulse in our veins.

'Now, Alec,' he went on, 'I think you understand why I believe there can be no god. It was not divine intervention that saved a life. It was just mere chance. Mathematical probability. Odds of one in six, lengthened considerably by my ineptitude with firearms.'

The fire was dying down. Rupert got up and tipped some coal into the grate from a brass scuttle. The chimney filled with blue smoke, a little of it billowing out beneath the mantel.

Peering into the smoke as if he might find some oracular message written there, he said ironically, 'The Peacemaker. This is what they call this weapon. A curious name.' He prodded the fire with a poker. 'And tell me, if all it takes to make peace is a gun and flimsy ethics, then what need have we for gods?'

5

Just as I am given access to the gardens, so, too, am I allowed to sit on the terrace outside my room long after lock up, weather permitting. This is a rare privilege. I never see any of the other inmates afforded such liberty. They are incarcerated in their rooms at nine o'clock, not to be released until the following morning.

It is during these quiet interludes that I study the world such as I have come to know it. I have no interest in the universe beyond the brick wall, but it impinges itself upon me. I can see nothing, but I hear sounds. Sometimes, distant children playing or a dog barking with hysterical canine joy. At other times, I pick up the noise of a train rattling rhythmically along a track. On Mondays, if the wind is in the west, I discern the unmelodious cacophony of church bells. If these distractions are absent, I find myself hearing memories.

Recently, sitting by the open french windows as dusk fell upon a summer's day, I heard men singing. The tune was 'Mademoiselle from Armentières.' I dislike it for its crudeness and sexual undertones, its degrading of women. The *mademoiselle* in the song is a snag-toothed whore who hasn't been kissed in forty years, whose face could stop a cuckoo clock, who has four chins and is knock-kneed from two decades of fornication. I only heard one verse clearly:

> 'You might forget the gas and shells, parlez-vous.
> You might forget the gas and shells, parlez-vous.
> You might forget the groans and yells,
> But you'll never forget the mademoiselles,
> Hinky, dinky parlez-vous!'

Closing my eyes, I saw a train accelerating away from the platform, the smoke from the locomotive gouting up towards the great arc of the sooty glass canopy of the station. It may have been Charing Cross or Waterloo. In the windows of the carriages were paper stickers upon which had been written: 'Boat train.'

From every carriage leaned a figure, dressed in uniform, some with cockades in their caps, all with buttons and regimental badges polished bright, all smiling, laughing, waving. All as proud as bantams.

Then, I was in the train, yet it was not the same train. The carriage was warm. I must, I concluded, be in first class, for there was a strong scent of leather, wood polish and Brasso. The floor was carpeted, the fabric of the seats soft and somewhat like velvet; had I been in second or third class, the material would have been coarser and itched the back of my legs. Behind my head was a lace antimacassar, above it a dim reading lamp in a crystal glass surround. The mirror above the seat opposite was engraved with the letters *LNER*. I was wearing a dark blue blazer and grey shorts and my feet did not quite touch the floor. To my left sat a handsome man with a trim moustache smelling faintly of Mr. Yale's hair tonic; on my other side was a woman dressed in a tight-busted cream blouse with a maroon hat upon her piled blonde hair. Her skin looked smooth and she had about her the faint perfume of gardenias, which counteracted and mingled most curiously with the musky smell of the man's hair preparation. When I looked at them, they smiled at me, the man ruffling my hair and laughing before giving me a shiny Victorian silver crown bearing the queen's head and a naked man on a horse, in a Greek warrior's helmet and cloak, running his lance through a dragon; the woman took my hand and tickled my palm with the long, perfectly manicured nail of her index finger.

Quite suddenly, without the warning of a cutting or embankment, the train entered a tunnel. There were no lights on in the carriage. The locomotive whistled loudly, the noise echoing in my head like a scream. There was a rush of black air which seemed to snatch my soul away. When the train came out of the tunnel, I was wearing long trousers and a jacket, a tie embroidered with a crest and knotted so tightly at my collar I could hardly breathe. I reached up and tugged at it, bursting the stud, tearing the tie off. Beneath the crest was a motto in Latin: 'Nihil Praeter Optimum.'

Looking round, I saw the man with the moustache was gone. The woman was wearing a plain white blouse edged with black lace. Her blonde hair had been cut shorter, and the aroma of gardenias had been replaced by a faint smell of camphor.

Gradually, the train slowed and pulled into a station. The platform signboard read either 'Scunthorpe' or 'Market Harborough.' I was not quite sure, for the lettering seemed to shimmer as if through rain. Whichever it was, it was an ugly name evoking flat, featureless land-scapes and pewter-coloured expanses of still water, bent reeds and muddy tidal estuaries. The door to the corridor opened and a second man entered. He was tall and, when he spoke, gruff, his every word curt and humourless. His eyes were grey and somehow suggestive of those of a vicious and wily guard dog, and his hands were extraordi-narily strong and large. He sat on the other side of the woman, his cold eyes searching hers.

The train set off once more, but now I found myself alone in the carriage. Where the adults had gone I did not know. In my hands was a drawing block upon which I was sketching the face of a woman in charcoal. Looking up, I found myself sitting opposite a small boy in a braided school cap and blazer. Outside, fields passed by, intermittently obscured by the smoke from the locomotive. Through the windows came the sharp tang of coal soot and steam. A bridge of iron girders went by, the grid of struts methodically flicking shadows across the carriage, across the paper upon which the face was half-drawn.

'Who is that?' the little boy enquired. 'In your drawing.'

I did not answer immediately.

'Is it your mother?'

'I'm not sure,' I replied.

The boy leaned forward, glanced at the picture and announced, 'Yes, that's your mother. She got off at Peterborough,' he added with the puerile surety of a precocious child certain of its facts.

Again, I did not respond but wondered how the child knew what I did not, that the woman who had been sitting beside me was my mother.

'Are you going to draw a picture of your father?' the boy wanted to know.

I pondered on this for a moment before shaking my head. Such a task was impossible, for, I now realised, I could not remember him. I assumed my father was the man with the moustache, but if that was the case, then what was the identity of the man with hands the size of dinner plates?

'The man with the big hands is your stepfather,' the boy answered with certain confidence.

'Is he?' I queried incredulously. It was unnerving. Somehow, this mere child was reading my mind.

Perhaps, I mused, the boy was me: it was a thought that, curiously, neither concerned nor interested me.

The train rattled over a level crossing in a country lane. A Lanchester saloon stood at the gate, the driver wearing a prim chauffeur's uniform, an old lady seated behind him dressed in mourning. In a nearby field, a traction engine with smoke pumping from its funnel was driving a long, loose belt which in turn was powering a threshing machine. The crossing gatekeeper's young children balanced precariously upon a barrel, waving. The shadows were long upon the field, a line of poplars by the lane casting bars over the stubble.

'Where is my father?' I asked the boy as the train passed under a granite bridge.

'Dead,' the child replied bluntly. He was not yet old enough to understand pathos. The truth had no passion, for it was stark and real. The artifice of tact and the grey tones of compromise and diplomacy were as yet unknown to him.

'And my mother?'

'She died of pneumonia.'

By now, the train was travelling through darkness.

'And what of my stepfather?'

'He is Colonel William John Kenneth Urquhart,' the precocious child continued with evident admiration. 'Hero of Bloemfontein. He killed ten Boers with his sabre. And he was awarded the Victoria Cross. It was in all the papers,' the child concluded unnecessarily.

I pondered this for a moment. The mention of Bloemfontein seemed somehow familiar. A bright light seared down upon me. It might have been the baking noonday sun of the Orange Free State. Mingled with the rhythmic clatter of the train wheels was the discordant sound of bridles chinking. For a fleeting moment, I saw a horse, its flanks polished with sweat and its mouth foamed, tugging a gun and limber up the steep bank of a desultory river of brown water. Its hooves scrabbled on the dry earth, kicking up dust which blew into my mouth, gritting on my teeth. To my puzzlement, I recognised the weapon. It was a standard Mark 1 eighteen-pounder field gun.

From somewhere nearby I suddenly heard a barely audible high-pitched squeal. I opened my eyes. It was night now. The duty nurse had yet to do her rounds. The moon was high, washing the garden and the brick wall with a neutral light which slanted through the stone balustrade running along the edge of the terrace, stark upon the flagstones by my slippered feet.

Second by second, the noise swelled until it reached a terrible crescendo in my head. I opened my mouth to shout, but no words formed.

A gentle hand touched my wrist. The squeal evaporated and upon my hand, its infinitesimal weight hardly telling, was a bat, a pipistrelle, its eyes like dark tiny beads, bright in the moonlight and filled with terror.

6

I remember it as if it were yesterday. Indeed, I would believe it had happened not more than a fortnight ago were it not for my gnarled fingers and the arthritis in my left hand.

The early evening was clear. It had rained in the afternoon, cleansing the city air of soot, smoke and the sweet but pungent clart rising from the damp horse dung. The cobbles in the mews glistened, the pavements before the houses washed by the downpour and subsequently swept clean by servants with stiff-bristled brooms. Even the sounds of horses' hooves, carters' and tradesmen's calls, carriage wheels, the occasional steam or internal combustion engine seemed somehow laundered, as distinct as the steel-edged notes I heard played on a saloon bar piano as I passed a public house in Floral Street.

It had not been on my way. A direct route to the house would have taken me along the Strand to Trafalgar Square, up Cockspur Street and Haymarket, then left into Jermyn Street. Yet I just could not bring myself to go straight to my destination. Instead, I walked a perambulatory route through the maze of crowded thoroughfares around Covent Garden, designed in mediæval times and still laid out as if awaiting the resurrection of Chaucer and his fellow pilgrims. With every step my heart grew heavier, a depression settling upon me like city smog. I found myself lingering in front of wholesale greengrocers' premises, studying the fruit and vegetables that had not sold in the morning and were now being offered at cut price to passersby or cooks from eating houses where the clientele were working-class and their palates undiscerning. In a futile attempt to delay longer, I entered a small ale house tucked away in the narrow confines of

Goodwin's Court: yet even this killed only a matter of minutes. There were few customers present; I was served almost immediately and, being on my own, tended to drink my pint of mild quickly. In less than a quarter of an hour, I was through and back on the streets, walking westwards.

Eventually facing up to the inevitability of my situation, I turned into Jermyn Street and approached the entrance to Marquand House with much the same foreboding as a French aristocrat must have stepped up to his rendezvous with Madame Guillotine. My grandfather's town house, and my father's after him, it would, one day, be mine, yet for the time being my stepfather had possession of it, granted him by my mother until his demise, the bequest angled for in their marriage settlement.

The porcelain button of the doorbell stared at me like a basilisk eye from its circle of brass which had been so frequently polished, for so many years, the engraved pattern in the metal was indistinct. As I pressed it, a sense of impending gloom fell upon me, only alleviated by the knowledge that I had a return train ticket to Oxford in my wallet.

Barlowe, my stepfather's butler, who had served with him in the South African War against the Boers, answered the door. A short, stocky man, his skin was still dry and dark, as if the tropical sun had not so much tanned as stained him. His eyes were close-set and narrowed as if, in the back of his mind, a part of his soul was still squinting against the stark glare of the high veldt, searching for a telltale glint of gunmetal. His hands were lean, the sinews running from his knuckles to his wrist as prominent as the ribbing on a pair of workman's gloves.

'Good evening, Mr. Alec.'

His voice was condescending, his accent a flat South London, ugly and without the idiosyncrasies of a rural dialect. 'The colonel will be with you shortly. If you'll follow me to the library, sir.'

As we ascended the sweeping staircase to the first floor, I recalled the pictures that had hung upon the walls in my childhood. They had been paintings collected on my grandfather's many trips to Europe on business, not of the usual subjects of the Grand Tour, the Rialto in Venice at dawn or the cathedral of Santa Maria del Fiore in Florence, but more eclectic—the temple to Poseidon at Paestum, the papal palace at Avignon and the Norman castle above Cefalù in Sicily. My favourite had been an impressionist watercolour study in the style of Turner of the Roman amphitheatre at Arles, the arched tiers of the walls seeming to tower above me, beyond the confines of the ceiling, the dust in the arena soaked, in my imagination, with the blood of wild beasts, religious innocents and slaves coerced to sacrifice in the name of entertainment. It was, I thought as I mounted the steps, perhaps those pictures which had triggered the allure of history in me and brought to me the sense of futility inherent in violence.

Since my mother's death, however, the pictures of my youth had been removed, sold at auction or stacked in the attic store beside the chambermaids' bedroom, to be replaced with oil paintings depicting seminal moments in the history of my stepfather's regiment. Gilt frames surrounded scenes of carnage, of Cossack horses skewered by lances in the Crimea, of men dressed in soiled bandages standing at the barricades during the Peninsula War to defend their position to the last bullet, of mounted generals in plumed hats on hilltops surveying the orchestration of their strategies on the fields of killing spread before them far below.

In the library, a huge portrait of my great-grandfather which had adorned the wall facing the windows was gone. In its place—indeed, in its very frame—was a newly commissioned painting of the advance for the relief of Ladysmith. Whereas the scenes on the staircase had been depicted using dark colours, the cavalry horses the colour of mahogany, the uniforms rich in blue, red and gold, and the sky filled with thunderheads and clouds of cordite smoke, this painting was one of light. An African sun glared down upon a world of bush veldt and brazen grass; a river ran in the foreground, beyond which lay tier upon tier of rolling hillocks punctuated by the occasional *kopje* and a hint of a trench or low stone wall. Across the river, lines of troops were advancing into machine-gun fire, men being cut down like scythed corn in August. The enemy causing this carnage was invisible. Somehow, the scene was all the more obscene for being bright: the tonal qualities were more suited, I considered, to the small watercolour by Boudin, of courting couples walking on the beach at Deauville, which my mother had had hanging in her drawing room and which, I was sure, would by now have also made that short journey to the auction house or the attic.

The travesty of replacing my ancestor's picture with this monument to human arrogance and the dubious values of glory and courage infuriated me. Yet I knew there was nothing to be gained from expressing my anger. My stepfather—the colonel—was intractable. It was better to grit my teeth, keep quiet and get the evening over with.

Stepping up to the painting, I looked at the title, engraved upon a small brass plaque screwed onto the frame where once my great-grandfather's name had been. It read: 'The Battle of Colenso.'

'They had Mauser action rifles.'

I turned to find my stepfather standing in the library doorway.

'The Boers,' he added by way of extrapolation. 'And a one-pounder Maxim gun. It didn't put our boys off. The Connaughts, the Inniskillings: the green and the orange, Catholics and Protestants. Side by side. The Royal Dublin Fusiliers and the Connaughts suffered the greatest.' He looked at the painting, reliving the mêlée. 'What was it Conan Doyle said in his history of the scrap? "In every fold and behind every anthill the Irishmen lay thick and waited for better times."'

'I presume,' I said with feigned naïveté, 'the better times did not come.'

He chose to ignore my remark and went on, 'Brooke commanded the Connaughts. Fine man. I knew him well. He fell with his lads. Shot through the throat. Pinned down by the river, they were. Hammered by the Boers and by British artillery shells falling short. You'll not see greater bravery.'

'Were there court martials for the gunners?'

'The gunners?' he repeated, clearly nonplussed.

'Those whose shells fell short.'

'Courts martial!' the colonel repeated, stressing the word to correct my grammar. 'Good God, no! War is war,' he added enigmatically.

'I suppose it doesn't really matter whose bullet kills you, so long as you stood your ground and did your duty.'

It was a futile attempt at sarcasm. No sooner had I spoken than I realised my irony was wasted on my stepfather. He might have been a man capable of skilled military observation, but he lacked imagination and a ready wit. As far as he was concerned, humour was not a subtle art but a dirty story told in the officers' mess over coffee and brandy and a thin Burmese cheroot.

'Quite so!'

There was a knock on the library door Barlowe entered.

'Remember Colenso, Barlowe?'

'Yes, colonel,' the butler replied. 'Blood bath, sir.'

'Lost some fine boys that day, Barlowe.'

'Lieutenant Roberts, sir.'

'Ah, yes indeed. Freddie Roberts. Fine lad! He was the only surviving son of Lord Roberts. Did his family proud. But we learned an important military lesson that day, did we not, Barlowe? No more frontal attacks. Terrier work. Go round the side and bite the buggers' ankles. Remember what Lord Dundonald said, Barlowe?'

'Yes, sir. "Better to harry than parry," ' Barlowe replied, then added, 'Supper is served, sir.'

As I followed my stepfather through the house, I pondered on how this was the pattern with which all our meetings invariably began. There was never a greeting, never a shaken hand or an enquiry into health, just a brief instruction in military tactics. Better harry than parry, I considered: the consequences of a massacre reduced to a catchy turn of phrase.

The dining room was sombre. On the shelves where my grandfather had kept a collection of Elizabethan pewter tankards and salvers there now ranged mementoes from the colonel's military existence, a *lathi* with a polished horn and brass boss, a small dirk in a moth-eaten zebra-skin sheath, a rhino-hide *sjambok,* a silver statuette of a native trooper, a bronze of a horse with a rifle hanging from the saddle in a case. In the fireplace, in lieu of the embroidered fire screen my grand-mother had sewn depicting a peacock, stood a Zulu shield held in place by two short *assegais*.

Once we were seated facing each other down the expanse of the table, Barlowe waited upon us. It was a simple menu such as might have been served in the colonel's field tent during a long and arduous campaign, the supply lines somewhat stretched. The French onion soup was weak, the fish course consisted of a very small trout and the beef, although cut thick, was strung through with strands of gristle. The wine, a merlot, was poured straight from the bottle. It had a bit-ter aftertaste, as if it was not quite corked.

As we ate, the colonel did not speak except to give orders to Bar-lowe. It was only when the plates were cleared away and a carafe of chilled muscat was placed between us that he spoke to me.

'So I understand you have now graduated from your university?'

His words carried a slight hint of disdain.

'Yes, I have. I was awarded an upper second,' I said.

'Remind me. The subject you studied?'

He already knew the answer and was, in his usual manner, being deliberately obfuscatory.

'I read for a bachelor of arts degree in history and archaeology.'

'And now that you are a qualified historian and archaeologist, do tell me what you intend to do with your newly acquired knowledge.'

'I have yet to decide,' I admitted, sensing I was already beginning to lose the battle of words. 'There are a number of options open to me.'

The colonel poured himself a glass of muscat. 'I cannot believe that a degree in history and archaeology qualifies you for very much. As I understand it, you can use the qualification for entry into the law, into the foreign service, perhaps. Into the church, no doubt. An upper second, I am told, does not open up a career in academic circles. For that, you would require a first class degree which . . . ' He tested the wine, the pause designed to emphasis his point. ' . . . you did not achieve. Of course, you can use it to become a schoolmaster, but, as such, you would be a second-class citizen of the educational world.'

As my stepfather had not exhibited the common courtesy of passing the carafe of muscat, I reached across the table for it and poured myself a glass. Where the merlot had been tart, this was sweet and syrupy with a sickly bouquet reminiscent of honey.

'I intend to make a career as an archaeologist.'

'Indeed,' the colonel responded. 'And with what as your capital? You have over the years since you left school squandered most of your mother's inheritance studying for your course.'

'I do not consider the acquisition of an education to be a squandering . . .'

'Under normal circumstances,' he interrupted me, 'I would concede that point, but you have hardly studied a practical subject. Engineering, medicine. Something of purpose. Even theology can have a limited use. But archaeology . . .'

'A knowledge of, an appreciation of, history is purposeful,' I defended myself. 'The lesson of history instructs us in the path of the future.' I sounded like one of my recent professors, pedantic but confident in my surmission. 'As you have already said earlier this evening, you learned a lesson at the battle of Colenso. Harry rather than parry. Is that not history instructing the future? Not information useful in another campaign?'

The colonel was silent for a moment, unused to being questioned. 'History has a value. I don't deny you that. It does instruct the future, as you so succinctly put it. Yet we are not talking here of history. We are talking here of archaeology. What is archaeology but a scrabbling about in the dirt for pieces of broken pot? What does that tell you? How does that instruct us? Or bones. What can a skull tell you? It can hardly talk, and if it did . . .' he smiled disdainfully '. . . you'd not understand it unless it spoke Latin or Greek.' He sipped his wine again, keeping his eyes on me. 'Tell me, how are your classical languages?'

I was tempted to tell my stepfather quite bluntly that he was wrong, but I knew from experience that polite argument was a better form of diplomacy.

'On the contrary, a skull can talk. A study of the teeth can tell one about diet, the standards of health. Lesions in bones can indicate injury or diseases prevalent in the past . . .'

The colonel sensed he was losing the argument. He slammed his hand down on the table. 'Who cares what a bloody Roman ate, whether he had the pox or not and how he died? More to the point, who's going to pay you to find out?'

'I already have a commission from a wealthy Scottish landowner,' I said, 'to conduct a survey of Iron Age settlement upon his land.'

'Rich men's hobbies! And how much is this spendthrift paying you to look for bones in his peat bog?'

'Twenty pounds a month with full board and lodging.'

The colonel pondered for a moment.

'It's a good sum,' he allowed, 'but, tell me, how long is this commission of yours to last?'

'Up to three months.'

'And then?'

'My reputation will build.'

'Your reputation as what? A gimcrack hireling pandering to the foibles of wealthy profligates.'

There was nothing more to be said. I reached for my glass. Barlowe entered with a mahogany tray upon which stood a silver coffee pot and two small cups. The pot bore the crest of the Marquands, well worn, like the doorbell, by decades of ardent polishing. From a sideboard he produced a cigar humidor with an ebony and silver lid, the body of the vessel fashioned from the foot of a pigmy hippopotamus.

As his butler poured the black coffee, to which there was no alternative, the colonel leaned back in his chair, reached for a cigar, clipped it and rolled it in his fingers. There was something about his gestures that unsettled me. Usually, when my stepfather realised he was losing an argument, he would momentarily go quiet, seem to surrender, to retreat, before coming back hard for the *coup de grâce*.

'Of course, in three months, you'll be looking for alternative employment once again,' he remarked, almost casually.

'Yes, I shall.'

'Well, don't you worry, my boy,' he said, patronisingly. 'You'll find work. As sure as hell is hot, there'll be a war with the Germans before the summer is out.' He smiled at Barlowe as if sharing with him an intimate secret which he was, nevertheless, going to divulge. 'And you may mark my words, sir. And mark them very well. A war is the best employer of them all.'

7

From time to time, fragments of my memory of my own life filter through to me. They are of themselves succinct but always without context. It is as if someone is flicking through the pages of the book of my life, pausing randomly to read a few paragraphs before running his fingers on for a few chapters.

Just such a shard of my past occurred to me only an hour ago.

I was standing by an ornate wrought-iron lamp on an island in the middle of a wide thoroughfare. At first, I thought it might have been a Parisian boulevard, but there were no trees lining the sides, the pavements were comparatively narrow and none of the buildings contained cafés or *bistros*. Instead, there were shops—bespoke tailors', a confectioner's in the window of which were racks of expensive chocolates decorated with crystallised violets and rose petals, a chemist's with retorts full of brightly coloured liquid as advertisement and a tobacconist's with a carved wooden cigar-store Indian standing at the door, his feathered war bonnet somewhat grimy. Perhaps, I wondered briefly, I was in New York, where, I have been led to believe, such shop mannequins are commonplace.

The street was pristine. It seemed as if it had been purposefully swept, the horse dung collected up, the dog shit swept down the drains, the litter spiked and disposed off, the kerbstones polished with beeswax. I reasoned that, possibly, there was to be a procession passing by later, a parade of carriages carrying crowned heads or persons of presidential grandeur, yet there was no bunting hanging from the street lamps, no flags suspended from windows and no gathering spectators.

That was the most puzzling thing of all. I was the only person present in the whole panorama. Nothing else moved, not so much as a dog dozing or scratching in a doorway or a pigeon roosting on a cornice. There was no wind, either. Everywhere was silent. It was as if time were in abeyance, holding its breath with apprehension.

I then seem to have realised where I was. In the distance, down the perspective of the street, which bent slightly several hundred yards in front of me, a column rose vertically into the air behind a building, topped with a figure. Halfway to the bend was a theatre, the marquee carrying the name of the current production in tall letters I could not quite read. To my left was a short cul-de-sac at the end of which was an imposing glass-roofed portico protecting doors of dark wood and gleaming brass. It was, I saw, the main entrance to the Savoy Hotel, I was in the Strand and this was London.

At a leisurely pace, I began to walk down the centre of the street. Still, nothing moved but me. I laughed aloud at the novelty that I was in motion whilst London, the city that never slept at the heart of the greatest empire the world had ever known, was frozen into immobility. My laughter echoed back from the buildings.

Crossing the junction with Carting Lane and Southampton Street, I became aware of a distant sound. At first, it was barely discernible above the noise of my steel-capped heels on the roadway. It might have been nothing more than a humming in my head, the resonance of my blood running through my veins. It had a certain liquid quality to it, like water in a fountain, rising and falling.

I continued on my way. In my left hand I discovered I was holding a cane made of ebony with a silver collar fixing the shaft to a handle made of amber in which a primeval insect had been imprisoned. Like a dandy parading himself, I swung the cane, passing it between my fingers as a drum major might his baton.

Down the Strand, towards Trafalgar Square, there appeared a haze on the road. At the same time, the noise increased in volume. I halted. The haze took shape. It was a throng of men, shoulder to shoulder, filling the wide street from side to side. Those at the edge brushed against the buildings, were swept back into the crowd to be replaced by others spreading out from the centre. It was as if they were a wall of human water surging forwards. They were all dressed in dull colours, undyed woollen vests, leather jerkins, moleskin trousers, black boots—the uniform of the peasantry. Some carried staves, others axes, scythes, pitchforks and shovels, the flat heads sharpened to make them more effective weapons.

As the throng reached the corner of Bedford Street, the leaders saw me. An incomprehensible shout went up, primordial and vicious, filled with the venom of festering hatred.

I turned to run. Nearby was an alley into which I thought I could escape. Reaching it, I was about to enter its protection when I saw the far end was plugged with other rioters. They, too, were advancing upon me. In the gloomy shadows, their eyes glowed like coals in an ash bucket.

In the Strand, the mob was not more than fifty yards away. I could see detail now—the beards framing baying mouths, the rank tangle of unwashed shoulder-length hair, the muscular, sinewed hands and the cracked teeth.

There was nothing for it. I had to flee ahead of the riot. Yet I could not. My feet would not obey. I stood transfixed with fear as the rabble accelerated towards me, as helpless as a deer transfixed by a bright light.

Over the growing clamour, I heard a click, as clearly as if there were no other sounds to be heard. At the head of the throng, a man was standing with a flintlock, cocking it, taking slow and deliberate aim. The weapon fired, the flash of the black powder quickly obscured by gun smoke.

I saw the lead ball coming towards me. It was turning lazily upon its axis, one side polished, the other scorched by the charge of gunpowder.

This, I thought, was how death came, taking its time, letting you know it was on its way, that there was nothing you could do to avoid it.

A figure stepped in front of me. Where it came from I had no idea. I had not seen anyone else in the street except for the rioters, and I was certain there had been no one behind me. The person was dressed from head to foot in a white garment that hung from his shoulders like a shroud. Putting a hand out, the figure caught the musket ball, crushing it to powder in his fist.

Something touched me on the shoulder. I grew dizzy and felt myself falling, unable to maintain my balance. My eyes closed until all I could see was the pattern of the blood vessels in my eyelids, illuminated by a strong light shining upon me from I knew not where.

After what seemed an interminable time, I opened my eyes to find myself lying on a hard surface. Far above me was a ceiling with an ornate plaster rose in the centre, from which hung an electric light assembly of six bulbs each contained in a glass shade tinted blue. The bulbs, which were switched on, were of a low wattage. A voice, disembodied but coming from a source close by, spoke succinctly in soft tones not much above a loud whisper.

'I do not consider war neurosis to be a form of mental illness any more than I believe that but a handful of the three hundred and six Allied soldiers executed during the years of the Great War were cowards, malingers or deserters, or anything of the sort.'

'Surely this is a mental illness, sir?' a second voice suggested.

'In the instance of mental illness,' came the response, 'the cause of the dysfunction is rarely known, but in the case of war neurosis the cause is overtly obvious. I prefer to consider this condition not as an illness but as a wound, not of the flesh but of the psyche. Of the soul, if you will.'

The words seemed to echo. I wanted to move my head, but instinct told me to lie still, make no movement.

'The victim of war neurosis, more commonly referred to as shell shock, need not necessarily have become so wounded by the sounds of actual gunfire, explosions of grenades, whistling of artillery projectiles and the like. Receiving any terrible shock whilst in combat is sufficient to trigger the condition, subsequent events only exacerbating the situation. In time, the seemingly never-ending turmoil of war, the horrors of battle and ever-present threat of an imminent, violent and probably painful death, drive the victim into a state of unreality. He can no longer accept normality as he knew it, and lives in permanent fear. His surroundings are so appalling, so incomprehensibly terrifying, that they replace whatever he previously knew as normality. In short, he accepts his present situation as the norm.'

The voice paused. Tiny sounds, of hands moving or sheets of paper turning, came to me. A third voice spoke, from farther away.

'You speak of the patient as a victim, sir.'

'Indeed I do. A patient is someone who has received an injury, contracted a disease through no fault save that of chance, of nature, if you will. A victim is he who ails as a result of another's action.' The voice became lighthearted. 'We can hardly lay the blame for catching a cold on a general or his adjutant.'

There was a muted ripple of laughter.

'Yet we can blame the general for war neurosis.' The tone of the voice was now hard, accusatory, louder than before. 'It was he who subjected his men to relentless conditions of terror without release, without hope, without support. It was he who decided a man spend up to a month at a time in the trenches, sleeping in water fouled with blood and excrement, without so much as an hour's leave, the corpses of his erstwhile comrades hanging on the barbed wire above the trench, gnawn by rats and shredded by bullets and the wind. It was he who ordered attacks against enemy lines in the full knowledge they would achieve no military purpose whatsoever. Can a man who has been exposed to this vile inhumanity be called a patient? I think not.'

The voice paused and returned to its quieter tone.

'The victim'—the word was stressed—'has no escape from his predicament except into his own mind. He is aware of his surroundings, but he gradually becomes unable to relate to them. They are simply too terrifying and alien. He accepts them, but he tries to negate them. In vain. How can one ignore the bone that sticks out of the dugout wall, knowing it to be Sergeant Jones's femur or Corporal Smith's ulna? To fight these awful truths, the victim withdraws from reality into fantasy.'

'He displaces reality with a substitute,' a disjointed voice interrupted.

'Exactly! And these fantasies can take many forms. They may be hallucinations, dreams of better times and places. Or the victim may go into a state of denial. I know a private who refused to believe there was any such thing as a German. He stepped out of his trench, in broad daylight, walking towards the enemy lines. His comrades begged him to return. He kept walking, whistling as if strolling through meadows. Fifty yards into no-man's-land, he halted, turned to face his comrades and called out, "See, chums! They ain't here." He set off walking back.'

The room was silent.

'I know what you are thinking, but the Germans did not open fire. They must have been bemused. The following day, the private refused an order to fire. He saw no reason. There was, in his mind, no point in shooting at a non-existent enemy. He was instead shot in the head by the major in command of his unit. He is not one of the three hundred and six. They were afforded the mockery of a drumhead trial. The delusionist was not.'

Footsteps crossed the ceiling above my head, heavy at first, then soft as they reached a carpet, loud again at the far side of it. A chair briefly scraped on the boards.

'In extreme cases, the victim withdraws completely from reality to enter a state of semi-catalepsy. To remind you, this is a condition of self-imposed trance, with or without a loss of sensation and consciousness, sometimes accompanied by the maintenance of an abnormal or convoluted posture. One cannot know what fantasies exist in the mind of the cataleptic who has completely withdrawn. He lives in a world that is closed to us behind many doors, and it is up to us to find the keys and unlock those doors. If this proves beyond us we must, as thieves, attempt to pick the locks in the hope of somehow springing the mechanism. Unless we succeed, the victim will spend the rest of his existence self-excluded from human contact, as surely as if he were marooned upon a desert island.'

With the last dozen words, the voice drew nearer. I still did not move my head but studied the periphery of my field of view.

'Such a one is Alec Marquand. Twenty-six years old, he is single and has no physical injuries. A brief précis of his case notes is in your folders.'

There followed a shuffling sound and a long period of comparative silence.

A shadow fell across me.

'You may notice that his eyes are now open and have been for the last five minutes or so. He sees and hears. He also comprehends the world around him, even at this moment, despite his fixated stare. You are observing him in his deepest state of catalepsy. This condition comes and goes. At other times, he behaves normally, sits up, looks out of the window, reacts to external physical stimuli. He also draws pencil sketches, the subjects of which either are his fantastic world or hark back to his life before. . . . '

I turned my head. At the far end of the room was gathered a small group of men. They were cast in semi-shadow and, for a moment, I wondered if they were the throng that had been approaching me up the Strand. Much nearer to me was a figure dressed in white. A hand was on my shoulder. The other had been that which had pulverised the musket ball. I glanced up the coat to the face. It was looking down upon me, smiling benignly. Had it not been a man's face, I should have thought it was filled with love for me.

'Hello, Alec,' he said soothingly.

Not for the first time, and certainly not for the last, I firmed my resolve and held my peace.

8

Over the first mile, the track wove among rocks, clumps of wind-bent heather, patches of wild thyme and coarse tussocks of grass, gradually climbing and veering into a valley between two sheer-sided peaks, the summits of which were bare of vegetation. Just before we entered the valley, I glanced back. We had already climbed several hundred feet from the shore of the loch, the waters of which were rippled by the offshore breeze and the wake of the paddle steamer which was now out of sight around a headland, only a rapidly evaporating drift of smoke marking where it had been. On the far loch side, the sun was shining weakly through the clouds, catching the rocks and forest of pine trees that stretched down to the water's edge. I could just make out the jetty at which I had landed from the vessel plying fortnightly between Glasgow and Stornoway.

Quite soon, the track grew steeper as it approached the head of the valley. In a short distance, it began to double back upon itself in a series of hairpin bends as it ascended towards a pass between the mountains. The horses maintained a slow walk. I had noticed they were unshod and now understood why: with steel horseshoes, they would have slipped on the rocks and fallen to their deaths, taking us with them. In places, the side of the track was a sheer drop.

With a final, torturous bend, the track entered a small corrie and reached the pass, levelling out over a plateau about two hundred yards long. On either side were two ruined buildings, little more than low stone walls with a lone standing gable. Beside one was a pool of still, black water. A stiff wind blew through the pass. Lowry, the guide who had been sent to show me the route over the pass, reined his horse in.

'We'll rest the horses awhile,' he announced, dismounting and letting go of the reins of the packhorse he was leading. It was the first time he had spoken since we set off.

I slid from my saddle. My back was stiff and the inside of my calves ached. Looking around, I searched for something to which to tether the animal, yet there was nothing, not even a substantial bush.

'Let the beast free,' Lowry said. 'He'll go no further than the water.'

On either side of the pass, the two mountains rose into low clouds. I reckoned the plateau was at an altitude of about a thousand feet; the summits, where they disappeared into the mist, were at least another four hundred feet above us. Strewn around were jagged boulders that had broken off from the peaks, and patches of loose scree. Between them was bare rock with only a few indentations holding any semblance of soil, a few diminutive tufts of grass and tiny alpine plants clinging to them. Although the scene was bleak, it had a majesty.

'Does this place have a name?' I asked.

'It's called Bealach na Clachan.'

'What does that mean?'

Lowry nodded in the direction of the ruins. 'The Pass of the Kirks.'

'They're churches?' I replied, somewhat amazed.

'Just cells.'

'For whom?'

'For monks.'

I walked towards the nearest ruin. It might have been a deserted croft, the meagre home of a shepherd driven from his land by the inhospitality of the barren place or the whim of an absentee landlord.

At the foot of one of the gable ends was an alcove, half buried by soil and fallen rubble, that had once been a small hearth. The stone lintel above it bore the cracks of having been continuously heated and cooled; an iron bar hung at an angle, rusted through at one end, the wall scarred with a raw gash of iron oxide. It was as if the stone had been wounded and metallically bled. Life for these monks, I considered, had been ascetic in the extreme, a matter of hanging onto existence on the side of the mountain with nothing more than their fingernails and their faith.

Following me, Lowry added, 'They say Saint Maelrubha built them. He was an Irishman, son of King Niall of the Nine Hostages. He travelled here on a mission in the year 671. It was he who spread Christianity throughout the pagan highlands.'

'What became of them?' I asked.

'Like all things in the mountains,' Lowry answered, 'they had their time.' He looked up, scanning the sky and mountains. 'This wind'll blow fair for the rest of our journey.'

As if to prove the point, the mist around the summits thinned and a weak sun shone through, yet insufficient to cast shadows from the boulders. In the very far distance, I could just make out the sea.

Lowry walked over to the pool where the horses were standing, heads down, drinking. The wind rippled their manes. He knelt and, cupping water in his hands, also drank, the horses raising their heads as if in deference to him. I followed his example. The water was utterly tasteless and bitterly cold, making my teeth ache. When we had drunk, we sat on boulders while the horses continued to take their fill.

'How much farther have we to go?' I enquired.

'Three hours, maybe more. If the weather sets well,' Lowry replied. 'Have you a mind to bide long there?'

One of the horses moved away from the pool and started to half-heartedly tug at a tussock of grass.

'A month or two. Maybe a little longer.'

'They don't get trippers here, as a rule. Sometimes a climber.' Lowry glanced at the packhorse. 'You'll not be a climber, though?'

'No, I'm not a climber,' I confirmed. 'I'm an archaeologist.'

'I was of a mind that archaeologists worked in Egypt and suchlike.' Lowry said. 'Do you mind my asking what your business is in these parts?'

'I'm to carry out a survey of the brochs.'

'Aye, the brochs,' Lowry repeated.

There was a hint of distrust in his voice, as if he believed the information was being given merely to cover a greater and more calculated mission. He was a man old enough to remember the deviousness of those absentee landlords, the eviction of crofters from their meagre land and the destitution of the Highland peasantry.

'For Mr. McGillivray,' I volunteered.

This seemed to lay Lowry's fears, for he answered tersely, 'Aye, McGillivray. The laird's a fair man. There's no doubting that.'

He put his fingers to his lips and whistled. It was a high, almost inaudible note. The horses looked up and started to move towards us.

'We'd best be on our way.'

It was early evening when we arrived at Breakish, approaching the village along a narrow path clinging to the top of a low cliff running along the shore. The tide was on the turn, the sea smooth with a low swell gently rising and falling, twisting the weed to and fro as if in slow motion. There was virtually no breeze at sea level and the air was warm from the rocks which, towards the mid-afternoon, had become bathed in sunlight. Although we had at no time so much as trotted the horses, letting them walk at their own leisurely pace, the reins slack, the animals were slick with sweat, the scent of their bodies mingling with the iodine smell of the sea and the perfume of the wild thyme growing beside the path.

The village consisted of a dozen or so small, low crofts made of stone, several of them protected by turf roofs, three or four slate-roofed houses, a tiny church little more than a chapel surrounded by a graveyard dotted with headstones crudely fashioned from slabs of granite, and an inn which, incongruously, was whitewashed. Only the inn and one of the houses were two-storeyed. All the buildings stood round a semi-circular inlet, a headland affording protection from the sea. The four single-masted fishing boats, moored to a short quayside wall, were utterly motionless. No people were to be seen moving about. It might, I thought, have been a photograph were it not for the smoke rising from several of the chimneys and a cat sidling along the quay, sniffing occasionally at lobster pots and stains of fish offal on the stones.

Without instruction, the horses headed for the inn, halting before it and lowering their heads. While Lowry unburdened the packhorse, I entered the building to discover the landlord, a stocky man with a beard, sitting at a table in the parlour. Before him was a black morocco-bound ledger in which he was writing with a tortoiseshell-cased fountain pen. The large gold nib gleamed in the light of the lamp. Around him, on shelves, was stocked the merchandise of a general store. The scent of shag tobacco hung in the air.

I offered my hand. 'I'm Alec Marquand,' I introduced myself. 'You've had a letter from Mr. McGillivray about me?'

'If you've a mind to go to sea,' the innkeeper replied, rising from his chair, 'watch for the windlass. A tightening rope's sharper than the surgeon's knife.' He held out his right hand. Only the index and middle finger remained, the other two digits and his thumb missing. 'My name's Duncan Ogilvy.' He gripped my hand between his two surviving fingers. It was like being held in a pair of pliers. 'Welcome to Breakish. The laird's instructed me to aid you in your endeavours. If there's anything you should want for, just ask. At least good fortune left me able to hold my pen.' He nodded at the ledger. 'I'm writing up my story.'

'Your story?'

'I was second officer upon one of the laird's clippers. Cotton, piece goods and a wee box or two of illicit opium from Calcutta to Canton; silver, silk, tea and porcelain on the return. Lost my footing in a typhoon off the Paracels. Grabbed for the nearest rope. It was either that or a long sleep at the bottom of the South China Sea. It saved my life, but it charged me my fingers for the favour. Mr. McGillivray was good enough to keep me on in his service. He owns this inn and store. In fact, as I'm sure you're aware, he owns Breakish, every stick and stone of it.'

The room into which I was shown, my lodgings for the coming weeks, was on the upper floor. Large, it was sparsely furnished with a table and chair, bed and chest of drawers. The window commanded a view of the village, the little harbour and, in the distance, several low, dark islands settling into a light sea mist. A fire of peat blocks was burning in the grate, the dusty grey ash spilling over onto the slate hearthstone. No lights showed in any of the houses and it occurred to me, as I unpacked my clothes, that I had still yet to see any living person other than the innkeeper.

9

It might be summer, but today it is cold. A sharp wind is blowing across the gardens, tossing the branches of the oak about and stripping petals off the dahlias and roses, to scatter them along the path and trap them in drifts against the bottom of the brick wall. The sky is cloudy and presages rain. I am confined to my room, my life interrupted only by the routine of meals and the visit from the nurse with my pills.

Let me give you three names.

They will mean nothing to you. They are of men long since passed on, all but forgotten except in the annals of a family history, a box of faded letters and sepia photographs—a tarnished uniform button, perhaps; a bridge scoring pencil made out of a brass .303 cartridge case, a pressed colourless flower, a lock of hair tied with faded red cotton—kept in an attic or a dark cupboard, treasured by descendants, rarely opened or seen yet handed from generation to generation with the strict instruction never to be disregarded, never to be surrendered, always to be considered an object of pride. Regardless of what the history books might say . . .

First, I shall tell you of Edward Tanner. His friends may have called him Ed. Perhaps Ted. Who can say? I never knew him myself, yet I've lived with him for most of my life. For several weeks, he had suffered from dysentery, shitting himself empty every hour, on the hour, his stomach muscles sore and his arse as raw as a side of bacon. By mid-October, although his guts were settling down, thanks to liberal doses of Dr. J. Collis Browne's Chlorodyne tincture of morphine and chloroform, he had reached the end of the line. No doubt aided by the opiate, and dreaming of a girl he had known, or a village street he could visualise in such detail he could almost smell the honeysuckle, or a black mongrel he had last seen watching him from the platform of Westbury station as his train pulled out, with its head hung down and its tail wagging feebly on the dusty stones, he took off his uniform to replace it with a nondescript jacket, a shirt without a collar, and a pair of serge trousers. This was not an act of deliberate intention. It was a vain search for something normal in an abnormal world, where death hummed like an angry bee, the starlight was obliterated by magnesium and the morning mist could be laced with invisible strands of chlorine.

Once dressed, he walked away from wherever he was, bidding no one farewell, telling no one where he was going; he was uncertain of his destination himself, sure only that it was somewhere else and he was meant to be there. After a while, he was discovered and brought back, asked to explain himself. He could not. All he could say was that his nerves were shattered. No one listened. The officers charged him with desertion, and, at dawn on the twenty-fourth, he was shot by a firing squad. As he fell against the ropes that bound him, age thirty-three, he couldn't know how the world was spinning uncontrolled towards a madness he could never have envisaged in his wildest nightmares.

And then there are Alfred Longshaw and Albert Ingham. Fred and Bert? The Two Als to their workplace chums? They were clerks in the Salford Goods Yard of the Lancashire and Yorkshire Railway Company. In the middle of a summer's day, they sat on a flatbed wagon to eat their chunks of bread and cheese with onion and cauliflower pickle, drink their mugs of tea and talk of the county cricket team. After their evening shift ended with the 10:50 down train from Blackburn to Manchester Piccadilly, stopping at Bromley Cross and Bolton, they went to the pub together, downed their pints of bitter, played dominoes and darts and shove-'apenny, openly cheated each other at cribbage and sang music hall songs to a tuneless piano in the public bar played by the barmaid's uncle. During the long northern winters, they huddled in a track-side hut, heating cocoa in an enamel jug on a Valour stove with a mica firebox window, which filled the place with the fumes of burning paraffin.

When the time came, they willingly accepted King's Regulations as their mistress and joined the Third Manchester Pals or, more correctly, they were assigned to No. 11 Platoon, C Company, the Eighteenth Service Battalion of the Manchester Regiment. From the rain-polished streets of terraced houses and back alleys, never far from the sooty smell of locomotives and the boiled cabbage stench of poverty, they were to go to Egypt, see the pyramids and the Sphinx, buy a photograph of a naked girl with a feather boa looking in a mirror from a man in a fez, and watch the sun set over the Nile.

Yet it did not last. Within a month or two, they were in the ditches of northern France, dreaming of warm sand and Salford, listening for birdsong and hearing only a hymn that stuck in their heads. 'Praise, my soul, the King of Heaven . . . Slow to chide and swift to bless . . .' If they were quiet, they could hear voices singing it from afar. Bert thought it was the lads and lasses from the Charlestown Congregational Sunday School, in which he often taught the Scriptures, but Fred, a Catholic, said it was the male choir at St. Sebastian's in Pendleton; they argued about it, in the way that friends do when they know nothing will shake their companionship. Sometimes, standing sentry duty with a Lewis gun in a salient, they might have hummed it softly together. For them, the third verse must have had especial meaning: 'Frail as summer's flower we flourish; blows the wind and it is gone . . .'

It took a year to break them, strip them of their dignity, turn them into dissembling liars. They were simple men, unable to accept the enormity of their actions and incapable of justifying what they were being ordered to do in the name of king and country and God. They just could not go on. To kill had become anathema to them. As for Fred, he had also received a letter from one of those grimy Lancashire back streets that told of his wife's illness.

As they had always done, together, they fled, headed for the coast and stowed away aboard a Swedish coaster in Dieppe. Perhaps, they must have reasoned, they'd be home for Christmas. Yet they were discovered. Fred lied, said he was a Yankee.

On December 1, the two pals were shot by a squad of Pals: friends killing friends in the cause of a warped justice which none of them approved of yet they dared not question. 'Died of wounds,' read the obituary in the Salford paper.

They are nothing more than dead names now, worthy sons of loving fathers, mothers' prides and sweethearts' favourites, their bones lying under a foreign sod with no one giving a damn.

In the quiet hours, when my fellow St. Justinians are asleep or medicated into acquiescent calm and the night duty nurse is sitting at a desk in the main ward office, the lamp shining a forty-watt glow onto the pulp fiction paperback he is reading, I think of them.

I can see them, though I never knew them. They are looking straight at me as if into a camera, their regimental badges gleaming, the peaks of their caps down to their eyebrows, their tunics buttoned to the neck. One has his cap on not quite straight. They are clean-shaven, serious, determined to see it through. And they are surrounded as if by light shone through samite, as should be those who carry no blame.

10

About two miles to the east of Breakish stood the ruins of the broch of Dùn an Làmh Thoisgeal, approached by a narrow path that clung to the coastline, sometimes dipping to the rocky foreshore, at others running along the rim of the low cliffs where the mountains slid down to meet the sea. From the littoral rocks basking seals slid into the water at my approach. Herring gulls noisily took to the wing, riding the breeze before dipping to the surface of the sea fifty yards out, settling on the light swell and surveying me with that quizzical avian suspicion common to their species.

Surrounded by heather and scrub, the broch was a circular fifty-foot-high dry stone tower, the outer walls of which were slightly concave. On the seaward side, they remained intact almost to their original height, but the inland-facing quadrant had collapsed to a height of about twenty feet. Between the outer and inner walls, which had been constructed as concentric circles, was a gap about four feet wide, in places filled with a rough stone staircase spiralling into the dark recesses of narrow, windowless rooms and passages.

Before I could commence my study, I had to clear the heather and bracken away from within the structure, and set to with a short handled hedging hook I had borrowed from Ogilvy. It was a vicious and efficient tool, as sharp as a scythe, and it reminded me of the ornate bladed pikestaffs carried by Chinese warriors portrayed on early Q'ing dynasty vases. I found a primitive pleasure in swinging it from side to side, slashing through the undergrowth.

It took the better part of an hour to remove the cover from within the broch, laying bare a tumble of stones that had fallen inwards. I piled the cut brush ten yards off, wedging the larger bushes into crevices in the rocks so as to anchor them against the wind. This done, I stepped back and, sitting on a smooth boulder, took stock of the place.

Typically situated on a rocky outcrop at the foot of a valley running down to the shore, the broch commanded a position over a small plateau which ended in the low sea cliffs. The flat area, perhaps fifteen acres in extent, was visibly devoid of large rocks and had, I surmised, been cleared not only to build the tower but also to provide arable land and pasture. Yet there were, I noted, no signs of field boundaries or demarcatory ditches.

Taking a quarto notebook from my leather satchel, I balanced it on my knee and began to meticulously sketch the broch as it looked from the west, noting every detail of the structure, outlining as best I could every crevice and stone. This task completed, I climbed into the broch and drew every detail I felt of archaeological importance—the solid slab used as a lintel to the low entranceway, the crude steps rising through the cavity between the two walls, the flat stones projecting into what had been the hollow central atrium of the tower, which I assumed had been installed to take beams for supporting floors, a partial roof or internal hoardings.

As I worked, as the features of the place took shape upon the page, I found myself being drawn into contemplating the life of the broch dwellers. Like the adherents to Saint Maelrubha's rule, their life would have been tenuous and brutal. Whatever they wanted, or needed, would have had to be won from the elements, from an enemy that might be of flesh like themselves or made of nothing more than the wind that blasted in from the North Atlantic carrying ice on its back. If they had time to pray, their gods would be have been those of vengeance, retributive deities that, like them, carried spears and took no quarter. Had they the leisure to tell stories, their narratives would have consisted of glorious sagas of blood, epics of victories won, heads decapitated and enemies routed. I could almost hear their voices whispering from within the stones—*and he smote him with great might, and the defiler of women and consumer of children fell, and he struck him*

*again and again with his blade forged of Aira's steel until the earth was mud-
died with his blood . . .*

It was early afternoon by the time I finally finished my preliminary
drawings. The sun was by now high and warm, and a lazy heat
emanated off the stones. A number of sheep, allowed to range loose
on the mountainside, had wandered onto the plateau and were grazing the patches of short grass. While the ewes fed with their heads
down, a ram with curlicued horns stood sentry on a hillock, its head
turning from side to side as instinct dictated, watching for the wolves
that were long expunged.

Leaning against a boulder, I removed a parcel wrapped in cheesecloth from my satchel, cutting the cord with my pocketknife. The
contents had been provided by Ogilvy—several chunks of coarse
bread, half a dozen slices of lamb, an apple wrinkled from being
stored over the winter and some salt in a twist of paper. Beside the
packet was a bottle of stout with a porcelain stopper sealed with a
brown rubber washer. Loosening my shirt, I started to eat, the breeze
cool on my chest. I had not until now realised how hot I had become
clambering over the ruins.

For a while, I lay in the sun and closed my eyes. The breeze hissed
in the heather and, as the sheep drew nearer, I occasionally caught the
scent of their shaggy coats as the wool snagged on a clump. Finally,
however, my conscience got the better of me and I rose to my feet.
This was not, I told myself, a vacation. I no longer possessed the
undergraduate's luxury of time to waste. I had work to do, a schedule
to keep to, money to earn.

With my leather-cased measuring tape, a one-pound mallet, a ball
of white twine and a pocketful of small sharpened wooden pegs, I
set about marking out the interior of the broch into a grid of one-
yard squares. When the corner of a square coincided with a rock, I
tied a knot around a small stone and used that in lieu of a peg. These
marker rocks were not taken from within the broch; every stone
there had to be archaeologically accounted for. I collected these from
the hillock upon which the ram had stood. It occurred to me that
it might have been a spoil heap formed by stone picking on the

plateau, the removal of small stones intended to make ploughing easier. Certainly it was not a natural feature, but there was no way by which I could date it. The broch builders might have cleared the land, but, I knew from my research reading, they also lived by fishing and raiding, so may well not have been such ardent agriculturalists as to bother.

As I worked, it became apparent that the stones that had fallen into the central area of the broch were far too few in number to have made up the entire structure. I therefore concluded that whilst the structure had fallen in at various times, it had also been robbed. The stones, I was sure, would have been taken to build elsewhere. As Breakish was the nearest settlement—indeed, the only settlement for at least five miles in either direction, except for a few isolated and now abandoned crofts—I guessed that most of the buildings would contain at least some material carted from the broch.

This realisation pleased me. It would simplify my work. The stones upon which I was laying my grid would almost certainly have been disturbed by the stone robbers and would, therefore, not be important to my study. I could, I decided, remove them without too much fear of disturbing the archaeological record. So long as I made quite certain that the stones I took out were present in a random distribution and not a part of an internal structure, I would not be destroying anything of note.

Nevertheless, once the grid was finished, I mapped out on a careful diagram the position of every stone larger than a loaf of bread.

So engrossed was I in my work that I was not aware of the passing of time, the lengthening of the shadows and the cooling of the air. It was only when the sun started to dip behind one of the distant islands that I realised it was late and I would have to move fast if I were to get back to Breakish by nightfall.

Hastily I gathered up my belongings and, checking that none of the grid pegs had worked loose, set off at a quick pace, ever mindful in the gathering gloaming of where I put my foot. A slip from the path might not have killed me, but it could have invalided me out of my employment. Rain and a twisted ankle are the archaeologist's greatest enemies.

About halfway to the village, the path turned towards the sea, dropping down a steep rocky slope into which attempts had been made to cut rudimentary steps, perhaps by the builders of the broch. Water, seeping from a spring on the hillside, had worn the steps and made their surface slick. In my haste, I lost my footing and fell the last ten feet to the rocky foreshore, sharply barking my shin. For several minutes, I sat on a rock by a shallow pool filled with limp bladderwrack, rubbing the bone to disseminate the pain and cursing myself for my stupidity.

At first it did not register in my mind, but then, quite suddenly, I recognised an outline against the last light in the sky. It was on a low island about half a mile out to sea. Beyond a doubt, it was another broch. Not as tall as Dùn an Làmh Thoisgeal, it appeared to rise out of the sea perhaps fifty yards from the shore. I stared at it for some minutes before I realised it had been erected on an islet attached to the nearby island by a short causeway. This discovery greatly excited me. Island *dùns,* as they were known, were not uncommon in the Hebrides, but close to the Scottish mainland they were rare.

As I was rising to my feet to get my bearings on the island and a better view of the broch, something else caught my eye. On the island, close to where I assumed in the closing darkness the causeway to the broch began, a dim orange light momentarily flickered, then disappeared. I wondered if it were a lantern on a fishing boat at sea beyond the island, but it had seemed too insubstantial. It was more like a firebrand than a controlled light, and although I could not account for my reaction, I felt the hairs on the nape of my neck rise. It was, I thought romantically, as if the men of the broch were signalling to me across the aeons.

On reaching Breakish, I found Ogilvy standing at the door of his inn, looking out for me.

'I was feared you might have got yourself lost. Or had a mishap,' he said. 'You'd not be the first Sassenach to come to grief along the shore.'

'I slipped on the steps . . . ' I admitted.

'Aye! That's the place,' Ogilvy interrupted me. 'You'll see how the steps slope down? Cut during the '45 Rebellion. And the water. Directed there from the spring above. Cumberland's troops tumbled there and, as the column slowed, the Jacobites picked them off one by one with their muskets. It was a sweet revenge, for the bonnie prince, our beloved Charlie, had already been defeated at Culloden and was on the run.'

We entered the tap room, lit by the glow of the peat fire and two lamps with tall glass chimneys blackened with soot. I put my satchel down on one of the chairs.

'I've heard tell if you grub about in the stones of the shore, you can still find the lead balls,' Ogilvy continued, 'disfigured by hitting bone as well as stone. They've a saying here the sea ran red for three tides, and you'll not find many a man hereabouts that'd walk that way in the darkness.' He picked up a glass and held it under the wooden tap on a small keg resting in a bracket on the wall. 'You'll have a wee dram?'

'Yes,' I replied, 'thank you,' and I sat at the long table, sipping the whisky. It was smooth and had an aftertaste from the oak cask. Ogilvy took a seat across from me, a glass clenched between his two fingers.

'Aye!' Ogilvy went on. 'They've a mind around here the poor souls of the soldiers linger in the glen nearby and on the rocks. Some say they wave their ghostly lanterns to lure unsuspecting fisherfolk onto the rocks. Of course, you and I know that's rubbish. We're men of science, not of superstition. The glen's full of peat and the lights are ignis fatuus. Marsh gas. Methane self-combusting on the cool night air.'

The door opened and a boy of about twelve entered carrying a tray upon which stood two bowls of thick mutton broth.

'This'll be Jamie,' Ogilvy remarked. 'His mother sees to my needs and those of the few guests that stay from time to time. Say good evening to Mr. Marquand, lad.'

'Good evening, sir,' the boy said, placing the tray on the table between us.

When he had gone, Ogilvy explained, 'His mother's Beth. A

widow lady. Her husband was a fisherman. Lost at sea a year or two ago.' He raised an eyebrow. 'She'd like to see to all my needs, if you get my meaning.' Picking up his spoon, he continued, 'So, tell me about the broch.'

As we ate, I explained that brochs were circular fortified stone houses with tapering walls containing inner galleries, thought to initially date from the late Iron Age as an extension of the tradition of small stone fortress building, which itself was a development from the hill forts to be found in England. Constructed without the use of mortar, they were the architectural wonders of their day. Their use was thought to die out in the fifth century, but no one was certain of this: it was, I said, one of the questions I hoped to answer. Dùn an Làmh Thoisgeal, I remarked, was one of the better preserved.

'Have you an idea what the name means?' Ogilvy asked.

'*Dùn* is the Gaelic for a small fortress or fortification,' I said.

'Aye! It is, and *làmh*,' Ogilvy translated, 'means a hand, but it can also mean an attack. *Thoisgeal* means left or sinister. And the left hand is the unlucky hand. Except'—he held up his damaged right hand and grinned—'of course, in my case.'

'The fortress of the unlucky left hand,' I mused.

'Or of the sinister attack. But,' he added, 'in this context, I'm inclined to concur with your translation and believe it means the left hand, for the left hand is the one that does no good.'

At that moment, the door opened and Jamie returned to remove the bowls, Ogilvy asking him, 'Jamie, this gentleman's come here to study the brochs. Do you know what the brochs are?'

The boy nodded and said, 'The towers of stones, Mr. Ogilvy.'

'Och! You're a smart lad and that's no mistake. And would you know, he's spent his day at Dùn an Làmh Thoisgeal. What do you make of that then, Jamie?'

'I'd not like it.'

'Why not?'

'*Tannasg*!' he exclaimed, and he quickly gathered up the bowls, avoiding my eye.

'*Tannasg*?' I queried after the boy had gone.

'Ghosts,' Ogilvy explained. 'Will-o'-the-wisps. Phantoms. Evil spirits. Call them what you will. It's said the *dùn*'s their home, that you can hear them of a winter's night when the gales blow. Of course, that might be the wind howling through the crevices. Then again, it might not. Whatever the case, they say there was evil done there.'

'Do you believe that?'

'Who can say what's happened in the dark hours of history when the chroniclers were sleeping?'

'The *tannasg* may account for something I saw on my way back,' I ventured, smiling.

'Indeed?' Ogilvy answered. 'You've not been here but a day or two and you're already turning into a credulous soul like the others hereabouts.'

'It was a red flame, like a fire,' I said.

'They say that Cumberland's soldiers' lanterns have a faint blue flame.'

'It wasn't on the peat moor above the broch or the path,' I said, 'but on that low nearby island.'

'Was it now?' Ogilvy responded thoughtfully.

'There's a broch on the island,' I went on, 'standing on an outcrop of rock in the sea, approached by a brief causeway.'

'And I suppose you'll be wanting to visit it?'

'Yes, if I can.'

'I suggest,' Ogilvy said, 'you put it from your mind. It'll not be easy. The tides rip by the island and there's no landing place. And Mr. McGillivray's not the laird over there. Your commission's to study only the brochs on his land, is it not?'

'I should still like to go there,' I replied.

'There's few'll take you.'

'Can you find me someone?' I asked.

'I'll enquire for you,' Ogilvy responded, 'but the fear of the place is great in Breakish.'

'Of the currents?' I enquired. 'Or the spirits?'

'Both,' he said matter-of-factly. 'And the rocks. Only a wee boat can manoeuvre ashore.'

'Who owns the island?' I persisted. 'I shall need to seek their permission.'

'No one owns it.'

I found this hard to believe and replied, 'Surely someone has the right of possession . . .'

'It's in its own possession.'

Ogilvy stood up to pour himself another glass of whisky.

'On the navigation charts for these waters,' he went on, 'the island's called Eilean Tosdach.'

'Meaning?'

'The Island of Silence. Yet there are those about here as call it Eilean Donas.'

'*Donas?*'

'Evil,' Ogilvy said bluntly, holding his glass under the tap on the keg. 'They say if you step on Eilean Tosdach, you'll not come back. It's a place of no return. They say the silence'll swallow you up.'

'These, I assume, are the same people who are lured onto the rocks by spirit lights . . . ' I began, slightly mockingly.

'No,' Ogilvy cut in. 'These are canny folk who are wise enough to pay heed to something they do not fully ken.'

11

I believe I may have what some radical psychiatrists call a residual memory. There is, left over on the bottom of the pool of my present existence, the silt of a previous life. Perhaps lives; who can say? These recollections do not so much concern people whom I have known but places which I suppose I must have visited. They invariably seem strange and yet, at the same time, uncomfortably familiar.

At times, these reminiscences come upon me like a pickpocket, with speed yet stealth, reaching into me without my being at first aware that they are present. It is only when I realise they are touching me that they make themselves known and carry me off on an involuntary yet never reluctant journey.

Usually, they arrive about an hour after I have taken a certain medication. Given to me only three times a week, it is a capsule no larger than a chickpea, coloured chrome yellow and coated with a hard shell of sugar. The coating, I assume, takes a while to dissolve, hence the time lapse between swallowing it and my departure.

It is said that drugs do not give access to new worlds; they simply open doors to those that already exist within us, veiled and unfrequented. It is only a matter of prying apart the padlocked box in which imagination has stored its seed corn. Yet as it is claimed imagination is constructed of the bricks of experience, it must therefore follow that whatever journey one embarks upon, it is somehow based upon what one has lived.

As usual, my lunch was served to me at ten minutes past one. The timing seldom varies more than a few minutes either side of this. I ate most of it: despite the fact that we live in a secular world, the *chef d'hôpital* still serves fish on Fridays. Or maybe he only does this for me, not knowing my religion and being keen to accommodate me in my silence on the off-chance I might be a staunch follower of Rome. Today, I was given a fillet of plaice poached in milk and butter, accompanied by a dozen crisply cooked *mangetout*. It was tasty and I ate everything but the grey skin of the fish marked with deep red spots like piscatorial stigmata. The dessert was custard and a sliced banana which I did not touch.

Shortly after my tray was removed, the nurse entered my room. Her name is Sister Cynthia. This is not information she has volunteered herself. A name badge on her breast, above where her nurse's watch is pinned, gives it. She is young, in her early twenties, not long qualified. Life is still full of potential for her, yet to be sullied by failure or sadness.

'Hello, Alec,' she greeted me cheerfully. 'Did you enjoy your lunch?' Her question was rhetorical: she expected no response from me, and I gave her none.

She busied herself about my room, smoothing creases in the cover of my bed, emptying the stale water in my glass and refilling it from a blue plastic bottle, adjusting the picture on the wall. Every so often, she cast a sideways glance at me.

'Time for your medicine,' she announced at last, stepping back to ensure the picture was straight.

From a dispensing trolley outside my door she brought a cod liver oil pill and the yellow capsule. Very gently, she raised my hand, placing in it a small plastic container holding the medicine, then fetched the glass of fresh water.

'Are we ready?'

I waited a moment before I slowly raised the cup to my lips. It was not procrastination on my part. I have all the time in the world. She put the glass to my lips. I took a sip and swallowed.

'All gone?' she asked.

She never grants me the indignity, as I have seen her do to other inmates, of opening my mouth to make sure. For some reason, she trusts me.

'Now, are you comfortable, Alec?' She reached down my back and, easing me forwards a few inches, rearranged the cushions in the armchair. 'I'll be back later to see how you're getting along.'

When she was gone, I closed my eyes, not to sleep but to wait.

It was not long before I felt myself slipping.

At first, I saw only bright colours marbling before my eyes, mixing like smoke curling in a beam of kaleidoscopic light. Gradually, this dissolved into a scene of a parched grassy plain under a brassy sun, the skyline rimmed with dark forest behind which, far away, a range of low hills shimmered in a heat haze. In the centre of the plain stood a ruined palace. Its walls were crumbling; several of its domed roofs were perforated with jagged holes, whilst a minaret in the centre leaned at an angle. I knew, although there were no means by which the information could have reached me, that the damage had been caused not by war but by an earthquake.

I drew closer. I was not on foot, nor was I riding a horse or vehicle, yet I came upon the palace at some speed. Near to it, I saw that the whole complex was surrounded by a curtain wall with battlements. To the west, the outer perimeter ran along the edge of a moat filled with stagnant water over which hovered huge emerald green-and-black dragonflies the size of small birds, whilst to the east there stood a pavilion looking out over the plain.

This structure was not a lookout or watchtower but clearly a building of pleasure. The roof, which had not suffered from the ravages of time and tectonics as badly as the others, was ornate, with a pointed dome reminiscent of the onion-shaped churches of Bavaria. On the pinnacle was a weather vane shaped liked a new crescent moon lying upon its back. At some time in the past, it had been gilded, as fragments of gold leaf still adhered to it and caught the sun. The six pillars still bore fragments of plaster which must have once been painted vermilion. Within the pavilion was a raised platform upon which the potentate of the palace must have lounged on delicately embroidered cushions, being fed dates from Arabia by handmaidens dressed in pearlescent silk.

More slowly now, I approached the walls to find a heavy wooden door knocked off its hinges and scarred by termites. Ghost-like, unaware of my feet touching the ground, I glided through the portal to arrive in a large courtyard to one side of which were steps rising to the pavilion. Ascending these, I reached the platform and looked out across the plain.

It was a scene that might have provided inspiration for a landscape study of the Garden of Eden. The seered grass teemed with animals— secretive deer moved leisurely through the landscape, grazing here and there between stands of ringal bamboo; peacocks strutted in courting circles, their tail feathers spread and vibrating as if charged with static; idle buffalo sat in mud wallows in a swampy area, chewing the cud and fanning their ears; macaques sauntered here and there, picking at the ground with their nimble fingers.

Suddenly, one of the deer raised its head and issued a short, sharp barking sound, as an excited terrier might on seeing a rat. On the instant, all the deer looked up in unison. The macaques began to chatter agitatedly to one another, the females picking up their infants and clutching them to their breasts. A few of the larger youngsters jumped onto their parents' backs, gripping tufts of fur as a jockey might the reins. The peacocks lowered their fans and ran through the grass. The buffalo stopped masticating, and one stood up, its flanks caked with dark mud that fell off in clots to thump onto the swampy ground. They must have been several hundred yards away, yet I could hear the thud.

It was then I saw the tiger. It was moving forward on its belly, infinitesimally slowly, barely visible in the dry grass. Its eyes were intently fixed on the standing buffalo, which raised its head to better test the air. Its flopping ears moved to and fro, trying to discern the slightest sound. The other buffalo clumsily got up. All of them faced in the direction of the tiger's advance.

By now, from my elevated position, I could see the tiger quite clearly. It was not fully grown, its coat as pristine and as colourful as a newly emerged butterfly's wings. Between the sharply defined black stripes, the fur was russet and gold. It moved by dragging itself forward with its front paws, the back legs tucked in and pushing. Behind, its tail stretched out, the black tip twitching slightly.

Perhaps it was the white signal flashes of fur on its ears, perhaps the tail, perhaps a taste of tiger on the air: whatever spooked them, the buffalo, as one, turned and stampeded away. They ran like old men, their backs rising and falling, their hooves kicking up first the mud of their wallow, then, as they reached solid ground, a cloud of dust that obscured their flight.

Thwarted, the tiger showed itself. The macaques ran pell-mell for the trees, shinning up the trunks. The deer followed the example of the buffalo, melting away into the forest. The peacocks took to the wing, flying in their ungainly fashion up to the walls of the palace, where they landed and began to preen themselves, confident and supremely arrogant.

I descended the steps to the courtyard. This time, I could feel the soles of my bare feet on the stone, hot at the top and cooler below in the shadow. I had no idea where I was going, but something told me I had a purpose. Diagonally across the courtyard was an archway. Beyond it was a durbar room, the roof caved in, and yet the floor, paved with pristine glazed tiles in geometrical patterns, was curiously devoid of any rubble. Without knowing why, I set off across it, heading for the rajah's throne, a large and ornately carved chair standing on a low plinth.

Just as I reached the middle of the room, I felt I was being watched and, stopping, looked round. In the archway stood the tiger. Its ears were flat, its tail flicking from side to side, its upper lips drawn back in a silent snarl and its teeth unblunted by age and killing.

I started to run. Now, I found the floor to be thickly covered in a débris of shattered roofing tiles, rotting beams, smashed furniture and twists of soiled damask. Here and there, weeds were pushing up from deep, uneven cracks in the floor which only moments before had been undamaged. Ahead of me a tapestry, shredded by the wind and termites, hung on the wall.

The tiger did not leap but continued to follow me, its head lowered, its every movement measured, its huge pugs making no sound on the loose rubble.

In less than ten steps, I realised I was cornered. The only door into the room was that through which both I and the tiger had entered. I halted and faced about. Where there had been one tiger there were now three, fanned out as if, in some instinctive feline way, they knew to block my only escape route. I could smell their breath, the scent of corruption.

Maybe, I reasoned, if I was to get behind the tapestry, they might think I had got away. Very slowly, so as not to prompt a charge, I began to step backwards. Reaching the edge of the tapestry, I was about to slip into its protection when it was flung aside to reveal a low door. It was open and standing it in and beckoning to me was a beautiful young woman dressed in a shimmering dark blue sari shot through with silver and gold threads.

The tigers saw her and emitted a deep purr of rage. She beckoned to me. I threw caution to the wind and ran. Infuriated at being robbed of their quarry, the tigers leapt. I stumbled through the door. The girl slammed it shut. The tigers, unable to brake their leap, smashed heavily into the other side of the door. The wood held.

Beckoning to me once again, the girl set off down a passage. I followed her. She stepped lightly, her feet encased in jewelled slippers: her bare shoulder was smooth, her sleek black hair hanging straight down her back to her waist.

The passage was enclosed in stone walls with a vaulted roof. There were no lanterns to guide our way and yet it was light. We reached a junction. She paused, as if to get her bearings, then set off down the right-hand way. Breathless, I followed her. At last, we came to another door, identical to that which had cut me off from the tigers. She clasped the handle and turned it, signalling me past her. I went through the door to find myself in my room in St. Justin's.

'Thank you,' I said.

The words seemed singularly inappropriate considering she had saved my life. I wanted to be more effusive yet somehow could not. Instead, I decided I should be gallant and at least kiss her hand. Turning, I saw her standing in the doorway. Yet, now, she was a crone, bent and wizened, bedecked in black rags. Upon her feet she still wore the same slippers, but the jewels had been cut or fallen off.

She smiled at me, her teeth grey and her lips bloodless. Then, still smiling, she slowly closed the door, the latch snapping softly shut.

My room was almost as I had left it. On top of the chest of drawers were my hairbrush and comb. The upright chair had my jacket draped over it. The only change was that it was now night and Sister Cynthia had been in, turned on the light by the bed and draped a tartan blanket over my knees.

It was good to return, but I was a little puzzled. I have never been to a far-fetched land of tigers and peacocks and yet I realised I had seen the palace, in this life. Or, to be more accurate, I had seen a place very much like it, in ruins and filled with unimaginable terror.

12

I woke an hour after sunrise to find Ogilvy already up and busy in the parlour, cutting the bread that had baked overnight in the oven, warmed by embers from the fire. The room was filled with the perfume of freshly risen dough.

'You've a fair day for your little expedition,' he said, folding thick wedges of bread over slices of hard cheese to fashion crude sandwiches, placing them in a small canvas sack with a hard, barely ripe pear.

'You've found someone to take me out?' I asked, delighted at the prospect.

I looked out of the window. The sun, already clear of the mountains behind Breakish, was coruscating upon the sea. On the horizon, those of the outer islands were etched against the western sky. The only clouds I could see were gathered above their summits, presaging rain on the easterly slopes in the late afternoon. The sea was smooth, with only surface ripples to catch the clean early morning light.

'Aye,' he replied, 'someone who needs the money more than most.' Cutting into the wedge of cheese, he added, 'There's not a chance I can dissuade you, I suppose?'

'None!' I exclaimed lightly. 'The pursuit of scholarship and the attainment of truth . . .'

'I thought as much and have arrived at the conclusion it's better I aid you than try to hamper you. That way lies a foolishness we could both live to rue. And, after all's said and done, you never know what valuable truths you might be finding.'

'Quite so!' I concurred.

He put down the serrated bread knife and pulled from his pocket a small apothecary's tincture bottle, made of dark blue glass, with the stopper secured in place by a leather thong. Holding it out between his two fingers, he said, 'You'll be needing this out on the water.'

'What is it?' I asked, accepting the bottle and noting the word Poison embossed on the glass.

'I was mindful of it last night, writing my story,' Ogilvy replied. 'I bought that wee bottle in a ships' chandler's in Tilbury. Must be thirty years ago. It was just before I took my first voyage to warmer climes. It cost me a florin and that was when I was only earning seven shillings a week. Yet it saved my life, time and time again.'

I shook the bottle. It contained an opaque, semi-viscous liquid.

'The sea's a perilous place, even when the waters are as still as stone. It's not only tides and currents you have to have a mind to.' Ogilvy nodded at the bottle. 'Coconut oil. You'll be needing that. Even as far north as bonnie Scotland, the sun can flay you.'

'Sunburn?' I ventured.

'Sunburn,' Ogilvy conceded. 'I've seen the skin peel off men like wallpaper in a damp room. A fire can do no more harm.' He poured some salt into a twist of paper, adding it to the sack of food. 'That's not for flavouring. It'll replace what you lose in your sweat. A man's done for without salt.' He pushed the sack towards me. 'You bide my warning,' he stressed, not releasing the bag. 'The sun can kill you. And,' he added, 'when you get to your destination, watch out for yourself.'

I smiled, assuming this to be a warning in jest, yet Ogilvy was serious and I felt somewhat foolish to seem to dismiss his advice.

'Thank you, I will,' I assured him, somewhat cowed by my folly and holding up the little bottle.

Half an hour later, I approached the quay alongside which lay the small vessel Ogilvy had hired to take me to the island. It looked frail, too insubstantial for use in northern seas, being little more than a rowing boat with a short mast carrying a square sail rolled tightly onto a spar. Standing by the worn mooring post to which the vessel was tied was the boy, Jamie.

'Good morning, Jamie,' I greeted him.

He nodded but made no other response. Taking my satchel and the sack of food, he placed them in the bottom of the boat beside two wicker crab pots and a folded fishing net.

Once we were in the little boat, the boy cast off the mooring rope and let the boat drift away from the quay. The tide was on the turn, the sea smooth, with no discernible currents. For a quarter of an hour, the boy rowed the craft out from the shore. The sun sparkled on the water. Already it was hot, the rays seeming to be concentrated by the water as if through a magnifying glass. I rubbed the coconut oil on my face and arms. It had a musty smell to it, like that of old, damp wood.

Half a mile out, a light offshore breeze struck up. The boy stowed the oars and rowlocks, hauled up the sail and settled himself at the tiller, taking a southerly course. The boat moved forward, gradually accelerating, cutting a crisp wake through the flat water.

Neither of us spoke. The boy seemed self-contained and withdrawn, unwilling to converse, and I respected his silence. Instead, I sat forward of the mast and watched as the coast slid by, looking out to recognise waypoints on the path to Dùn an Làmh Thoisgeal but only positively identifying the treacherous steps.

Gradually, the outline of the island rose from the sea, coloured in different hues of grey according to the undergrowth or the rocks. I preferred to think of it as Eilean Tosdach, rather than Eilean Donas. I could not see how such a tiny shard of land could be the repository of sufficient evil as to warrant that name. The island seemed innocuous, of little interest save, perhaps, to botanists, marine biologists and archaeologists like myself.

The boy steered for the channel between the island and the coast. The tide now running, the current moving through the strait was in our favour, and he lowered the sail. I glanced at my watch and was surprised to note our journey had taken over an hour.

I had assumed Jamie was going to drop me off near the island *dùn*, from where I believed the broch builders must have come and gone, but we sped past it.

'Can we not go ashore at this end of the island?' I enquired.

'We'd best go further, sir,' he opined without offering a reason.

The little craft ran along the entire length of Eilean Tosdach, the rocky shore offering not so much as the least possibility of a landing site.

As the southern tip of the island came level, the boy swung the tiller hard over. The boat leaned sharply to one side, the momentum gained from the current keeping it moving forwards. It looked as if we were heading straight for the rocks and I grew anxious, praying that the boy knew what he was doing. Yet, as we came almost onto the rocks, so close I could see the sharp barnacles, I realised there was a tiny narrow cove, not much over thirty feet across, hidden behind a natural breakwater.

'Well done, Jamie!' I exclaimed as the boat rapidly slowed.

The boy half-smiled at the compliment and said, 'This'll be your place, sir.'

Although there was a shingle bank up which he could have run the boat, the boy chose to bring it alongside a flat rock shelf into which had been sunk, at some distance time, an iron ring. It was now rusted firm to its shackle.

I picked up my satchel and tossed it onto the rock.

'Are you coming with me, Jamie?'

'I'll abide in the boat, sir.'

I lifted myself ashore and looked down at him.

'I would certainly welcome your company,' I said, adding, 'There is nothing to be afraid of.'

'We've to be away on the rising tide, sir,' the boy stated with adult authority, ignoring my invitation.

'Three o'clock?' I suggested.

'Aye,' the boy concurred. 'Will you push me off, sir?'

'You're not staying here?' I replied, surprised that the boy was not going to wait in the boat, perhaps tying it up to the iron ring.

'I'd rather be away, sir. But you need not fret. I'll be here on the hour to take you up.'

Obliging him, I pushed the prow of the boat with my foot. It glided backwards out of the cove. The boy gave a brief wave, turning the tiller and picking up the current. Immediately the boat gathered speed, heading southwards.

As I watched it go I suddenly felt apprehensive, as if I had been marooned. What if, I considered, the boy was unable to return, to get his little vessel into the cove. What if something happened to him during the day? No sooner had the thoughts come, however, than I realised how illogical they were. The boy was obviously adept at handling the boat: his mother would hardly have permitted him to undertake the task had she no confidence in him. Besides, Ogilvy and, no doubt, by now most of the population of Breakish knew where I was. If I did not return, someone else would come to find me. Shouldering my satchel, I set off up the slight rise from the shore. Only at the top did I look back. To my consternation, the boat was nowhere to be seen.

The island was covered in low scrub, but, to my surprise, I found a narrow and intermittent—yet well-worn—path which, from the occasional pellets of dung that littered it, I guessed had been made by sheep. I had not expected to find any livestock on the island, and as I walked I wondered if they might have been descended from the beasts kept by the broch builders. It was a quixotic notion.

The path ran along the leeward side of the island, just below the skyline of the spinal ridge that stretched from north to south. Here and there, it deviated from its course to skirt boulders or outcrops of rock, but otherwise it seemed to follow the same contour. In places, it was heavy going, for the path all but disappeared in the scrub and I had to push my way through knee-high bushes, gnarled and bent by Atlantic storms.

Eventually, I reached the start of the causeway that led out to the broch and paused to survey it. It was made of stones piled together with the flatter on top, forming an uneven pavement. As I was about to set out upon it, something erupted from the cover at my feet, startling me and setting my heart racing. I jumped back with as much alacrity as I might had it been a venomous snake. It was a rabbit: the droppings I had believed to be those of sheep, I now recognised, must have been leporine. Shaken by its sudden flight, I laughed aloud at my timidity and started to cross the causeway.

The broch was characteristically circular, the walls not more than fifteen feet high at best, yet they were complete, the single main entrance not facing the causeway but out to sea, offering additional protection against invasion. Within, the layout of rooms was evident from the stone partitioning, and the steps built into the outer walls rose to a sort of rampart. Climbing to it, I realised that this broch had probably never been taller. It seemed not to have been erected as a defensive structure but more as a watchtower or lookout, standing guard over the approach to the island. If, I reasoned, this was the case, then there must have been a settlement elsewhere on the island, perhaps a larger, defensive broch.

For several hours, I measured the ruin, drew sketches and diagrams of its salient features and made notes. At last, satisfied that I had done all I could without actually excavating the site, I packed up my satchel, returning to the rampart where I sat on the low outer wall. Feeling the sun hot on my face, I re-applied the coconut oil then, taking out the food Ogilvy had prepared for me, started to eat, quartering the pear with my clasp knife and sipping water from a beer bottle. It was lukewarm from being in my satchel. In deference to my host and his advice, I even dipped my finger in the salt and sucked it off, finding the bitterness refreshing.

As I ate, I gazed out to sea, trying to imagine what threat the broch builders had faced. They had lived here long before the emergence of raiding Norsemen and must, I thought, have sought to defend themselves from neighbouring tribes or clans rather than maritime invasion. Looking at the sea tired my eyes, so I turned my attention to the island at the end of the causeway. If this broch was a lookout post, then it followed that it might have been within view of the settlement it was guarding.

Carefully I studied the hillside and the end slope of the island's dorsal ridge. The sun was high, it being not long after noon, and there were few shadows. This made identifying features difficult. It was always easier to see patterns on the ground when the shadows were long. Yet an outcrop of boulders drew my attention. Although most had clearly tumbled at random, a few seemed to me to have been positioned by design rather than by chance. This, I knew, could mean that they had been either tipped or rolled there deliberately or were indicative of a collapsed structure that lay behind them, beyond my vision.

Almost without recognising it, my eye was drawn by a movement. It was slight, measured, cautious. A wary rabbit, perhaps. It was a moment before I realised it was a person hiding in the scatter of boulders. The motion had been their head, ducking down.

For several minutes, I scrutinised the rocks. The head appeared again, some yards off to the right, peeking round the base of a boulder. It was too far away to discern the features clearly, but I assumed it was the boy. Having plucked up his courage, he must have landed on the island out of curiosity to see what the Englishman was doing: or, alternatively, he had arrived to chivvy me along. It was nearing the time when I would have to set off back down the island to make my rendezvous with him and the tide race.

I waved. The head instantly vanished.

'It's all right, Jamie!' I called out. 'I'm on my way now.'

Packing my satchel and wearing it with the strap across my chest like a bandoleer, I set off down the broch and across the causeway, keeping my eye on the outcrop. There was no further sign of the boy's presence, so I assumed the lad had doubled back in the direction of the landing point.

Although, logically, I knew the head must have been Jamie's, it still unnerved me slightly. As I walked, I became conscious that my step was quickening. I recalled, then, the orange light that had first brought the island to my attention. An involuntary chill ran down my spine.

The bushes twenty feet from the path shivered. Rising out of the scrub was a human form. Desperately I swung my satchel behind my back, out of the way of my arms and in readiness to defend myself. Yet the other did not attack me. It stood quite still, the sun above it casting it in a narrow shadow. It was dressed in a kind of brown sackcloth coat, without buttons, a dark woollen undergarment showing through the open front. The sleeves were long and rolled back at the cuff. From the waist down, it seemed to be wearing a lengthy kilt, dyed grey. Its hair was long and tangled in matted curls which shone like metal in the hot sun.

For some seconds the figure watched me before moving away, walking backwards with slow, small steps, always facing me. There was something astonishingly primeval in its movement. Despite it standing upright, I was reminded of the way a cat moves away from a dog, every muscle tight, its eyes not moving from the threat.

'I'm sorry I startled you,' I said, acutely aware of the irony in my remark: the figure had clearly had the advantage.

At the sound of my voice, it froze.

I took one step towards it. Instantly it fled, running fast over the rocks, moving with a bestial agility.

'Wait!' I called out, and I set off in pursuit, my fear evaporating.

It was hard going. The ground was rough, the scrub snatching at me, the rocks under my boots slippery with water leaking from springs in the hillside. Twice, I stumbled. After a hundred yards, having lost sight of the figure, which had passed over the line of the ridge, I gave up and halted at a spring. My head pounded and my mouth was dry from both the exertion and my initial terror. Bending to the water I saw, in the mud, the fresh imprint of a bare human foot, the water still oozing into it.

Gaining my breath, I set off back down to the path at a stiff pace, aware that both time and tide were now pressing. I had not gone two hundred yards when the figure re-appeared standing on a sheer rock above the path, not ten feet from it. I stopped. The figure had removed its coat. It was slimly built. What I had assumed was a kilt was, I now saw, a sort of loose smock reaching down to the ankles. From beneath the hem protruded two sets of prehensile toes that gripped the edge of the sheer rock as a diver's might the end of a diving plank.

Assessing that the figure felt protected by the sheer rock, I decided to approach nearer and walked slowly on, keeping my hands in full view in the hope that this might be interpreted as not posing a threat.

When I was not quite beneath the rock face, I halted again. The figure was motionless, looking down upon me, the face in shadow, the long hair hanging down on either side.

'I don't mean any harm,' I ventured, keeping my voice soft and low, unthreatening. 'I'm an archaeologist. I've just come to study the broch.'

The figure still made no reply but leaned forward a little, at the same time sweeping its hair aside and back over its shoulder.

I caught my breath. The face looking down upon me was that of an exquisitely beautiful young woman. Her eyes were dark, her features fine, her skin white, as if the sun and salt-laden wind had never touched it. She reminded me of the paintings of the Pre-Raphaelites, of girls with flesh the colour and translucence of funereal alabaster, their faces ringed with innocence.

'What's your name?' I asked.

She looked at me, her head angled slightly as if the better to catch my words.

'I'm Alec. What's your name? Do you live here on the island?'

Her lips parted, but instead of speaking she growled. It was the low, sustained snarl of a bitch defending its puppies.

A rush of terror ran through me. I was immediately afraid but could not understand why. I was in no danger. She was a girl, in her late teens. I was older than her, heavier than her, stronger than her. Nevertheless, I moved my hand down towards my pocket in which I had put my knife.

The moment my hand entered my pocket, she was gone. I did not hear her go. She simply vanished, dematerialised.

I continued on my way at a jog, wanting not only to be on time at my rendezvous with Jamie but also to put as much distance as I could between myself and the girl. Her beauty had struck me, yet she also terrified me.

At the entrance to the cove, the boy was sitting in the boat a few feet off the rocks. When he spied me, he sculled the craft in, and I scrambled on board, a sense of relief washing over me. In a matter of minutes, we were out in the tidal race, the sail up to give us more speed. In less than a quarter of an hour, we had sailed the length of the island and were heading for Breakish.

In the bottom of the boat, one of the wicker traps was filled with a dozen or so large crabs, blowing bubbles of air and clicking, their pincers wound round with twine. Next to them, already gutted, were several large herring.

'You've had a good day,' I remarked to instigate a conversation.

'Aye, sir.'

'Will you sell me one of your crabs?'

'Mr. Ogilvy's accounted for all of them, sir.'

'What will he do with them?'

'You'll be getting one for your tea, sir. The rest he'll sell to the fishermen from Kyle.'

With the conversation under way, I asked, 'Tell me, Jamie, do you believe in the ghosts that live on Eilean Tosdach?'

The boy did not immediately answer me. Breakish was coming in sight and he busied himself lowering the sail.

'You know, Jamie,' I pressed him. 'The *tannasg*.'

Holding the tiller steady in the current, the boy looked me in the face and replied, 'You've seen one, sir, have you not?'

13

What do I, who have no past—at least, no immediate past, and that is what counts—need of the world? I have at my fingertips the universe of the garden.

Whenever the weather is set fair, those patients deemed not to be of undue risk to the others or themselves are permitted access to the grounds. Those on crutches, confined to wheelchairs, or, to be charitable, no longer occupying all the rooms of their mind, are attended by a nurse or orderly. The remainder can wander as they please at, they think, their own leisure. However, one or two members of staff keep watch from the terrace, eternally vigilant like schoolmistresses on playground duty.

During these hours of comparative liberty, I always choose either to walk the pathways through the flower beds and shrubberies or to sit under the shade of the large oak, the grass sparse under its canopy, the earthy humus warm and dry, scattered with the husks of the previous season's acorns and a litter of twigs. My favourite position is between two buttress roots, gnarled and worn to a polish. As if they were the sides of an armchair, they hold me in place.

It is good to have boundaries, to know one's limitations, to be aware of one's position in the order of things. That, I have decided, is another aspect of my presence that confounds the staff: they cannot understand how I can be contented in my silence.

A number of my fellow inmates are lost in their discontent. Some cry out, bestially, some moan and rock backwards and forwards with the frustration of elephants in a concrete pit at the zoo, their arms swinging loose, like trunks. Others are violent and forever pushing at the limits of their existence, as if trying to escape, to free themselves.

I, who have seen pain, felt sorrow, suffered true incarceration, react differently. I sit tight, within myself, taking things as they come and accepting them as they are.

The garden gives me all I need. It has beauty, tranquillity, boundaries I know and am willing to be contained within. It has a life, a vibrancy that cannot be affected or destroyed, a stability in that greater universe of chaos that lies without, from which I have divorced myself.

Despite this insularity, the garden can still hold surprises. Today, for example, whilst walking in the garden, I found a hedgehog in one of the shrubberies.

Quite possibly, it has been here all along, one of a small colony of its kind that has gone undiscovered ever since the walls were built. Certainly I cannot reason how it might have just arrived, for the security here is tight, there are no gates to the outside and hedgehogs do not, to the best of my knowledge, tunnel. Furthermore, there are plenty of places in which it and its comrades may have hidden—the dark corners of the shrubberies, up against the walls, the compost heaps behind the gardener's potting and toolshed, the crannies of the various rockeries.

At the moment I first saw the creature, it was routing about in the litter beneath a rhododendron bush, turning leaves over with its snout, pausing occasionally to investigate a stone. I watched it for some time before Sister Cynthia, seeing me standing immobile, approached to see if I were in need of her assistance.

'Are you all right, Alec?' she asked tentatively, peering around the edge of my peripheral vision as a child might peep round the side of its parents' bedroom door, afraid of bursting in on an embarrassing moment in the inner sanctum of their lives. 'What are you looking at?'

Following my line of sight, it was a moment before she saw it. Her drawing near had caused it to freeze, and it was only when it decided it was safe that it continued its activity.

When the hedgehog moved, it did so with a scurry. Its tiny feet, invisible beneath its skirts of spines, made a rustle in the dead leaves.

'*Erinaceus europaeus,*' Sister Cynthia said, keeping her voice low. 'It is classified as an insectivore although it is really omnivorous and eats not only bugs but worms, invertebrates and even frogs and birds' eggs.'

The hedgehog reached a piece of broken roofing slate lying under the bush. Pausing for a moment, it sniffed along the edge, then, getting its snout and head under the rim, lifted it up and nudged it aside. Beneath lay several worms, which the hedgehog immediately began to devour, chewing on them with swift bites.

'When a hedgehog is first born,' she continued, 'its spines are fully developed, but they are hidden under the skin, which is bloated with liquid. Gradually, the liquid is absorbed by the muscle and the spines push through. They are as white as the flesh of an apple. Within a day or two, darker spines appear. Later, a third coat develops.'

She looked into my face.

'Can you guess how I know so much about hedgehogs? When I was a little girl, I wanted to be a naturalist.' She laughed ruefully. 'Another dream dissolved in the acid of adulthood.'

I kept my eyes on the creature, which had now moved on, discovered a snail and was crunching on its shell.

'They are solitary little fellows. They keep themselves to themselves.' She cast me a sideways glance. 'He's not such a cute little fellow, though,' she went on. 'Hedgehogs can carry ringworm, influenza, the yellow fever parasite, food poisoning bacteria and leptospirosis, not to mention an abundance of ticks and fleas.' She glanced at the animal. 'Like so much in life, he is not all he seems.'

For the first time in many years, I felt the vague urge to reply, to agree with her and congratulate her on her acuity. Yet I did not. I dared not. For once I start to speak, I know that it will be like uncorking a never-empty bottle containing all the evils ever devised by man, and would not wish to subject her to the torrent of despair and degradation to which I have been privy.

Her presence and our concerted concentration on the hedgehog drew the attention of several other inmates who sauntered or loped over. They stood in a semicircle behind us, pointing, laughing, several cowering behind their attendants. To amuse his charge, one of the orderlies found a long garden cane and prodded the hedgehog's back. Until then, it had chosen to ignore the small crowd gathered to observe it hunt for food. The moment the stick touched the creature's spines, it hugged itself into a tight sphere, its stubby and vulnerable legs tucked away, its head folded into its belly.

'It does that,' Sister Cynthia remarked to me, 'by tightening two muscles that start on either side of the head and run the length of its body.'

Gingerly picking the hedgehog up, the orderly held the creature out for everyone to see. This caused increasing consternation amongst the onlookers. One fled, terrified.

Satisfied that I was not in need of her, Sister Cynthia left me, patting my arm as she departed. The attendant returned the hedgehog to the shade of the bushes, the other inmates drifted or were led away one by one and I continued my observation of the animal. After a while, it unrolled itself and, momentarily checking that any danger was passed, moved farther into the shrubbery and was gone.

I welcome the creature, my fellow prisoner-by-choice, for it asks no questions and makes no demands. It is merely present, doing what it does in its own fashion. In many ways, it is like me, mute and small, always ready to curl into a defensive ball when someone prods it with a stick.

14

The fine weather did not break. For three days, I woke at dawn and made my way in the early morning sunlight to the broch. With the loose stone cleared from the interior of the broch, I could see more clearly the layout of the interior rooms around the walls.

It was apparent that the broch had first been built with no accommodation in the centre at all. This, I believed, had consisted of a courtyard, which was only later reduced in size by the construction of a number of small apartments around its periphery. I drew this conclusion from the fact that the walls of these little rooms were not keyed into the main structure but simply abutted onto it. Working carefully with a bricklayer's trowel, I excavated three of the rooms down to the base of the walls.

In the smallest, I discovered a number of potsherds of crude manufacture, seashells and round pebbles from the shore, many splinters of bone and a much-corroded iron pin about four inches long, with a flattened head. As the broch builders had not used nails in the construction of their towers, I assumed this was a pin to fasten a cloak or some other garment. The scatter in the room suggested to me that the finds I uncovered had been put there for a purpose, perhaps to give substance to the beaten earth floor, which would otherwise have been churned up; for this reason, I decided the room had been a domestic animal shelter possibly, judging by its dimensions and the bone splinters, a kennel for hunting dogs.

The floor of the adjacent room showed two postholes which had, presumably, held up a roof of thatch, whilst the third and largest room contained not only four postholes but the site of a hearth, a thick layer of burnt charcoal surrounded by a square of five fire-scorched flat stones.

These discoveries convinced me that the broch was not a place of refuge in time of strife but a permanently occupied homestead belonging to a family or clan of some social position in the locality.

Yet whilst my archaeological inquisitiveness was somewhat sated by my work, my curiosity concerning Eilean Tosdach increased by the hour. I could not look up from my work, take a break to slake my thirst or pause to stretch without seeing it lying half a mile away: and whenever I looked at it I had the uneasy sense that I in turn was being watched.

On the afternoon of the third day, I completed my excavations at about four o'clock in the afternoon. My back ached from hours of bending and my eyes seemed to be fixed permanently to a focal length of about two feet. I bagged up my finds, completed my notes and left the ruin to sit on the boulder where I had eaten my midday meal on my first visit.

The sky was studded with clouds, which ran their shadows over the mountains at my back and the sea before me. I waited until I was in their shade, then slid from the boulder, removing from my satchel a seafarer's telescope I had borrowed from Ogilvy on the pretext of wanting to survey the island for ruins.

For twenty minutes, I covered the far shore with the telescope. I saw nothing moving. There was also no sign of any habitation, either ancient or modern, save the causewayed *dùn* about which I came to the conclusion that it was not actually an outstation for an insular settlement but for the settlement in which I was working.

'I shall have to return to Eilean Tosdach,' I said to Ogilvy that evening as we sat on benches outside the inn, a jug of ale between us and the twilight deepening, watching the fishermen return with their wicker baskets filled with herring, sild, sardines and assorted crustaceans.

'Is that so?' he replied, tapping a briar pipe out against the heel of his foot and filling it with shag from a tobacco pouch in his pocket.

'I need to visit the *dùn* again,' I explained by way of excuse, mentioning my theory and going on, 'If I can find potsherds on the island similar to those in the mainland broch, it will support my hunch.'

'Aye, I suppose it will do that,' he replied noncommittally, tamping down the contents of his pipe bowl and lighting it with a Swan vesta, the air suddenly tinged with the blue smoke and aroma of rum-soaked tobacco.

The following morning, Jamie took me out to the island, dropping me off at the same landing place and instructing me to be back there not after four o'clock. As before, he cast off as soon as I was ashore, sailing ahead of a stiff breeze down the coastline.

In truth, I did want to see if my thesis held up to archaeological scrutiny, yet I was far more fired by the thought of seeing the girl again. It was not then a matter of love, nor had I any carnal desire for her; it was her exoticism that drew me. I regarded her as I might a priceless Etruscan vase or a piece of Roman glass: just thinking of her somehow reminded me of a delicately blown fourth-century amber-coloured jug I had once been permitted to handle, with a tre-foil mouth and exquisite turquoise handle, the rim decorated with intertwining spirals. Just as with that exquisite artefact, I was intrigued by her, by the mystery of her past, enchanted by her appearance.

Setting off along the path, I walked slowly, scanning the way ahead carefully, watching for any movement I could not attribute to the breeze. I even checked the direction of the wind, to make sure it was in my favour. Every few yards, I looked round but saw nothing.

Approaching with caution the boulder upon which I had last seen the girl, I noticed a barely discernible track heading up the ridge behind it. It was little more than an indentation in the scrub, but I found it to be well worn. There was no doubt in my mind that the boulder was one of the girl's vantage points, and, looking over to the mainland, I realised that if she had chosen to observe me working in Dùn an Làmh Thoisgeal, it would have been from here, almost directly opposite across the strait.

Not knowing what lay over it, I crouched low as I reached the top of the ridge. The track I had ascended here joined a very obvious and well-used path at least a foot wide that appeared to run the length of the island, keeping just below the skyline on the seawards side.

For some minutes, I sat down in the scrub. It was, I thought, like being on the far, unseen surface of the moon, and I wondered, remembering Ogilvy's comment on the fishermen's loathing and avoidance of the place, how often men had cast their eyes upon the landscape before and below me.

On this side of the island, even the scrub was wind-bent, as if ordered by a gigantic brush combing it towards the top of the ridge. There were no trees; indeed, the tallest bush was not above four feet high. Boulders were strewn about the slopes, affording ample cover to anything that might choose to hide from view. The girl could have been behind any one of them, observing my progress over the ground, yet I did not feel her presence.

Sitting on the bare earth, my head just above the top of the scrub, I gave her much thought. I could not come to terms with what she was doing on the island, how she survived there with no contact with the mainland. I had seen no signs of domestic stock, no indication of any agricultural activity, not so much as a bush with an edible berry. And the loneliness. How, I wondered, did she survive the solitude.

At the semi-crouch, I pressed on. Abandoning the path, I moved like a hunter from boulder to boulder, keeping my profile as low as possible whilst, at all times, assuring I was not silhouetted against the sky. It was slow going and I saw not a sign of any human activity. I even began to wonder if, perhaps, the girl had been a figment of my imagination, that Ogilvy's coconut oil had not been as efficacious as he had assumed and that I had, after all, suffered sunstroke and one of its commensurate hallucinations.

Rounding a small spur coming off the ridge, I was suddenly aware of smoke. I could not see any indication of a fire, but the scent of burning wood was strong. With the stiff breeze blowing, I assessed that I must be quite close to the fire, so, lowering myself to my belly, I edged forwards, pulling myself through the brush by my elbows.

After some yards, I came to the side of a steep combe. Had it not been for the smoke giving me warning, I would almost certainly have stumbled upon the place, giving away my presence in a spectacular fashion with an ignominious tumble down the slope.

About thirty yards across and forty long, the combe was strewn with boulders around which the soil had been tilled, worked by a foot plough that lay against a rock. Several narrow raised beds of vegetables, formed by turning over two layers of turf and fertilising the depression between them with dried kelp, were growing in what must have been the only sheltered place on the island. Irrigation channels ran between the rows of plants, fed from a spring at the head of the combe. A pen of interwoven wicker panels contained a number of hens and a gaudily plumed cockerel. At the seawards end of the combe was a tiny shingle beach upon which was drawn up a craft not unlike a Welsh coracle. So much, I thought, for the talk of there being no landing place on Eilean Tosdach. On a flat boulder near the water's edge, gutted fish were laid out for drying. A net was strung between two poles.

For a while, I lay on my belly looking at the scene through the cover of a low bush and marvelling at how anyone could survive so successfully on the island. Even the broch builders had not, it seemed, sought to tame the place but just used it as an outstation, supplying its occupants from the mainland.

The smoke, the product of very dry wood, was hardly visible, but a faint wisp appeared every so often from a dense clump of bushes close by the beach. I retreated some yards, then, still on my stomach, edged my way towards the sea for a better view.

Tucked into the protection of the undergrowth and boulders was a croft. The low walls were made of stones, neatly fitted together in the manner of the brochs, without mortar. The roof was covered with living turf, only a circle of stones at one end breaking the uniformity of the tough grass: through this escaped the drift of smoke. There were no windows, but, facing away from the sea, a low door was hung with a heavy curtain of hide, the bottom hem sewn with stones to keep it closed.

A little way from the door was the site of an outdoor hearth in which a charcoal fire was burning. It was exactly like that which I had excavated at the broch, a rectangle of flat stones with a space between two of them to allow air into the embers. A large earthenware pot, the sides blackened by smoke, stood on one of the hearthstones, simmering. To one side of the croft was a pool surrounded by boulders and fed by the spring. A wooden ladle, carved from one piece of bleached driftwood, lay by the water's edge.

As I gazed down from my hidden position, it was as if the whole scene was a reconstruction of life as it had been lived two millennia ago. It reminded me of the sort of tableaux imaginative museum curators erected. All it lacked was a tailor's dummy dressed in rags, wearing a claymore in a leather scabbard and holding a spear.

For ten minutes, there was no movement or sound other than the scratching and clucking of the hens. The breeze died down somewhat, the sun shone intermittently as the clouds blew over and the sea lapped gently at the shingle. I grew uneasy. The absence of the girl made me wonder if she was there. If she wasn't, she could have been behind me, her hands holding a rock with which to cave my skull in, or a spike to drive into my spine. I bent my head over my shoulder. I could see up to the ridge and scanned it carefully. Nothing was out of the ordinary. A herring gull perched upon a rock preening itself told me I was at no risk.

When I returned my attention to the combe once more, she was there, crouching by the pool, the earthenware pot at her feet. She had her back to me, her hair falling forwards as it had on our last meeting, showing the nape of her neck. After a moment, she raised her hands and, in one motion, pulled her upper garment over her head. Her skin was white and unmarked save for the faint shadows of her vertebrae. Naked to the waist, she dipped the wooden ladle in the pot and tipped the hot water over her hair. I, not ten yards from her, watched the water run down her back. She shivered as it touched her skin.

I felt guilty, secretly watching her, yet I could not take my eyes from her. Her every movement, no matter how prosaic, had a defined beauty. Where the water wet her back, her skin glistened. The sunlight seemed not to shine on her so much as be absorbed by and radiate from her.

After a few minutes, she began to sing: it is the best I can describe the sound. It was not a tune, exactly, nor had it words. It was a grotesque and whimsical melody of twanging, plunking notes, discordant and yet imbued with primitive rhythm, rising and falling in muted crescendos. It was as if she were strumming a simple stringed instrument inside her head, her mouth echoing like a sound box.

When her hair stopped dripping, she ceased her music, stood up and turned to face me. Her breasts were small and white, her nipples dark. With almost delicate steps, she went to the hearth and, scooping up a handful of cool ashes from the periphery of the fire, started to work them into her hair, massaging her scalp with her long fingers. This done, her hair caked with a paste of ash, she went back to the pool and rinsed it out.

So entranced was I by her activity, I did not see the curtain to the croft lift and a mongrel appear. I was first aware of it when it gave a short, sharp yelp. The sound startled me and I must have moved my head. This alerted the dog further. It remained silent, but its hackles rose, its lips lifting in a snarl.

At the dog's bark, the girl had jumped to her feet and turned about. She made no attempt to cover herself, quickly brushing her wet hair behind her head.

The dog was set, staring in my direction. It tilted its head to one side, the better to hear if I moved. She did likewise. The cockerel, alarmed by the dog's bark, raucously called out once. The hens fell silent and crowded together under a ledge of rock in their run. Even the breeze seemed to die. The only sound to be heard was the hiss of the sea on the shingle.

I knew I should leave, that I was intruding upon the girl's world and had no right to impinge myself upon it. My motives were selfish, almost voyeuristic. Yet I had to stay. The girl's loveliness held me.

Looking upon her brought a deep calm over me. I could not explain it. It was as if being near her was almost spiritual. Had I been religious, not a modern man of science with a training in logic, I would have said that either great goodness or great evil dwelt in her. It was, I considered, no wonder that the people of Breakish were afraid of this place, of her, the *tannasg*. She possessed a power that they dared not face and I could not resist.

The door curtain was flung aside and a man appeared. Dressed in a leather jerkin and a dark-coloured kilt, he had shoulder-length hair and the full beard of a patriarch, grey with age. Although not tall, he was stocky, powerfully built. Behind him came an elderly woman wearing a long brown skirt and woollen shawl, her hair scraped back into a tight bun. He looked at the girl, then at the dog.

I kept still, my heart pounding, my pulse beating in my brow.

None of them spoke.

The man began to survey the side of the combe. I could tell he was staring at the base of the slope, slowly and methodically working his way up. The girl remained at the pool side, making no effort to hide or run for cover. She, too, scanned the hillside, yet whereas the man had a scowl upon his face, a soft half-smile seemed to play upon her lips. The woman moved quickly over to the girl's side, picked up her discarded clothing and folded it over her arm. Such a domestic act seemed so incongruous in the circumstances.

His study of the hillside complete, the man entered the croft to return a moment later carrying a broad pouched belt and a long-barrelled flintlock musket of some antiquity. As the woman scanned the bushes, he opened the pouch, took out a powder horn and primed the weapon, tamping the charge home with the ramrod. This done, he took a musket ball from the pouch and, with a wad, rammed that down the barrel. I could not help wondering if the weapon had been used on Cumberland's soldiers as they fell down the wet steps.

So mesmerised was I by the man that I temporarily ignored the girl. When the gun was charged, I shifted my gaze. She was looking straight at me. Like a wild stag on the mountains, she knew exactly where the stalker was even if she could not see him. It was, I thought, only a matter of seconds before she gave away my position, yet she made no attempt to communicate with the old man.

And, now, she was unequivocally smiling.

The man put the musket to his shoulder. I heard the distinct click of the flintlock as he thumbed it into the cocked position. The breeze picked up, agitating the undergrowth. Under cover of the movement, I began to worm myself backwards as quickly as I dared. When out of sight of the bottom of the combe, I rose to a crouch and ran for the cover of a tumble of boulders just below the ridge. As I reached them, I heard the distant report of the musket. The ball struck one of the boulders fifteen feet from me. I felt safe. Either his aim was poor or the weapon just did not have the range. No other shot was fired.

I looked back down at the combe, which was, from the ridge, barely discernible, and I knew that, despite the risks, I had to return to be with her.

15

In my silence, I possess the rarest of assets, of which others would be immensely jealous were they to know of its secret, for my silence places me out of the reach of common harm. There is nothing the world can do to me now, for I am cosseted in my security, safe within the room in which I have existed for longer than most men live and sound in the knowledge of the shelter of silence. Because I do not speak, I am beyond argument, beyond reproach, free of blame and released from the dictates of convention or society.

The worst reality can throw at me it already has, and I have, in retrospect, caught it or deflected it with the consummate skill of a professional cricketer who, with a mere flick of the wrist and turn of the bat, can send a well-aimed ball bouncing off to the boundary of the pitch, with no more effort than it takes to whisk an egg.

This fact is lost on Sister Cynthia and the rest of the staff of St. Justin's. They think because I am forever silent I must forever be in some form of mental anguish, my mind a confusion of anxieties and doubts, fears and repressions which they see it their duty to release, like squeezing the pus from a boil, cutting out a tumour or opening a door in the skull.

Five thousand years ago, the same was true of the shamans and witch doctors who called upon the sun for help, the moon for guidance and the gods of the seasons for results.

When I was a first-year undergraduate, eager-eyed and keen to unravel the mysteries of prehistory, I was set a vacation study topic and sent by my tutor to the British Museum to study the morphology of early hominid skulls.

I had often gone to the museum throughout my boyhood, spending my afternoons wandering the galleries of Roman armour and Greek statuary, Egyptian sarcophagi and Sumerian tablets, always frustrated that between me and my goal there was a sheet of glass or a knotted rope suspended from brass-bound poles over which a museum guard stood sentry. I did not want to passively observe but, like all children, actively touch. If my finger could have followed the indecipherable script on a pressed mud tablet I would not have translated it and yet I would have communicated with its creator. I liked to think that some tiny fragment of him, a flake of his skin or a strand of his hair, might have still been wedged in the cracks at the edges where the sun had dried the tablet, and my being would touch his and a spark would be lit over the hazy centuries.

Now, armed with a letter of introduction from a professor in my university, I was to go beyond the glass.

I recall quite clearly mounting the steps to the front façade of the museum, the tall pillars rising above me like polished menhirs, the bronze doors moving silently open on their well-oiled hinges as scholars entered to go about their work. Going to the reception desk, I presented my credentials and was ushered through a door marked: "Strictly Private." Following a guard, I was taken through a labyrinth of narrow corridors piled high with shelves of books, glass cases of exhibits yet to see the light of public display and sealed boxes of artefacts. The air had that dry, enticing mustiness of scholarship and the unknown.

My destination was a small room in which a laboratory bench stood under a grimy window looking out onto Russell Square. It was winter and the trees were stark in the gardens. Upon the table was an oblong wooden box, the lid of which was fastened by brass hooks. I was greeted by a curator, a thin man wearing gold-rimmed *pince-nez* and a waistcoat of faded brocade.

'This is, I assume, your first visit to the department of palaeontology?'

I confirmed that it was.

'Then there are a few ground rules I must explain to you. These boxes contain specimens that are quite unique and, being so, are invaluable. You must at all times wear these. . . . ' He turned to the bench and handed me a pair of white cotton gloves, somewhat soiled by usage. 'When handling a specimen, you must use both hands at all times. Specimens removed from the box must be placed upon the india-rubber mats provided,' he indicated a pile of them at the end of the bench, 'and not directly onto the worktop. You may not walk about the room carrying any specimen. Furthermore, you may not write up your notes with anything but a lead graphite pencil.' He smiled condescendingly. 'We cannot risk the spilling of ink.'

When, at last, I was left alone, I slid open the catches and lifted the lid off. Surrounded by cotton waste in individual compartments the box contained three Neanderthal skulls, the eyebrow ridges as prominent as a modern ape's, the mandibles solid and heavy, the teeth ground down. My hands shaking with the excitement of it, I pushed my fingers down the sides of the cranium of the first and lifted it onto a mat. Its empty orbits seemed to stare at me. With my set of callipers, I started to make measurements and draw the specimen.

The second skull was much like the first, but the third skull had been trepanned, a square hole punched in the right centre of the parietal bone. It had not been the cause of death, for the rim of bone was rounded off, indicating that it had healed.

When language was in its infancy, before the invention of the smelting of bronze, men had worked out how to set their demons free with a sharp flint and a hammer stone. The doctors of St. Justin's are just the same except that they wear white coats instead of a wolf-skin cloak and rely upon a pharmacy to anaesthetise rather than a bunch of smouldering herbs. And they may have science on their side, but they are still dabbling in mystery.

Just today, I watched them at their magic.

There is a young man who occupies a room on the second floor and goes everywhere carrying a large doll. It is an androgynous mannequin about two feet high from which he will not be parted and which he dresses, much as a little girl might, in some children's clothes. When in the garden—he is one of those who is at all times accompanied by a member of the staff—he sits with the doll on a bench beside him, occasionally pointing out something that catches his eye which he feels might interest his inanimate partner. This might seem not unduly abnormal: he has a fantasy friend to share his fantasy world. It is only when the orderly with him suggests they go in that one wonders at his sanity, for he always carries the doll by its neck.

This morning, there must have been a lapse in security, for as I watched the rain falling out of my window he appeared on the lawn, unaccompanied. In place of his doll, he was carrying a grey cat often to be seen stalking sparrows in the garden or sunning itself on the roof of the gardeners' shed. The cat was dead; he was carrying it by its neck, swinging it back and forth as he walked.

It was only a matter of a minute or so before four or five orderlies appeared with a doctor. At a distance, they surrounded their quarry before they moved slowly in on him. He pretended not to notice them, but as they came closer he made a dash for it, waving the cat round his head for all the world like some grotesque mediaeval weapon, holding his foes at bay. After a brief chase, however, they cornered him. The doctor advanced, talking to him and catching his attention. When the orderlies pounced, the young man was taken completely by surprise and resorted to spitting and biting, his free hand clawing at his captors' eyes. I saw a hypodermic syringe appear, to be plunged into his thigh. Once the drug was in, the orderlies retreated. Gradually the young man grew dozy and sat on the ground, letting go of the cat. When he was finally almost comatose, a burly orderly picked him up and carried him like a child into the building. Another scooped the dead cat up with a spade and threw it into one of the gardener's wheelbarrows.

There was no question that the young man was going to do anyone any harm, even himself. He merely wanted to walk in the rain with his new friend. Yet they had to save him, had to bring him back from his world into theirs, where they believe he is the happier.

This they will never do to me. They cannot, for I give them no means of achieving their aim. They have no handle on my life. If they were to drill a hole in my head, not a single demon would escape, for they, like me, are hidden, deep out of reach. Even when I am dead and my skull an empty void, they will still be out of harm's way, out of the range of those who would rescue me from them, yet still going about their evil business in the world of men.

16

It seems as if every day of my life I have faced death. This is true for all men, for death is only ever a moment away; we are not to know it until the second hand jumps and the blade scythes down on the wheat of our existence. Yet, in my case, it is more so, for I have watched for it, seen it arrive for others, awaited my turn, which has yet to come.

Not a week goes by but one of my fellow inmates shuffles off into the great unknown, gibbering or stamping his feet or, as in the case of the most recent one, dancing the light fandango hanging by his boot laces from a hot water pipe in the nurses' sluice room. How determined he must have been, saving up and weaving laces for months for just that one insignificant event.

I wonder, as he kicked away the medicine trolley upon which he stood, as he took the short drop to eternity, if he recalled the same scenes as I do whenever I think of dying.

Childhood: I revisit specific moments, at random, in the years in which I lived in innocence, unaware of the corruption of humanity even if still subjected to it in my puerility. For one must accept that if the boy is the father of the man and no matter how angelic the child, there lingers within him the seeds of fascistic brutality.

On the day they cut down the weaver-of-laces, I remembered the dame school I attended at the age of five. In a tall, imposing terrace house in a leafy suburb of south London, it was called Stream Valley School. Operated by a middle-aged spinster, Miss Violet Holland, and her widowed younger sister, Hyacinth, it provided the basics of a good education, preparing pupils for entry into the better preparatory schools of Surrey. The building was divided into two. The school occupied the ground floor rooms whilst the top two storeys were taken by the sisters for their accommodation. A downtrodden maid lived in the basement, in a room between the coal cellar and the scullery. The pupils shared her small lavatory, the stink of which I can smell now, singeing my nostrils like the taint of acid: the linoleum-covered floor around the water closet was stained with years of little boys' ill-aimed urine.

Lessons were arranged in three areas of academia: scientific, artistic and spiritual. The former consisted of playing with levers, discovering points of fulcrum, measuring liquids into jugs and doing simple mathematical problems, often involving coppers, sixpences, shillings and florins made out of cardboard. Economics and trade drove the Empire, we were told by Mrs. Hyacinth, who had lived in India and who, my father said, had married a poodle-faker. I had no idea what this meant and assumed throughout my childhood that he had been some kind of dog breeder. Artistic lessons involved elementary French and Latin, making table mats out of coloured raffia, reciting Wordsworth's pastoral poetry by rote and studying the history of southern Britain by copying pictures of castles, hill forts, palaces and other architectural subjects of historical interest into a black-and-red cardboard-bound exercise book. A seed was planted in me in those classes. Spiritual education centred upon the well-being of the soul and the body, two factors often intermingled. We were steeped in the Bible, chapter and verse, with emphasis upon what happened to sinners. The Ten Commandments were dinned into us with Miss Violet adding a few of her own, one of which was the strict instruction that when the boys went to the little room in the basement they should touch their willies only for so long as it took to use them. We were not to abuse, she said, the temples of our bodies, the development of which, in turn, was addressed by physical training sessions on the playground at the bottom of the garden, a cinder-covered oblong surrounded by a wicket fence. Here we jumped on the spot, touched our toes, swung our arms and I discovered the inherent cruelty of my species.

At exercise time, the girls tucked their long dresses into their knickers, giving themselves the appearance of wearing water-filled balloons around their waists. The boys removed their jackets and rolled up their sleeves, as if in readiness for some manly toil or battle. Mrs. Hyacinth, who took responsibility for our bodies, was insistent on our preparations, helping those who could not to roll their sleeves up so that they did not unravel.

There was one boy, a newcomer, who asked to leave his sleeves rolled down. He was neither belligerent nor insolent. Indeed, he was polite in his noncompliance. This was, of course, out of the question. Not being given leave, he then refused. Mrs. Hyacinth boxed his ears. It knocked him off balance and he had to grab at the wicket fence to stay on his feet. Yet even then, he refused. She stepped forward and grabbed him, fumbling at the buttons of his cuff. He squirmed and she boxed his head again. As his sleeve went up his arm, we saw his flesh was emaciated, little more than bone covered with pallid skin, which was heavily blotched with the livid pink scabs of eczema.

I felt for him, my classmate in distress, but could do nothing to save him from his plight. It was not cowardice on my part. I knew instinctively that I was up against a greater force in Mrs. Hyacinth than I could ever hope to counter.

She was momentarily taken aback at the sight of the boy's condition, but she had her position to maintain. As in India, she could not weaken in front of the natives for fear of another mutiny. The boy's sleeves were rolled up to his armpits. Six weeks later, he was dead.

It is strange how I remember such a trivial incident. Yet it has haunted me down the decades, has been retained in my memory whilst so much else has been eradicated—a turning moment upon which I based so much of my philosophy.

17

It took me an hour of studying the density of stones lying on the ground around Dùn an Làmh Thoisgeal to discover the site of the community's midden. Fifteen yards from the northeast quadrant of the broch, a pit about three yards in diameter had been dug, this showing on the surface by a complete absence of any stones bigger than a golf ball. The surrounding ground was littered with far larger stones. Knowing that middens were a rich source of finds that would do much to establish the lifestyle, status and cultural identity of a community, I set to excavating it immediately.

Marking off an area of about three square feet, I began scraping the soil away an inch at a time with my trowel, piling the earth behind me. It was slow but invigorating work: whereas much excavation was anticipatory, in that one never knew if one would find anything of worth, digging a midden was a certainty. Furthermore, because the pit had been originally filled with a good deal of organic matter, the soil was often friable and more easily removed.

By the time I had gone down eight inches, I had unearthed over a dozen potsherds, half a fragile bone comb decorated with a series of carved whirls and arabesques, a spindle weight etched with two concentric rings, a rib from a seal that had been notched and used, I surmised, to card wool, two smooth but cracked pebbles that might have been potboilers and a piece of metal, probably iron, corroded out of all recognition. This surprised me, as the broch dwellers seldom threw away metal; it was more usually melted down and recast. The finds I carefully placed in my satchel, padding the comb and seal's rib with moss to protect them from breaking.

From these finds I deduced a good deal: that the broch dwellers were of sufficiently high status to have possessed luxury items, that they herded sheep and spun cloth, hunted on both land and sea and were wealthy enough not to worry about accidentally throwing away a piece of metal with the rest of the domestic detritus.

The deeper I went, the more I uncovered—the teeth of sheep and cattle, shells, a bone needle and, at about a foot's depth, a section of red deer antler with a hole drilled through it—and the more I became engrossed in what I was doing to the exclusion of all else. Even the onset of a light sea drizzle did nothing to distract me. I continued to work, my clothes gradually becoming saturated, and it was not until it began to rain in earnest that I called a halt and hurried towards the broch to take shelter.

My boots slipping on the wet boulders, I entered the broch and headed for one of the chambers in the wall, easing myself into it and sitting on one of the steps that rose up through the wall. The rain grew heavier, but the walls were so thick, no water seeped through them.

I had been sheltering for about ten minutes when a small pebble the size of a child's marble bounced off a step above me and struck me on the shoulder. I looked up. If the rain, which was now torrential, was capable of dislodging a pebble from the wall, there was a chance that the structure, although seemingly robust, was in fact unstable. As I studied the wall for a widening fissure, another pebble dropped onto the step and ricocheted over my head. If the wall was crumbling, it was doing so higher up than I could see.

Despite the heavy rain, I stepped out from my shelter and moved as quickly as I could away from the wall. If it were to collapse, I would need to be some yards off to be safe. Scrambling over the ruins, another pebble hit a boulder by my side with a sharp crack. I glanced round, expecting to see the wall leaning towards me as it fell.

On top of the lower, inland side of the broch was the girl.

I was so taken aback, I stopped dead in my tracks, a wave of first fear then bewilderment rolling over me. How in the name of hell, I thought, had she got there from the island? And why?

Twenty feet above me, she was squatting on the edge of the wall, the loose shift she was wearing as sopping as my own. As I spied her, she lightly tossed another pebble into the air. I saw it coming through the rain and caught it. At this, she laughed. I could hear her through the din of the rain. It was not a human sound, more the playful chatter of a small primate, a marmoset or tamarin, but it somehow put me at my ease.

'What are you doing?' I called out, my words dulled by the rain. Now that my initial fear was gone I was, although I was already soaked through, somewhat annoyed at being driven from my refuge and made to look if not cowardly, then at least foolish.

She dropped the remaining pebbles in her hand and disappeared down into the cavity of the broch wall. I waited for her to reappear at the foot, but she did not show herself. I quickly checked around the ruins to be sure I was not being lured into a trap, to be sprung by the old man with the antique firearm, yet there was nobody there. She seemed to be alone.

Returning inside the broch, I saw her in the shadows of the chamber in which I had been sheltering. At first, I wondered if I should approach her. I was frightened. She was, in effect, cornered, and a cornered animal is a dangerous one.

Without speaking, she looked at me and tentatively held her hand out. Her fingers were long and thin, the nails smooth and rounded. I copied her, stepping nearer and bringing my own hand up, stretching my own fingers until the tips touched hers. The moment we made contact, she gripped my wrist, not tightly yet sufficiently firmly to prevent me from moving away. A surge of terror ran through me. I looked over my shoulder. The old man would be there with a bludgeon. Yet he was not.

Pursing her lips, she uttered a soft blowing sound. It bizarrely reminded me of how my nursery governess had blown upon food that was too hot before handing it to me.

With her other hand, she spread my fingers out, one by one, pushing in on my palm as if my flesh were made of clay and she was shaping it into a concave vessel. All the while, she watched my face, her mouth slightly open, her breath misting in the damp air. When I returned her look, she averted her eyes. Outside, the rain began to ease.

For some minutes, she toyed with my hand; then, twisting my wrist, she moved my palm to press it against her breast. Through the flimsy material of her shift, her flesh was firm but pliable, her nipple hard against the centre of my hand. I did not know what to do, how to react. Her action was confusing, both lascivious and yet at the same time completely natural and unerotic. It was as if she was not seeking sexual contact but something else I could not deduce.

I sat on the step next to her. At first, she did not move; then, relinquishing my hand, she started to run her fingers over me, slowly and gingerly, as a blind man might feel a delicate tropical flower. I made no attempt to stop her. Her behaviour was as fascinating as her beauty infatuating.

'Tell me your name,' I said.

She did not respond. Her hands were by now exploring my chest, her fingers feeling inside my shirt.

'You must have a name.'

She made no attempt to unbutton my clothing, preferring to feel through the material. On reaching my waist, her exploration stopped.

'How did you get here?' I asked, keeping my voice low so as not to alarm her and trying another tack to get her to speak to me.

Again, she chose not to answer, but moving her hands up my torso, she put her arms around my neck. I was filled with a moment of intense terror. She was lissom, but she was strong, her biceps well developed and her forearm muscles taut. It would have been simplicity itself for her to break my neck. Drawing me close, she kissed me on the cheek. Her mouth close to my ear, I could distinctly hear her purring, her breath warm on my damp skin.

I made to return her kiss, but she moved her head and, letting go of my neck, stood up. The tip of her tongue appeared a few times in slow succession, forced out between her closed lips. I was reminded of how contented dogs lying before a fire, or having their stomachs tickled, made this same action of canine ecstasy and pleasure. Moving past me, she stepped out into the rain. Combing her hair back with her long fingers, she looked at me. There was at that moment an intense sadness about her which cut me to the quick.

'You don't have to go,' I said.

I wanted her to stay. There was so much I knew she could tell me if only I could break down her shyness and get her to converse with me.

After pausing as if to consider my words, she walked away without a glance back, her body moving with the lithe grace I had observed at our first meeting, her clothing adhering with the rain to the contours of her body. I thought to go after her but decided against it. Instead, I waited until she was out of sight, then followed in her footsteps. I expected to find her down on the shore, getting into the little coracle I had noticed on the island, but when I reached the edge of the low cliff there was no craft to be seen drawn up on the rocks and she was nowhere in sight.

Collecting my satchel and tools, I set off for Breakish. Every so often, I looked back in the half hope that I might see her following me at a distance, yet she did not appear.

As I made my way along the path, my mind was filled with a confusion of thoughts to which I struggled to give some logical order.

First, considering the girl's predicament, I came to several possible solutions. She lived on the island with an elderly couple; they were either her parents, her guardians or her captors. That said, she had somehow come to the mainland to meet me but had chosen, I assumed, to return to them. Had she escaped from them, she would surely have come with me, especially after her display of such naïve intimacy. I wondered if, perhaps, she were under some kind of spell, yet to accept that premise was to subscribe to the superstitions of the people of Breakish.

Second, I pondered her identity. If she was the couple's daughter, much could be explained: the father's shooting at me was his way of driving off an unwanted suitor. Another possibility, which seemed a little more credible, was that she was their granddaughter. And yet if this was so, why did they not want her to meet others, perhaps a young man who might love and cherish her? As their years advanced,

I reasoned, surely they would want her to develop her independence, for if she remained on the island after their deaths, she could have little future alone.

Third, I faced the quandary of her coming to me. How she had crossed the strait was a puzzle; her skill with the coracle must have been prodigious. Or, it then occurred to me, had the old man brought her across, permitting or instructing her to meet me. Perhaps I was being chosen to be her suitor.

Finally, I tried to come to terms with her actions in the broch. Her tossing of pebbles had been almost playful, teasing, and yet she might have had another motive. By giving herself away, she had succeeded in not startling me as she had on our first meeting. Then there was her pressing of my hand to her breast and her kiss. Were these, I wondered, her way of showing friendship and trust or indicative of a desire for love. They were not, I was convinced, carnal in intent: my attempt to return her kiss had been rejected.

By the time I reached Breakish, I was no nearer to coming to a conclusion. I went up to my room and stood at the window. Behind me, the peat blocks in the grate burned with an intense glow, the air close and warm. The rain was coming in again from the sea, moving like grey curtains across the water.

18

'What an exquisite day!' Sister Cynthia announced, pulling back the curtains and opening the french doors of my room. 'Just right for a stroll in the garden. I daresay I'll take one myself when my chores are done.' She laughed. 'When! If there's no rest for the wicked . . .' She leered at me '. . . I must have been a very naughty girl once upon a time.'

She said nothing more but, swinging the doors wide as if to entice me out, collected up my clothing to be laundered and left. I listened as her footsteps retreated down the corridor.

I determined to go to the oak tree, but, as happens sometimes, I was swamped by a terrible, unassailable apprehension. Usually, when sitting under the tree, I make every effort to empty my mind, to concentrate only upon that which presents itself before me: a groundsman mowing the grass, an inmate chasing one of the squirrels that occasionally appear or, as I observed the other day, eating the blooms of a rose bush. I consider the tree not so much a sentinel over my being as a guide into my future, before which there was no past. Yet there are times when I believe the tree neither protects nor guides me but taunts me with its age and knowledge, tests me, attempts to break my resolve and, by doing so, possesses my spirit.

With tentative steps, holding onto the door frame as I moved across the lintel, I edged outside. The flagstones of the narrow terrace were warm, even though the sun had yet to touch them. Around the pots of geraniums were damp patches. One of the gardeners, I surmised, must have already done his rounds. With studied care, as if stepping to avoid treading on something fragile, I made my way to the steps at the end of the terrace.

On the path below, a man in a grey woollen dressing gown, his head encased in overlapping bandages, was being led by an orderly. I paused to let them pass before heading off in the direction of the oak. I did not walk straight to the tree but took a circuitous route, occasionally sidestepping a tussock of grass or a stone embedded in the ground. Anything out of the ordinary worried me. I cannot say why. It was an illogical reaction, yet there are times when I behave in this way, almost instinctively, as if programmed. Something deep within me, beyond my consciousness, drives me. How this condition came to be I do not know. It was born in the past I no longer possess.

On reaching the tree, I checked around the base of the trunk for anything that might arouse my suspicion, although what I could not say. Satisfied, I then sat down between the roots, my back to the rough bark and my hands loose in my lap. I was tempted to doze but dared not. Yet I felt relaxed. Birdsong in the branches above me reassured me that all was well.

I had sat under the tree for about an hour when a dove flew onto a bough directly above my head. I looked up at it. Its feathers were a soft grey, like the sky just after dawn on a misty autumnal morning. Around its neck was a thin black ring, its eyes sharp and black. They reminded me of a necklace of jet, perhaps one my mother had worn, the beads contrasting in my imagination with her white skin. When the sunlight caught the bird's head, the feathers took on a faint purple opalescence. Once it had come to terms with my presence, it began to coo softly, almost inaudibly. It was a fluid sound, warm and viscous like tepid oil or new, thin honey. The calls soon attracted another dove. Side by side, they perched on the branch, bobbing at each other in avian friendship.

Some yards away, the gardeners had recently reset a patch of the lawn which had been invaded by moss and raked out. Rain had thinned out the topsoil, exposing the seed over the possession of which half a dozen sparrows and a gaudy goldfinch were contesting. I ignored their clamour, but it did not escape the attention of the doves.

When, suddenly, they took flight with a clatter of wings, I was startled, yet a quick survey around the sides of the oak, and the fact that the doves headed straight for the seed patch, put me at ease once more.

Landing on the grass, the doves began to peck at the soil, hardly bothering to look up. The smaller birds pranced about them, chirping indignantly. In a matter of minutes, the doves had devoured most of the visible seed and were down to competing for the remnants. I watched as one of them set about the other, pecking at its neck to drive it off. With every jab of its beak, tiny wisps of downy under-feathers drifted away on the breeze. The victim retreated, only to return again from another direction, only to be repulsed once more. After four or five of these ambitious forays, the dominant bird launched a determined attack. It ran at the other with its wings half-opened. The sparrows, gleaning what they could on the periphery of this contest, took to the air in fright. With one vicious stab, the offensive dove gouged out its opponent's eye. The injured bird shook its head. Tiny specks of blood spattered the grass. The victor, ignoring what was left of the grass seed, flew over the wall and out of sight. The sparrows returned to squabbling over what remained.

The wounded bird did not move, made no attempt to fly or disguise itself. Its head was slick with blood. The sparse grass and soil beneath it was smudged. The bird had, I knew, surrendered to the inevitable. Its life was over. There was no point in making any effort. Fate had clapped its hands and the bird's number was up.

I felt nothing. Not anger, not compassion, not sorrow. All I could think of was the irony of the little drama I had just witnessed, staged as if for my benefit: the traditional bird of peace savagely pecked to death by one of its own kind.

'Good morning, Alec.'

I jumped. This was not good. I should have seen someone approaching. My defences had been down. Standing to one side of the oak, in partial shade, was a man dressed in a tweed jacket and slacks. Around his neck, suspended by a red rubber tube, hung a black-and-chrome stethoscope, At first, I took the figure to be that of the doctor who had rescued me from the fantasy rioters in the Strand.

Only when he stepped into the sunlight did I see it was the young doctor.

'I'm sorry. I didn't mean to startle you.'

He glanced in the direction of the dove that was now hunkered down on its breast, its blood congealing.

'Nature in the raw, driven by urges.'

The young doctor moved nearer and sat on the ground beside me.

'They are ruled by instinct, their actions governed by ingrained behavioural patterns, whereas we possess the ability to reason.'

He snapped his fingers. The sparrows were immediately alert. Several took to the wing.

'Those sparrows,' he continued, 'have no free will. Have you ever read T. H. Huxley? He would have called them conscious automatons. They lack any means to break the physiological conditions of their bodies.' He readjusted the stethoscope, which was slipping from around his neck. 'Huxley conducted an experiment. He decerebrated frogs, yet their bodies continued to swim. They were automatons. Extrapolating from this, he wondered if men with damaged minds were similarly automatons, their thoughts governed no longer by reason but merely by an automatic response to a given action. I wonder if that is true.'

He let his words hang in the air.

'Would you agree, Alec? I, myself, would not. I believe that so long as one has free will, one is not an automaton.'

Casually, the young doctor glanced sideways at me, looking for a sign that his words were getting through. I just stared at the dove, which was now breathing in shallow gasps, as if hungry for air.

'I wonder, are you an automaton, Alec?'

The dove's head very slowly sank down to the earth. The sparrows returned to feed, oblivious, close by.

I did not move, yet tears started to run down my cheeks, to slip from my chin to strike my hand as plainly as raindrops might have done. I looked down, puzzled by them, for I could not justify why I was crying. I have seen far worse than a mere bird die.

The young doctor produced a handkerchief from his top pocket, wiped my tears away as if I were a child and, taking my arm, raised me up.

'Come inside now, Alec,' he said as he gently eased me into a first step. 'You may be locked in a prison within yourself, yet you are still free.'

19

For three days, Breakish was lashed by rain. The little houses closed their doors and shutters against the elements, and people ventured outside only if necessity drove them, to tend their animals, bail out their small craft or visit the dunny. What in sunlight had been dark rock scars on the surrounding mountains became jags of white water tumbling to the glens below. The little brae which entered the bay to the northwest of the village became a fierce torrent that spread its delta of peat-coloured water as far out to sea as it could go before the tidal currents dissipated it.

I spent much of my time in my room cleaning, cataloguing and drawing my midden finds. The fragment of comb, I discovered, was not decorated with an abstract pattern but the image of a mythical beast not unlike an Oriental dragon. Its head was plainly visible, a bulging eye staring out above a frill of reptilian wattles. More exciting than this, however, was the spindle weight upon which I found a faint runic inscription.

On the second evening, I sat before the taproom fire with Ogilvy. He was intrigued by the runes and took a wax impression of them to send to an acquaintance in Inverness who he thought might be able to translate them for Mr. McGillivray.

As we drank what Ogilvy referred to as nippy sweeties and talked about his life at sea, I considered whether or not to confide in him my experiences of the girl. Finally, I decided to broach the subject, but only after Jamie and his mother had departed in the rain for their own small home along the quay, leaving Ogilvy and me alone with the bottle of single malt.

'The island's a strange place,' I said as he placed a piece of pale driftwood on the fire, the salt catching almost immediately, tiny orange flames spurting from cracks in the timber.

'The island?'

'Eilean Tosdach.'

'Oh, aye,' he replied, as if there had been more than one island of which I might speak. 'Eilean Tosdach. And how do you find it strange?'

'It has an air of its own.'

'That is has. An atmosphere as unique as any island you'd find anywhere on God's wee planet.'

'The *dùn* is all but unique,' I added. 'I believe it may have been an outpost of Dùn an Làmh Thoisgeal, for I cannot find a settlement site on the island of which it might be a part.'

'Can you not now?'

'Not that could be archaeologically associated with the *dùn*,' I continued.

'I daresay,' he answered, 'but I think you've found one that's a bit more—how shall I put it?—contemporary.'

I was startled at his prescience, but, attempting to mask my surprise, I replied, 'What do you mean?'

'I think you've already caught my drift. You've been to the island and you've stumbled upon the wee croft there. It's just as well you've not spoken of it to anyone in Breakish.'

'How do you know I've not?' I asked, my reply tantamount to an admission.

'Oh!' he exclaimed. 'If you had, you can be sure I'd've heard about it. You'd be the talk of the town! You'd also no longer be welcome except, perhaps, in my humble abode here.' He waved his arm to encompass the room, the oil lamp smoking in the corner, the driftwood burning brightly and the rain lashing at the shutters closed over the window.

'I'd not be welcome in Breakish?'

'Well, let me put it another way. Would you want a man staying in your home that had, in the most likely eventuality, kissed Satan's arse, formed a pact with him and sold his soul for a ha'penny kipper? Like as not they'd've run you out on the first available nag. If you were lucky.' He paused and continued, 'Jamie's daddy did not drown in a storm. He spent a night on Eilean Tosdach when his boat lost half its rudder on a rock off Sgeir Ghlas. To the north, about five miles. He was trying for Breakish but dared not attempt the strait's currents in the dark.'

'What happened?'

'On the island? Who knows. Probably nothing. He spent a fearful night on the shore and the folk as live there will have kept their distance. It's not in their nature to be inquisitive.'

'I mean in Breakish,' I said.

'It's best I don't speak of it and you don't know of it.'

'You mean they chased him from the village?'

'In a manner of speaking,' Ogilvy replied ambiguously.

'But they know I've been there. Jamie took me.'

'Aye! And they're suspicious of you, but they think you're just a stupid Sassenach with an interest in brochs.'

I decided to cut to the quick.

'I have seen the croft in the little valley,' I admitted, 'and the girl.'

'Och!' Ogilvy said, leaning back in his chair and stretching his arms. 'I know that.'

'How could you . . . ?' I exclaimed, no longer disguising my astonishment.

'When a man comes back from a spot like Eilean Tosdach, he's changed. In tiny ways. I've sailed around the world and I've worked with men. Sailors. You can always tell when the cabin boy's lost his cherry ashore, or the boatswain's caught the clap or a junior officer's had a letter from an errant girlfriend. You don't need to be told. You just know.'

I drank my whisky and accepted another dram from Ogilvy.

'What do you know of her?' I asked.

'Not a deal more than's common knowledge hereabouts.'

'So people know of her?'

'They say she's a siren, a mermaid who'll steal your mind with magic and such.'

'And the elderly couple with her?'

'Ah! So you've seen them, too. They are the trolls who bore her, who taught her the black arts.'

The thought that there were men in an age of reason who believed in trolls was so ludicrous, I laughed aloud.

Ogilvy looked away from the fire at me. 'Aye! You know it's poppycock and I know it's balderdash, but the people of Breakish haven't seen the world as I have, haven't had the education you've received. If they don't understand a matter, it has to be the work of God if it's good, and Beelzebub's doing if it's not.'

'So what is the truth?' I said.

'The truth's just as bizarre as the myth. I heard the story some years ago when I was in Kyle. Even as far away as Loch Alsh they've heard of her, but they don't know exactly where she is, which is perhaps just as well, for her sake.'

'For her sake?' I queried.

'They might be honest folk in Breakish,' Ogilvy replied, 'who'd not steal a crust if they were starving, but they're still riddled with their superstitions. It's not beyond them to burn a *briosag*. That's a witch,' he added bluntly.

'You can't mean if they caught the girl, they'd'—I paused at the monstrosity of the thought—'murder her.'

Ogilvy looked at me for a long moment, then continued, 'The laird before Mr. McGillivray was Robert MacIntyre. He was a master of the old school, ruled the people with an iron hand, evicted half the crofters and doubled the rents on the rest. What he said was law, and if you didn't like it you could die or be damned as far as he was concerned. Now, like many an autocrat, he was a very religious man. I've found that to be the case the world over. Perhaps they need to think their god's on their side in order to justify their actions. Now, I've a question for the historian in you. What is the language of God?'

'There are many gods,' I replied.

'The Christian one.'

I cast my mind back to lectures I had attended in my first year at university.

'According to Talmudic legend,' I said, 'Abraham, who had been hidden in a cave at birth so as not to be killed by King Nimrod, came out of it speaking Hebrew. As this was also considered the original language of the Scriptures, it was deemed to be the language of God Himself.'

'Good!' Ogilvy congratulated me. 'Now, in the early 1490s, King James the Fourth of Scotland, just before he supported Perkin War- beck, the pretender to the English throne, is said to have conducted a grotesque religious experiment. The king acquired two newborn infants, barely dry from the womb, and put them in the charge of a deaf mute spinster who lived alone on an isolated island called Inchkeith. The king hoped that, as the infants grew up without con- tact with the common spoken word, they might naturally come to speak in the paradisiac language that was instinctive to mankind. That is, the language of God, for, as we all know, we are made in the image of God'—he raised his eyebrows before going on—'and so there must be divine instincts hidden in us someplace, although I have to say, from my experience, I've not seen great proof of it. Be that as it may. Now, whether this was done or not is uncertain, although the Isle of Inchkeith exists in the Firth of Forth. The legend goes that the chil- dren were silent for many years, then, miraculously, they began speak- ing in Hebrew.'

He paused to poke the fire with a pine log. The driftwood had burned quickly and was almost gone. Having stirred the embers, he dropped the log into the centre of the grate. Almost immediately, the bark commenced to spit.

'Of course,' Ogilvy went on, 'the good people of Fife wouldn't know Hebrew if it was to jump up and punch them on their nose. The king's detractors, who were not in favour of his support of War- beck, declared the children merely imitated the sounds of the natural world around them. They no more spoke Hebrew than the Wild Man of Borneo.'

'I fail to see what James the Fourth and the Talmud have to do with Eilean Tosdach,' I said.

'MacIntyre was a true dyed-in-the-wool Auld Kirk Presbyterian bigot,' Ogilvy said, with some feeling. 'He was also a Celtic revivalist. About twenty years ago, or so they say, he had a bastard by one of his maidservants. It was a girl child. . . . '

He left his words hanging in the air.

'And that is the girl on the island?' I asked.

'Aye. He could not resist repeating the royal experiment.'

'So the elderly couple . . . ' I began.

' . . . were young then. Both of them are deaf mutes.'

'From Breakish?'

'No. From an isolated croft in the mountains. MacIntyre set his bailiffs on them, then made them an offer that they had to accept. What else could two such afflicted souls do? He put them on the island with some hens, a few sheep and the babe.'

'And so she cannot speak,' I said.

'Not a word of English or Gaelic. Or Hebrew, come to that.' He smiled ironically. 'Like the children of Inchkeith, she speaks only in the words of animals.'

'How would you know?' I asked.

'Like you, I've seen her,' Ogilvy confessed. 'When she's been on the mainland.'

He drained his whisky in one and poured himself another. I assessed everything he had told me. It was a monstrous tale, depraved in the extreme. The girl had been condemned to a life of virtual imprisonment, on an island, without words. I tried to imagine what it must be like not to be able to speak, to possess only the bark and call of a dog or a seabird.

'I saw her twice on the island,' I said at last. 'Once on her own and once with the elderly couple at the croft. The old man fired a flint-lock musket at me.'

Ogilvy laughed quietly and replied, 'That's his way. How far did he miss you by?'

'Some yards.'

'That's his way, too. Now. But be glad you didn't come across him when he had his eyes. I've heard tell he could bring down a gull on the wing.'

'And I saw her two days ago. She came to me at Dùn an Làmh Thoisgeal.'

'So long as you're in Breakish, Alec, I'd keep that fact to myself if I were you.'

'How did she get to the mainland?' I asked. 'I saw a small boat of sorts at the croft but did not see her rowing it.'

'She swam,' Ogilvy said. 'Once a year, the man used to come to the mainland, to the shore near your *dùn*, to collect supplies left there for him by MacIntyre. Usually just the basics he could not acquire otherwise—gunpowder, perhaps some seeds, a bolt of cloth, an axe or hoe blade. Three years ago, the girl came in his place, but MacIntyre was dead and there were no supplies waiting. For a week, she came daily. Word spread that she was in the *dùn*, mewing like a kitten for its milk, but no one dared go close. I was newly arrived here and reported the matter to Mr. McGillivray. He instructed me, secretly, to take what I thought the lassie needed. So I did, at night, without the villagers' knowledge.'

I warmed my hands on the burning pine log. The room was filling with the heavy scent of its resin, which bubbled from a split in the wood.

'What's her name?'

'She's got no name that I'm aware of,' Ogilvy responded. 'Leastways, not that her surrogate parents have given her. If you can't talk and you can't hear, what's the point? The men call her Meigead, and then only in an undertone in case their voices drift upon the wind, she hears it and uses it against them.'

'Meigead,' I repeated.

'It's Gaelic for the bleating of a kid. The way she talks, you see. Yet it's also the word for a she-goat. And who wears a goatskin?' He did not wait for an answer. 'Auld Clootie. Belial. Lucifer himself, the

Laird of Darkness whom you must never allow to touch you. Ironic, is it not?' he went on. 'MacIntyre thought she'd speak in the tongue of the angels and everyone else thinks she speaks Satan's Esperanto.'

'Have you touched her?' I asked.

'No, I've been ten feet from her but no nearer.'

'She took my hand and kissed me.'

Ogilvy leaned forward, the whisky glass clamped between his two fingers. 'And did you return her kiss?'

'I tried. She backed away.'

Ogilvy made no comment.

'My mind's not been stolen,' I continued, as if attempting to justify my action.

'No,' Ogilvy replied, 'your mind's still your own, but, like me, a piece of your soul's been given away.'

20

The young doctor's name is Belasco, a graduate of the medical school at the University of Bristol, where he studied for five years. His father is a general practitioner in Herefordshire, his mother is the deputy headmistress of a primary school in Ross-on-Wye and his sister is currently studying dentistry at the University of Cardiff. He has only been qualified for three years, and St. Justin's is his second position. Prior to coming here, he was on the staff of a big hospital on the outskirts of Birmingham. During his time there, he wrote a paper on schizophrenia. He lives in a small house in a village three miles away which he shares with his partner, Louise, a mathematics graduate who works as a loss adjuster for a commercial insurance brokerage firm. They have a black Labrador-cross-collie dog called Pliny, so named because he has the long face of a thoughtful sage, and a Siamese cat called Cardinal Sin. The latter is named after an ethnically Chinese Catholic prelate to the Philippine Islands, the irony of it lost on neither the good doctor nor me, although I make no indication of appreciating the joke.

I know all this because Dr. Belasco has told me.

For three days now, he has come to me in the early afternoon, sat at my side and prattled on about his past, his life and current affairs. From him, I have learnt such diverse information as the fact that the United Kingdom is still governed by a parliament of fools, there has been a serious flood in India and the price of petroleum continues to rise at an alarming rate.

On every topic upon which he has touched he passes a comment or takes a stand that is intended to excite or arouse me. He has made outlandishly racist remarks about "niggers and wogs," attacked the hypocrisy of the Roman Catholic church over the matter of contraception and revelled in the downfall of an arrogant and oversexed politician jailed for perjury and perverting the course of justice.

Throughout each diatribe, he has watched me. Not obviously, but astutely, in such a manner as he thinks I have not noticed. He looks especially at my hands and face, hoping to catch a twitch in my fingers, a flicker of an eyelid or a momentary parting of my lips: any sign that I have registered what he is talking about and might be willing to communicate through the curtains of silence he believes I must want to part and in which he must assist me.

What I find touching in his display is the fact that he is willing to betray himself to try to cure me. I know he has no racist attitudes. Watching him converse with several of the nurses who happen to be of black or Asian extraction, I can tell he harbours no animosity towards them. In the instance of one Chinese nurse, I would even suggest that Louise the loss adjuster might, one day, have to adjust to her own loss.

He does not realise he is wasting his time and merely helping me to pass mine on my trip down the road to oblivion. There is nothing he can do, or say, that will shock me. I am old; I have seen the world spin, and men spin with it. There is nothing left that can provoke anger in me. My rage is spent, its flame extinguished and its anguish veiled behind my quietude. All I have left are a few unexpurgated and unexpungeable regrets.

21

The day after the rain lifted, I returned to Dùn an Làmh Thoisgeal. The sides of the midden trench had caved in, but the rainwater had mostly seeped away into the surrounding soil, permitting me to continue with my excavation. I worked steadily, carefully, finding more animal bones, shards of pottery, another small section of the carved comb, a corroded bronze arrowhead in the shape of a thin leaf and a shaped fragment of pale green glass. The latter were most exciting. The arrowhead was not barbed and of the variety designed not for hunting but for military use, suggesting that the occupants of the broch had been involved in defending their settlement from incursion or, conversely, were belligerent towards their neighbours. As for the glass, the surface was covered in a silvered patina caused by the chemical reaction of acids in the earth. Even a cursory look confirmed to me that it was of Roman origin, possibly the neck of a *lachrymonum,* the delicate bottle frequently placed in Roman burials, into which had been collected the last tears of the deceased.

Cleaning the piece of glass in a pool of rainwater, I sat on a boulder and held it to the sunlight. Tiny bubbles of air, trapped in the matrix, seemed to move as I tilted it this way and that. Knowing that the Romans had never penetrated as far north as the Western Highlands suggested to me that the broch builders had been traders, perhaps maritime merchant adventurers who had sailed south in search of business, dealing in hides and luxury goods such as the comb. An alternative theory, that I might be in the region of the final resting place of the lost Ninth Legion, which it was rumoured had been sent north from Hadrian's Wall in the first century, never to be seen again, was too fanciful to be entertained: yet I could not help thinking it was within the vague realm of extreme possibility. To discover the legion's fate would be the making of my reputation.

Although involved with my dig, I kept looking up in the vain hope of catching a glimpse of the girl. When taking a rest, I sat in the ruins of the broch in case she had surreptitiously swum ashore. I scanned the island through Ogilvy's telescope yet saw nothing save scrub and rocks, only the low bushes moving in a strong onshore breeze.

At the end of the day, somewhat disappointed that I had not at least seen the girl from afar, I packed up and headed for Breakish.

Approaching the village, I saw a steam yacht riding at anchor in the bay, her woodwork highly varnished, her brass fittings gleaming in the late sunlight. A red ensign fluttered from a flag staff at her stern whilst, from a gaff on her mainmast, a short yacht club pennant snapped in the breeze. Gathered on the quayside was an animated group of villagers, mostly men and teenage boys. At their centre was a figure dressed in a gold-braided yachting cap, a dark blue blazer and immaculately pressed grey trousers. On the periphery of the gathering stood Jamie, a fishing rod in one hand and a wicker basket in the other.

'What's going on?' I asked him, reluctant to barge in on the meeting. I was conscious of Ogilvy's warning that the villagers regarded me with some misgiving.

'Someone's been shot, sir,' he said. 'Someone important.'

'Where? In Breakish?'

'No, sir, a-ways.'

I hurried on to the inn, to meet Ogilvy coming out.

'Someone's been shot,' I told him.

'Shot dead,' he replied.

'Down south?' I asked.

'You might put it that way,' Ogilvy said. 'Archduke Ferdinand of Austria and Hungary has been assassinated in Sarajevo by a Serbian nationalist. It happened a week ago Thursday. The German army has marched into Belgium and we are at war with Germany. The gentleman with the grand boat is touring the villages, spreading the news and asking for volunteers.'

I felt an immense apprehension wash over me and my stepfather's words returned to me: *A war is the best employer of them all.* A vision of the slaughter at the battle of Colenso came to me, of men killed by the shortcomings of their own artillery.

'There's a letter for you,' Ogilvy continued. 'Special delivery, brought from Mallaig by the boat there. It's in your room.'

The envelope was propped up on the mantel shelf above the grate. Although the address was typed, I knew from whom the letter came: the paper was cream with a discreet black regimental crest embossed upon the flap. I slit it open with my knife.

'Dear Stepson,' it stated with characteristic impersonality, *'As you will by now be aware, we are at war. I have spoken to the adjutant of the First Battalion, the Connaught Rangers, with whom I fought against the Boers He has generously arranged for you to receive a lieutenant's commission in the regiment. You are to contact him, Lt. Col. . . . '*

I read no more and, taking my pad of drawing paper and a pen from my satchel, went quickly downstairs to the taproom. There, at the table where most nights Ogilvy wrote his autobiography, I sat down and replied, my hand tense with anger and my jaw set.

It was a curt note and dispensed with the usual greeting: *'The value of history is that it instructs. Warfare has never justified its morality. I have no intention whatsoever of accepting a commission and shall not be seeking to enlist in either of the armed forces.'* I signed it *'A. Marquand.'* Not having an envelope, I folded the letter over and in on itself, hurriedly scribbling my stepfather's address on the outside. This done, I ran out of the inn and along the quay to where the gentleman yachtsman was preparing to depart for his pleasure craft in a dinghy. Handing him my letter and sufficient money to cover the postal charge, I requested he mail it for me at the first opportunity.

That evening, the mood in Breakish was sombre. Small groups of men sat on the quay, talking in subdued voices. Several repaired nets. One occupied himself by carving a wooden belaying pin. A number of boys in their late teens were gathered at the top of the landing steps, discussing in animated fashion how they saw their immediate future serving in Scottish regiments of the line. Just as their forebears had committed themselves to fighting the English, so did they now view the Germans.

I walked up and down the waterfront, my thoughts turbulent and bitter. My stepfather's letter had unnerved me, for it had, in its stark way, told me that whatever direction it took, my life was soon going to change, unequivocally and, probably, irrevocably. Beyond this apprehension, however, was a terrible fury I wanted to suppress yet could not. My dislike of my stepfather, until now little more than an aggravation in my life, was now matured into an abiding hatred. His presumption that I would want an officer's commission, his effrontery at arranging it without so much as a word to me, staggered me. By the time I had passed the carver of the belaying pin for a fourth time, I was seething, my fists bunched in my pocket and my jaw so clenched the muscles were beginning to ache. I wished the tyrant dead and concocted a number of ways by which I should like his death to happen. It was quite dark by the time I returned to the inn, exhausted by my ire.

'You've read your letter then,' Ogilvy said as I entered.

'I have.'

'The said contents of which have had you marching up and down Breakish as if you were softening a new pair of shoes. Or,' he added, 'readying yourself for the parade ground.'

'The latter is not an option,' I replied tersely.

'So you're not for this war?'

'Not this war. Not any war.' I felt my anger rising once more. 'I have studied enough of history to know that wars are the invention of politicians and princes, not people. No one benefits save the munitions makers and the warship chandlers, the gunsmiths and the steel magnates. The rulers survive. The ruled fall and rot'—I thought yet again of my stepfather's benighted painting—'in the long grass of a battlefield forgotten by everyone but the generals who oversaw the slaughter from a ridge behind the artillery lines.'

'So the defence of your motherland is of secondary relevance to you?' Ogilvy suggested.

'We live in an age of reason,' I almost exploded. 'Can we not find a better way to talk and settle differences, without the massacre of thousands of men to satisfy national pride? What are we?' I continued, my emotion now in control of my rhetoric. 'Visigoths? Vikings? Vandals coming over the hills of Rome with blazing pitch brands and broad-bladed axes? We are civilised, for Christ's sake!'

'If there's one thing I've learnt in my sailing the oceans of the world,' Ogilvy said, 'it's that what you call civilisation is a very thin veneer upon the soul of any man. As for anything being for the sake of Christ, may I give you a wee word of advice? It's got nothing to do with Christ—or Jehovah, or Buddha, or Mohammed or a painted totem pole in the jungle—and as soon as a man brings his god into justifying his own actions you can be sure the devil's got his hand in the matter.' He smiled. 'Beth's left a piece of pie for you. I'll fetch it from the pantry.'

Sitting at the table, I consciously calmed myself down, counting my pulse and trying to decelerate its racing. By the time Ogilvy returned, I felt calmer and more prepared for logical thought or discussion.

'It's cold,' he said, putting a plate and cutlery before me. 'Venison, from the hills behind, and pickled walnuts of my own devising. I pick the young nuts, before the shells have formed, and soak them in saturated brine for three weeks, changing it every third day. When they're as black as a witch's armpit, I put them in sweet vinegar with a sprig of rosemary. And I'll bet you'd like a wee dram with your food . . . '

I thanked him and began to eat. My anger had, like a day's strenuous exercise, given me an appetite. The meat in the pie was dense and heavy, the pastry hard, the walnuts aromatic and a perfect complement; the whisky was smooth after the richness of the meal.

'I see you penned a reply before the yacht departed,' Ogilvy observed.

Taking my stepfather's letter out of my pocket, I handed it to him. He read it slowly, folded it and gave it back to me.

'I've a fair mind I can deduce what your reply was.'

'I shall not fight,' I said.

The refusal had been in my thoughts ever since I slit open the envelope and took in the contents, but now, as I actually voiced them, the stark reality of my stand hit me.

'That's as brave a decision as loading your rifle,' Ogilvy remarked. 'You'll not find it an easy road.'

'You think I should?' I asked.

'I think you should follow your conscience,' Ogilvy answered. 'It's not for me to say how another man should be.'

'Will you join up?'

He held up his right hand. 'I think I'm a few digits short of a trigger finger.'

I finished the pie and pushed my plate aside. Ogilvy lit his pipe with a splint from the fire and poured out two measures of whisky.

'*Slàinte!*' he exclaimed, holding his glass between his two fingers.

'*Slàinte!*' I replied.

Shortly after, I went up to my room, taking a candle with me. It was dark by now, the walls a dance of shadows.

22

There has arrived in this place at some time during the last month a poor deluded character who believes he is someone whom he is not.

One of those considered to be of low risk, he is permitted to wander the garden and building more or less at will. Depending upon who he thinks he is on any one day, so he acts accordingly to all those whom he meets. On occasion, he has regarded himself as some sort of holy man, benignly blessing all who have crossed his path, offering consolation to those inmates he deems far worse afflicted than himself and redemption to those few who, misguidedly taking him at his word, have bowed their heads before him. The doctors and nurses have smiled at his fantasies, which he has acknowledged with an episcopal wave or exaggerated marking of the sign of the cross in the air before them. At other times, the holy boot has been on the other foot and he has been the one seeking the balm of salvation.

Today, he has considered himself to be a sinner.

As I was sitting beneath the oak, he came up to me, kneeling on the ground before me.

'Forgive me, Father, for I have sinned,' he said, his face downturned, his fingers interlinked and his hands hanging before him, palms upwards, as if to catch any drops of benediction I might care to scatter his way.

'I have sinned,' he repeated, 'against the Lord my God. I have dishonoured my father and my mother, have coveted my neighbour's property, stolen from him and given false testimony. . . . '

His first admissions were of lesser evils, but as he progressed his wickedness escalated, each sin vying with the last in the quality of its depravity and iniquity.

'. . . I have desecrated my own flesh and fornicated with whores, with children, even with the beasts of the field. I have slain women, ripping the unborn infants from their bellies and casting them into the flames, have put to death men whom I have emasculated whilst they were still alive and consuming their genitals, have sent to the rendering ovens of slaughterhouses mothers and babies, have electrocuted . . . '

I could take no more of his self-indulgent fantasies, nor could I accept any more of the images he was crowding into my mind, triggering off memories of my own few, petty sinnings, and being sinned against, which I know lurk within me but which I seek to abjure with all the strength I can muster.

To shut him up, I placed my hand upon his head. His hair was short, curly, coarse and slightly greasy. To make contact with it revolted me, yet I had no other option. Such is the drawback of being a messiah: you have to deal with all kind and condition of the human animal.

At my touch, he stopped his blathering and his shoulders began to heave as if he were an asthmatic trying to catch his breath. I placed my hand under his stubbled chin, raising his face up. There were no tears in his eyes. He was, like me, past crying.

Salvaged from his pit of degradation, at least for the time being, he got to his feet, brushing the detritus of the oak tree from his knees and sauntering off. He had not reached the far side of the garden before he was transmogrified into a man of the cloth once more.

He knows not who he is, yet I . . . I know who I am. I am the man who, because he does not speak of obscenity, can not deny it.

23

For two days after the arrival of my stepfather's letter, Ogilvy tried to persuade Jamie's mother to permit her son to take me back to the island, but she was adamant. There was talk in Breakish of submarines, which in turn engendered a report that one had been seen off Eilean Tosdach; that a school of dolphins regularly visited the area, chasing the mackerel and herring shoals, did little to diminish the rumour. Even my offer of thirty shillings would not sway her. She had lost her husband to the powers of evil and she was not going to risk her only child any further.

My despair grew by the hour. I had to see the girl again, yearned not so much for her company as her presence. Lying in my bed on the second night, I could not sleep for thinking of her and tried to recall her appearance in the smallest detail. In the small hours, I imagined her in my lodgings with me, not by my side but across the room, sitting in the chair with the moonlight playing on her hair.

It was comparatively easy to reconstruct her in my nocturnal imagination; to actually meet her again was as impossible as climbing one of the moonbeams cutting through the casement, casting the shadows of the window bars on the rug at her feet. I could no more sail a boat to, and land on, the island than build a bridge to it.

On the third day, I walked at dawn to Dùn an Làmh Thoisgeal. There was a light mist on the sea, killing the sound of my footsteps upon the stony path. The mountains were shrouded in fog, the air damp and cool and still.

Reaching the broch, I removed a white shirt from my satchel and, going to the edge of the low cliff, spread it out upon a rock, the long sleeves splayed as if the wearer were being crucified. To keep it in place, I weighted the corners down with stones. It was the only signal of which I could think. I had considered calling to her, but my voice would not have travelled through the mist and, had it, might have alerted the dog and, consequently, the old man. Lighting a bonfire was another option I had contemplated, allowing the smoke to drift over to the island; the lack of a breeze put paid to that idea. All I could do was let her know I was here and hope she would see my sign and correctly interpret it.

By eight o'clock in the morning, the sun had burned the mist away. The clouds on the mountains had dissipated, the day set fair and hot. To pass the time, I climbed the mountainside behind the broch, sketching the view in detail to set the ruin in the context of the landscape, yet all the while I watched the island and the strait before it. My anticipation rose when a head appeared briefly in mid-channel, only to dissolve into disappointment upon my realising that what I was seeing was a seal riding the current.

Late in the morning, I descended to the broch, pausing on the way to cool myself at the spring that must once have supplied the settlement. As I bent to the peat-tinged cold water, sluicing it over my face and wiping my brow, I sensed she had arrived. I could not say how I knew. There had been no sign of her presence: no bird had called, no rabbit broken startled from the undergrowth.

The realisation of her coming set my nerves on edge. It was as if some exotic drug were working its way through me, driving my blood faster, sharpening my nerves, setting my skin into a state of intense sensitivity that was not pain yet was, briefly, almost as unbearable.

She was not in the broch but making her way towards it from the shore, keeping low and moving from boulder to boulder. It was a moment before I realised she was hiding her progress not from me but from the island. As she passed it, she snatched my shirt from the rock, quickly folding it into a tight ball and hugging it to her chest.

When I reached the ruins, she was waiting there for me, sitting on one of the low interior walls, my shirt folded neatly beside her on a flat stone. She was stroking it, much as a furrier might a treasured pelt.

At my approach, she looked up and I heard her faintly mew.

'Hello,' I greeted her, keeping my voice soft. I was aware now that my speaking to her was redundant, but she was, I considered, talking to me in her bestial way and I should at least reply in my fashion.

Sitting beside her on the wall, I let her make the first move. For at least a minute, she just looked at me in silence: then, gradually, she moved her hand to cover my own, pressing her fingers down between mine. Her hands were strong, those of a person used to manual labour, and yet they were still very feminine, delicate almost. They reminded me of a charcoal drawing I had once seen of the hand of Michelangelo's *David*. She might have been made of white marble.

As long as she held my hand, she sat quite still, listening. Every so often, she tilted her head and glanced in the direction of the shore although, from where we sat, we could not see it. Her caution unnerved me. If the old man were to come ashore, there would be no escape from him. After a quarter of an hour, she suddenly relaxed, let go of my hand and, reaching down, picked up my satchel. Unclipping the buckle, she commenced removing the contents one item at a time, turning each object over in her hands as if it were some rare antique before laying it down next to my shirt. My knife, trowel, tape measure and the small corked bottle of Indian ink I took on field expeditions elicited little attention, yet my fountain pen greatly puzzled her. She studied it intently, holding it close to her face. I took it from her, unscrewed the cap and, across my palm, drew a thin line. She started back at this, a horrified stare on her face. I held my hand out to her, palm upwards. She took it and touched the line. With her thumb and index finger she then attempted to part the line, and it was then I realised she thought I had deliberately cut myself, that the pen nib was a blade. At the discovery that my skin was whole, she uttered a high-pitched whine of delight and ran a line over her own hand. She then giggled, drew another and handed the pen back to me. I replaced the cap and she put it on the flat stone beside the other items.

The interior of the satchel emptied, she undid the buckles on the outside pocket and found my leather-bound sketchbook, the covers of which were kept shut by a brass catch, opened by depressing a small button. As she was unable to work out how to operate it, I released the mechanism for her. She tentatively opened the book at the first page, a sketch of the broch from the sea. For several seconds she could not comprehend what she was looking at—then it dawned on her. Gasping with amazement, she stood up and looked around, pointing to certain features in the broch, comparing them to the sketch.

Realising she did not know how to turn the pages, I took the book and, holding it up that she might see it, showed her a series of drawings, culminating in the one I had most recently completed, of the broch with Eilean Tosdach in the distance. This she studied very closely indeed, holding the book herself and angling it to and fro as if, by doing so, she might see round an angle in the drawing. Finally, she placed the book next to my other possessions and, crossing the broch, climbed into the stair cavity in the walls. When she reappeared, she was halfway up the wall, on a narrow ledge upon which interior roof beams had once rested. She was naked, white and bleak against the dark stone. The bright sun shone on her, casting a dense black shadow on the ancient wall.

There was nothing erotic in her nudity. It was as if being devoid of clothing before a stranger meant little to her. She put out a hand to steady herself as she sat on the ledge, her legs dangling over the edge. Once comfortable, she held her arms out as if in supplication to a deity of which only she possessed any knowledge. All the while, she looked down upon me, smiling.

I was enraptured by her. Her innocence seemed both wonderful yet simultaneously compelling and primitive, even terrifying. I wondered if this was how men felt in the presence of the oracle at Delphi, seated in her grotto in the bowels of Mount Parnassus. The temptresses of legend must have been like her, exquisite in their beauty but horrifying in their power. I thought of Duessa, in Spenser's *The Faerie Queene,* who could change her form and appear beautiful to seduce unwitting men but who, in her true shape, had the tail of a fox, the claws of an eagle and the paws of a bear. To acknowledge her was to admit the essential truths of nature, of the passing of youth into old age, of growth declining to decay: in her was both the generation of life and the taking of it.

My inactivity seemed to make the girl grow impatient. She uttered a few little yelps; then, with her arm outstretched, she pointed down at me. It was as if a goddess were aiming her finger at me, reminding me of William Blake's painting *Ancient of Days*. At any minute, I thought, a bolt of divine energy might spark off her fingertips, to scorch or measure my soul.

She yelped again, a little more insistently, and I saw she was pointing not at me but at the sketchbook: she wanted me to sketch her. I picked the book up and opened my pen. She fell silent and sat gazing hard at me as I positioned myself on a rock and commenced to draw her.

For nearly two hours, as the sun passed its zenith and began to dip towards the sea, I worked assiduously on re-creating her likeness, attempting to capture the essence of her. It was not easy. I was a competent and exacting artist but used to drawing artefacts, not portraits.

After several studies of her on the ledge, I signalled her to come down and she obeyed, posing for me on the tumble of stones within the broch. She made no attempt to approach me and see the results of my labours but seemed contented just to sit or lie in the sun, the object of my undivided attention. Only once, when an eagle soared overhead and called, did she seem to suddenly waken and move quickly to a hole in the broch wall that faced seawards. It was as if the bird had spoken to her. Yet a few moments observing the shore put her at her ease again and she returned to sunning herself like a feline.

Eventually, I put my pen down. My hand was aching and I had run out of ink, having drained the little bottle.

Seeing me stop, she stepped down off the boulder upon which she had been sitting and came across to me. I watched the perfect orchestration of her muscles as she drew closer, unabashed by her nakedness. From a few feet she held her hand out, and I gave her the sketchbook. One by one, I turned the pages for her, she running her forefinger over the drawings.

'Do you like them?' I asked.

By way of reply, she took my hand and, as before, placed it against her breast. Very slowly, I put my other hand on her shoulder and drew her to me. She did not resist. Her skin was warm from the sun. I kissed her cheek. It was salty, perhaps from sweat, perhaps from her having swum from the island.

With her free hand, she unbuttoned my shirt, pushing it open and very gently pressing her breasts to my chest, at the same time letting my hand go.

I could have seduced her, lowered her to the spongy grass that grew between the debris of the walls, lain upon her and been her first lover. Of that I am sure. Yet I did not. I just stood with her in that ancient place, the stones of the broch our only witnesses, and hugged her closely, feeling her breath on my neck and listening to her sigh. Nor was it that I did not want her. I yearned for her, fantasised as I held her of bringing her to Breakish, of dressing her in real clothes, of taking her away with me. Of saving her. No sooner had I thought it, though, than I knew such a plan was impossible. I would not have been her salvation. It would be like capturing a beautiful wild creature—a cheetah, say, or an iridescent hummingbird—and keeping it as a pet, out of its natural habitat. To lie with her would have been to destroy her, to have given her a memory she could not repeat, imbue in her a longing she would never be able to satisfy without leaving Eilean Tosdach. To have seduced her would have been to devastate her innocence, corrupt her world by dragging her unknowingly into my own.

After a long while, I slid my arms from around her. She smiled as I let her go, stepped back and looked at me. I am sure, now, she was thinking what I was thinking. To have gone with me was simply too great an adventure.

The last picture was the third of three head-and-shoulders portraits. Picking up the sketchbook, I reached onto the flat rock and, taking up my knife, opened it in her full view so as not to alarm her. Carefully folding the page as close to the binding as possible, I cut it free, offering it to her. She did not accept it. Instead, she returned to the stairwell, collected her clothes from the shadows and dressed herself. She wore only the long, coarsely woven skirt I had seen before and an upper, shiftlike garment that I noticed had once been a man's shirt but was now devoid of its collar, with the front fastened by a length of twine laced through the stud holes.

Dressed, she came back to me and, fumbling in an inner pocket in the waistband of her skirt, pulled out a small packet wrapped in a square of dark leather tied with a thong of gut. This she undid, producing from it what I assumed was a twig of bleached wood not much bigger than a match. My first thought was that it might be some sort of charm such as gypsies tried to press upon one on busy market days whilst their scrofulous offspring surreptitiously inspected the contents of one's jacket or wallet. It would have been in keeping for her to posses such a thing. Unfolding my hand, she lay it along the axis of the line I had drawn on my palm, closing my fingers around it. It was so insignificant, I could barely feel it.

'Thank you,' I said.

At my words, she grinned mischievously. I felt momentarily uneasy. It occurred to me that this was how she cast her spell upon those who landed upon her island. Perhaps Jamie's daddy had been presented with such an object and it had twisted his soul, driven him from his wife's bed, from Breakish. Yet the feeling passed. It was illogical and I was not one to believe in talismans and sympathetic magic.

Opening my hand, I saw that what she had given me was not a wooden splint at all but a minute smooth bone. It was fragile, the colour of buttermilk, with tiny condoyles at each end.

Linking her thumbs together, she waved her fingers up and down, all the while lifting and lowering her hands, uttering a bubbling noise following by a curious warbling and pointing to my hand. The sound was immediately recognisable.

'It's a curlew's bone,' I said, and, taking out a pencil, drew a quick sketch of the bird in the corner of her portrait, its prominent needle-like beak curving away and down from its high-domed head.

When I showed it to her, she smiled again, then, reaching out, plucked the paper from my hand, folding it carefully and placing it in the pocket. This done, she abruptly turned and, without so much as half a glance back, walked out of the broch and off towards the sea.

The delicate bone still rested in my hand. Rolling it between my finger and thumb, I realised that this brittle object was not a means of casting a hex upon me but a token to me of her friendship, perhaps of her love, which, in her simplicity, she knew no other way of expressing.

I waited for a few moments, then, gathering up my possessions and satchel, walked down towards the shore, to pick up the path back to Breakish. Looking towards the island, I caught a brief glimpse of her. Naked once more, she was swimming against the current, keeping low in the water. Behind her, just breaking the surface, she towed a semi-translucent sheep's bladder containing her clothes.

24

Last evening, far off over the wall to the garden, a storm was brewing. Although I could not see them, I imagined hills with their patchwork of fields bright in the last of the day's sunlight, the sky in the distance beyond them the colour of tarnished gunmetal. Occasionally, lightning flashed deep in the clouds, yet there was no accompanying thunder.

I sat at the french doors of my room, my hands relaxed in my lap, my shoulders a little hunched and my head slightly downcast, the muscles in my neck slack. My feet were planted firmly on the floorboards, several inches apart. This was how, long ago, it had been suggested I should handle moments such as this.

Had I obeyed the instructions to the letter, I should have shut my eyes, not screwing the lids tightly but just letting them close as if waiting for the benediction of sleep or a kiss from someone I loved. Yet although I tried hard to comply, I could not, for I just had to watch, be alert, be on my guard in case the lightning struck too near. In my mind, I knew this was obtuse. There was no way by which I could avoid a bolt of lightning. It would come quicker than a blink. I would still have my eyes open as the million volts turned me into charcoal. One moment I would be watching the rain bouncing on the newly mown grass of the lawns; the next I would cease to exist. This would happen in the matter of a millisecond.

Such is mortality.

Against the backdrop of the storm, I envisaged a village on a hill, the surrounding farmland strangely pristine, like a landscape painted in oils by an artist who preferred to use primary colours, for whom there was only truth and lies, light and dark, reality and falsity. I wondered if the clarity was due to a brief rain shower that had passed by as the storm's vanguard, cleansing the air of the dust of summer, or positive electrical particles caused by the proximity of the storm somehow affecting the refractive index of the sunlight.

As if the latter theory were correct, I felt the hairs of my forearm rise, as though a charge of static electricity or a cold draught—perhaps the finger of death—had just touched me. In response I shivered, and, as has happened so many times before, with this came my fear.

It rose from somewhere deep within me, somewhere I cannot plumb: a fear I know to be unjustified, unsullied by reason, unadulterated by intellectual analysis. If I had had to describe it, I would have said it was a fear as pure as terror could be.

For half an hour, I watched as the storm edged inexorably nearer, the sky darkening, the sun slanting lower and setting. As the evening drew in, the lightning became more apparent and I began to hear the rolls of thunder, muted but increasing in volume.

Gradually, I became resigned to the storm and, although my fear did not diminish, I came to terms with it. In my mind's eye, I personalised it, visualising it as a small and hunched gnome with a hideous, distorted face, lingering in shadows which I knew I could dispel at any moment by the flick of a light switch.

Yet even with this reassurance, there was something else I dreaded about the storm, even more than my own loathing of the gloomy sky and its promise of primeval violence. Once it broke, for those in the other rooms, the storm's brutal drama would bring fresh terrors of their own. To every clap of thunder and flash of electricity there would come an accompaniment of screams and groans, incoherent shouts and the sad, muted orchestral rhythms of sobbing.

I knew that these sounds, in their turn, would be certain to spark off visions in my mind which I could neither refuse nor refute, and that they would stay with me throughout the long hours of the night, tormenting and teasing and testing me.

On each occasion I have heard the agony of the anonymous men beyond my door, I have felt the urge to respond. It is in my nature to call out to these tortured voices. I have desperately wanted to respond to their shouts with consoling whispers, and yet I knew no matter how loudly they called out in pain, I could only meet their anguish with my abiding silence.

Sometimes, after the lights are dimmed and before I surrender to sleep, words crowd into my head, like bees in a hive, churning round in a humming swarm, yet never finding my mouth, never discovering a way out. I press my hands to my ears or try to muffle my head with the pillow to quell their incessant clamour, but it is never any good. They continue to swirl around within me, marbling like the heavy smoke of a fat Havana cigar in a still room, only gradually subsiding into the silence in which I now dwell and which I have come to accept unequivocally.

When the door opened, I displayed no sign whatsoever that I was aware of the fact that someone had entered my room, yet I was fully conscious of it. My nerves were steeled as I listened, attentive to the quiet footfalls, the rustle of the sheets on my bed and the soft hush as my pillows were pumped and rearranged. After a few moments, I picked up an indistinct scent of apple blossom, which permitted me to lower my guard somewhat. Unless I were being bamboozled, unless this was some indiscernible trial to which I was being subjected, I knew the identity of the person behind me.

The quiet footsteps approached me.

'Hello, Alec.'

The voice was feminine, tentative, little more than a whisper and yet, at the same time, gently authoritative and confident. The fumes of apple blossom perfume grew stronger.

'It's Sister Cynthia, dear.'

I knew as much and, for a moment, I did not shift my gaze from the gathering storm, noting that one black cloud in particular was positioned at ten o'clock from the apex of the oak.

'How're you doing?' She looked out of the window, briefly following my gaze. 'We're in for a bit of rain. Still, we're all snug as a bug in a rug in here, aren't we?'

The cloud was not moving. It was not up to something. I risked turning my head a fraction.

'Nothing to get fret up about,' she said, as if agreeing with my interpretation of the cloud's possible motives. 'My grandmother used to say that rain was God's tears of laughter. His happiness made the flowers bloom.'

Very slowly, she put her hand out and, taking one of mine, raised it to her lips. My eyes followed my hand as if I were watching a magician conducting a particularly clever trick.

'Nothing to be worried about. Nothing at all.'

She kissed my hand and lightly patted it before putting it back in my lap.

'I'll be coming round with your supper soon. Poached haddock tonight. It's Friday. And'—she leaned forward a little bit—'sherry trifle.'

I gave no indication that this news meant anything to me.

'Bye-bye. I'll be back shortly with your tray.'

Her face moved away. My eyes remained fixed on the point where her lips had met my hand. Beyond was the bottle green velvet curtain, out of focus.

Perhaps a minute passed before, suddenly, I realised I had let my attention slip. I jerked my head back and stared out of the window. The black cloud was now at one o'clock to the oak. It had not moved with speed but gradually, stealthily. Perhaps, I thought, it might have an ulterior motive. There was no alternative but to observe it in case it should disclose its intentions.

Night fell and the storm arrived. A jag of lightning seared downwards behind the wall, momentarily silhouetting it, lending it an air of destruction. It looked for all the world like another wall I had known, in what seemed to me another life, before silence settled its dubious blessing upon me.

25

From the barred window of my cell I could see a corner of the exercise yard and, beyond it, a bleak granite tor with a scatter of rocks on the summit. At night, a single light sometimes burned from a small farm on the southern slope, a beacon pointing the way to freedom. The area of the cell was precisely six feet by nine. It contained two narrow bunks that were bolted into the wall with fittings for another two above them, a small shelf that made do as a sort of table, similarly affixed, a chair with a metal frame and wooden seat and two buckets, one of fresh water and the other for use as a latrine. Upon the bunks were canvas palliasses filled with straw and two coarse blankets which invariably smelled slightly musty even after recent laundering. Despite the available accommodation, I occupied the cell alone.

My daily routine was as predictable as the motion of the stars. I was woken at six by the jangle of keys unlocking the door and, queuing outside my cell with the other criminals, took part in the ritual of slopping out. This consisted of carrying my bucket of effluent to a manhole in the courtyard, emptying it down the abyss, swilling the bucket out at a standpipe and also tipping that down the drain. The task accomplished, I went back to my cell and waited for half an hour before being summoned to go through the same ritual with my fresh water bucket, refilling this at the same standpipe. Going to and from the yard was done at the double, and great care had to be taken not to spill anything. If a prisoner spilt water, he had to mop it up: if he spilt shit, he had to collect it up with his bare hands and take it to the sewer entrance.

At seven o'clock, half a loaf of bread and a chunk of hard cheese were delivered to the cell door by two prisoners drafted for the task. At seven-thirty, we lined up again and filed out to the yard to collect sledgehammers and pickaxes. Equipped for our day's work, we marched out of the prison with a detachment of warders and, arriving at the village of Princetown, were taken to a yard close to a railway line where large boulders of granite had been delivered. For the remainder of the day, we broke these into chips of hardcore. Our only respite came at noon, when we were permitted half an hour to collect a mug of water from a barrel and eat two ship's biscuits which were so hard they had to be soaked for ten minutes before becoming pliable enough to chew. At five o'clock, we were marched back to the prison, surrendered our tools, collected an apple, a plate of hot food and a mug of tea, then went to our cells. The doors were locked at half past six for the night. Only Sunday was different, when a chapel service was held at nine o'clock, after which groups of prisoners were permitted to exercise in the prison yard. At no time, except during exercise periods, were we permitted to speak to anyone but our gaolers. When not praying or stretching our legs around the yard, we were locked in our cells with our thoughts.

Every evening, despite myself, I could not stop mulling over the circumstances that had incarcerated me.

They had come for me as I was taking my breakfast of porridge with Ogilvy. A police constable, an under-sheriff and a soldier, the three of them had set off on horseback for Breakish several hours before dawn, risking the ascent to Bealach na Clachan in the dark. They were polite, almost diffident, but they had their duty to do. The wording of the arrest warrant was ambiguous, accusing me of conduct likely to engender a breach of the peace. I was given half an hour to pack my belongings; then, seated upon a horse they had brought with them, my baggage distributed among the other mounts, I was led out of the village towards the mountains.

Not until we reached the monks' cells in the pass did I look back. Far away, I could just make out the bay upon which Breakish stood while, to the south, Eilean Tosdach was little more than a smudge upon the sea. I had only been there a matter of weeks and yet I knew

I was leaving much of myself on that isolated coast. With every step the horse took, the emptiness in me grew deeper and more profound.

We rode throughout the day, stopping only twice to water the horses. It was after dusk when we reached a small railway halt close to a hamlet of less than a dozen houses. Here we discharged the horses, had a mean meal in what served as an inn for travellers and, shortly before midnight, caught a train for Inverness. Once we were seated in the carriage, the police constable took out his handcuffs and secured my right wrist to the leather strap hinge of the carriage door. As the train made its slow way across Scotland, weaving along river valleys and through glens, under towering mountains and forests of fir darker than the night, my companions took it in turns to guard me. The soldier kept his rifle well out of my reach by placing it on the luggage rack above his head.

Arriving in Inverness just after daybreak, I was escorted through the empty streets to the police station, where I was given an enamel mug of tea and some rashers of grilled bacon and toast, then placed in the local lock-up. That evening, with an escort of three soldiers, I embarked upon a journey that ended, two days later, in a courtroom in a suburb of west London.

My case was heard by three magistrates seated behind a table on a dais, surrounded by oak panelling into which was inscribed the coat of arms of the county of Middlesex. I was led in between two police officers and positioned in the dock, facing the justices. After I had confirmed my identity, I was told to remain standing. A lawyer had been appointed by the court to represent me, but my two short meetings with him prior to my appearance were sufficient to show me that, for a reason I could not fathom, he held me in contempt and would do nothing more than the minimum required of him.

'Alec Sebastian Marquand,' the chairman of the trio said after he and his colleagues had perused the documents before them for a minute or two. 'We have reason to believe that you have expressed the intention of avoiding military service at a time when this country is at war with Germany. Is this correct?'

My lawyer made to stand up, to go through the motions of defending me, but I signalled to him to remain seated.

I replied, 'I have been led to believe that the charge laid against me is one of seeking to carry out a breach of the peace.'

The chairman, without recourse to his colleagues, answered, 'That is the charge upon which you were arrested. This was for your own protection and to avoid undue publicity being given to your case. For this you should be grateful. Were the actual charge known, you may have'—he paused to consider his words—'experienced some discomfort from those whom you encountered, particularly at such a time as this.'

Ignoring his remarks, I said, 'I do not consider it just that I be arrested on what is essentially a trumped-up charge with no validity whatsoever, only to be accused of a totally different misdemeanour when appearing before the bench.'

At this point, I looked round the court. The public seating was empty except for my stepfather. It was then I understood. He had used his influence and, as he saw it, was teaching me a lesson. In the face of authority, he was convinced, I would surrender to his will, accept the commission he had arranged, become a soldier like him. Become a man. I wondered with which of the magistrates he had attended school, or military academy, or fought alongside in the African bushveldt.

'I have expressed no such intention,' I continued, addressing the magistrate's question. 'I have not been called upon for military service and so the matter has not arisen.'

'We have documents before us that show you have been generously offered a commission in the First Battalion, The Connaught Rangers.'

'This is an offer. It is not an order,' I rejoined.

The magistrate on the right, a thin-faced man with a tic beneath his left eye, said, 'Do you not consider, at a time of war, that such an offer is tantamount to an order to show your patriotism?'

'No, I do not,' I answered. 'The commission was not requested by me but was arranged by my stepfather without consultation with or recourse to me.'

'So it is not your wish to accept this commission?'

'It is not,' I said firmly, at the same time looking in my stepfather's direction. He was, I noticed to my discomfort, smiling faintly.

'If you are rejecting this opportunity for a commission, are you nevertheless prepared to accept military service?'

I should have considered my answer carefully, yet I did not. I was infuriated by that faint smile.

'I have not considered the matter . . . ' I began.

'Not considered the matter,' echoed the thin-faced magistrate, 'when men like you—young, fit men—are lining up at recruiting offices in every major city in the land, eager to serve in the defence of our great empire?'

I made no response.

'You mentioned you had not been called upon for military service,' remarked the third magistrate, an elderly man with a neatly trimmed full beard. 'By this,' he went on in an almost benign tone, 'are we to assume that you intend to take no steps to come to your country's aid until requested so to do?'

'You may assume that,' I confirmed.

They exchanged glances and, not to my surprise, the chairman looked briefly at my stepfather as if to either gain his acquiescence for what was to follow or to ensure that the proceedings were taking the path upon they had previously agreed.

'Are we to assume, Mr. Marquand, that you wish to consider yourself a pacifist?'

My lawyer got to his feet, whispered in my ear, 'Consider carefully how you reply,' and sat down again.

I had not considered such a question before. The concept of war was almost academic, something I had studied in tall-ceilinged rooms, the sun shafting through the windows to agitate motes of dust into a giddy, microscopic dance, or had looked upon with distaste in the painting of the Boer War massacre so admired by my stepfather. Now, I was being coerced into making a moral decision, taking a stand for what I believed to be right and just, and by which I could demonstrate my loathing for that which the self-righteous Colonel regarded as so manly and magnificent. It took me little more than a minute to reach my decision and compose my response.

'There are those,' I began, 'who consider war to be a glorious matter, filled with comradeship, honour, valour and loyalty. For them, to go to war is a gallant action which they justify by claiming right to be on their side. These noble sentiments are admirable and I do not seek to demean the memory of those who have upheld them in the firm belief that they were doing right. However, I consider war to be futile.'

The chairman of the magistrates leaned forward as if the better to hear me. The thin-faced one leaned backwards, as if already bored with what he was predetermining would be a tirade, whilst the bearded one looked hard at me.

'This futility,' I continued, 'lies in the fact that whilst national borders may shift and kingdoms expand or contract, there is little else of benefit to be gained. Merchants may trade more widely in one land and less in another. A political or religious ideal may come to the fore at the expense of another declining, but, for the general citizen, war is nothing more than a change of master earned at the expense of human life and misery. War is the playground of kings and presidents, not of people.'

By now, I was warming to my theme, but, my head filled with the enormity of my subject, I was having to struggle with myself to remain succinct.

'Whenever war is declared, the antagonists proclaim divine right on their side. No soldier has gone to war without the sure faith that his god is behind him, justifying his cause. The priests have condoned the killing in direct contravention of the holy commandment that all human life is sacred. Can the killing of a Muslim at the fall of Jerusalem in 1099 be claimed as a holy act? Or the death of a Christian crusader at Acre in 1291? The First Crusade had nothing to do with religious ideology. That was a hypocritical excuse, expressed by Pope Urban the Second. The real reason for the crusade was the fact that the population of Europe was expanding rapidly, causing the increasing demand for trade and the control of trade routes to the

East. Religious zeal was merely used as a tool to mobilise fighters in the name of mercantile progress.'

'We are not here,' the thin-faced magistrate interrupted me, 'to be given a history lecture. Kindly answer the question.'

The moment had arrived. It was, I suppose, the one for which I had been waiting all of my life, although I had not known it until then. Now was the time to declare myself, to state unequivocally where I stood on matters of common morality. Across my mind flashed a series of brief images, of the men cut down by their own guns at the battle of Colenso, of the bronze arrowhead, of Eilean Tosdach 'and the girl, of her innocence that knew nothing of such things, and I thought how good it would be if the world were like her, unknowing and unwise in the artifice of destruction.

'We are waiting for your answer, sir,' the chairman said brusquely, cutting into my thoughts.

I looked at my stepfather. He, too, was waiting to hear what I would say, for my capitulation.

'I believe,' I said quietly, 'in the value and sanctity of human life, irrespective of nationality, creed or colour. Therefore, I will not place myself in such a position as to take life.'

My statement was greeted by a brief but profound silence, broken only when the chairman of the magistrates looked at me and said, 'Mr. Marquand, I will afford you the privilege of withdrawing your statement.'

'I have no intention of doing so,' I replied. 'I wish to state formally my status as a pacifist who will not take up arms against another man.'

The response seemed to flummox the magistrates. They conferred in whispers before the bearded one asked me, 'Do you mean to say that were a German soldier to enter your home, rape and mutilate your mother or sister, you would raise no hand against him?'

'I would try to restrain him,' I said, 'yet I would not kill him. I should allow the law to judge him, not me.'

'In other words, you would abnegate responsibility for his punishment to others,' said the chairman.

'I would not take the law into my own hands,' I said, 'That is not the behaviour of a civilised man.'

'And the act of rape is civilised?' the chairman asked, adding, 'Would you say you are a religious man, Mr. Marquand?'

I thought for a moment and answered, 'No, I would not say I am a religious man, but I would say I am a moral one.'

'And what,' asked the thin-faced man, going back to the theoretical German military rapist, 'if there were no law? If this were war and the power of the law was in abeyance.'

'I would seek to restrain him,' I repeated.

'What if your restraint was ineffectual?'

'I would continue until such a time as he killed me,' I replied.

'So you would let your mother or sister be raped and killed, and yourself, when a swift act on your part could prevent it.'

'If by this,' I said, 'you mean my killing of the rapist, then yes.'

From behind me I heard footsteps on the floorboards and the door to the court being wrenched open, then slammed shut, the latch rattling.

'In this case,' said the chairman of the magistrates, 'you leave me with no alternative but to remand you in custody until such a time as either you come to your senses or you appear before a higher court. You will, therefore, be taken from this court and held in a secure place pending further action.'

He signalled to the constables to step me down, but I held my ground

'I wish to know,' I said, 'under what authority you are remanding me. I am not aware that I have broken any law.'

The magistrate, who had turned his attention to the file on the desk before him, looked up.

'You are being remanded, sir,' he said curtly, 'under the Defence of the Realm Act, 1914, ratified by His Majesty's government but a week or so ago and empowering me to act in accordance with its provisions, which afford me the discretion to imprison any individual who declares against the war effort on ethical grounds.'

I was escorted from the courtroom and down a narrow stairwell the walls of which were decorated with dark green tiles. The portal to Hades, I thought, must look like this, the sides slick so as to offer no handhold to the fearful sinner or penitent screaming for mercy. At the bottom, I was led along a subterranean corridor and pushed into a windowless cell containing only a table and chair.

'Right, mush!' exclaimed one of the policemen, entering the cell whilst his colleague remained outside. 'Take off yer belt an' shoes.'

I obeyed. He passed the belt out of the door, removed my shoelaces, then handed my shoes back to me.

'Don't wan' yer t' get cold feet, do we?' he said.

This comment was met with a loud snigger from the corridor.

'An' we don't want yer to 'ang yerself, neither,' he went on. 'Not that there's much chance of that, wot with yer aversion to killing.'

'More's the pity,' came the retort from outside.

The door closed heavily, the key turning smoothly in the oiled lock. I listened as the footsteps died away.

I am not sure how long I was left alone, my watch and other valuables having been taken from me before my court appearance, but after some time the footsteps returned.

'Visitor,' said a voice as the door was unlocked.

I looked up to see my stepfather standing in the doorway.

'Have you anything to say to me, sir?'

I knew he expected a recantation, that he thought a few hours' incarceration might have destroyed my resolve, brought me to my senses and made me acquiesce to his will.

'I have nothing to say,' I replied.

'So you are content to be a bloody coward, are you?'

He wanted an argument, but I had, perhaps for the first time in my life, the better of him. I made no further response, which riled him further.

'A bloody coward!' he reiterated. 'Wherever you go from here on, you'll be known as a milksop, a spineless man with no guts, with no loyalty to his fellows, no love of his nation and no pride in himself.'

Still, I said nothing, allowing his anger to mount.

'You're a funker, sir.' His cheeks were reddening; his right hand had formed a fist, the fingers of his left flexing themselves. 'I have only one consolation,' he muttered through clenched teeth, 'that whenever you are in the company of men, you will be hounded, sir. They'll know you for the milquetoast that you are, and if they've any spunk in them, they'll beat the shit out of you.'

My continued silence was more than he could bear. He desperately wanted to draw me out, yet the more his determination grew, so did mine.

'You are a disgrace, sir,' he growled. 'To your family, to your country. I am only glad that your mother is not alive to see this pretty pass.'

It was a clumsy ploy. He should have known I would not fall for it. He might have once been in command of men, yet, I realised then, he could not judge them. To him, they were either imbued with courage or cowardice, obedience or insubordination, loyalty or treachery. There was no middle ground; his world was simplified to that of friends and enemies, all those who were not for him being by definition against him.

'God damn you!' he muttered. 'I hope you rot in hell.'

I could not resist it. I had to play with him, had to have the last word.

'But not in a ditch on the veldt, shot in the back by accident,' I said quietly.

My remark must have struck a raw nerve. His face darkened, his right eyebrow twitching, and it occurred to me that, were I to research into the regimental archives of the Connaughts or the Inniskillings, I might find his role in the skirmish to be somewhat less than exemplary.

'Fuck you!' he muttered, and, with that, he was gone.

I never saw him again.

Early the next morning, my feet manacled and my wrists fastened by handcuffs, I was taken under military escort to Paddington station and put on a train for Exeter. Two soldiers travelled with me, the blinds to our compartment kept closed the whole journey. Arriving in Exeter, I was transferred to a local train, part of which consisted of a carriage containing a number of barred cages. I was placed in one of these, two of the other cages being already occupied by an elderly man in a shabby suit and a youth wearing a cloth cap and moleskin trousers.

As night fell, we arrived at our destination, His Majesty's Prison: Dartmoor.

26

I have inhabited ruins all my life—ruins of stone, ruins of steel, ruins of skin and skeleton. There has been no example of devastation that I have not witnessed during my journey through the twentieth century, from which I have sought to escape, from which I still try to run, but in vain. One would think I would have learnt my lesson, but such is the indomitable spirit of even a silent man that he goes on trying.

Diametrically across the lawn from the oak there stands an old cherry tree. It being summer, the fruits are ripening and the gardener has covered the tree with a fine green net and hung strips of tinfoil from the branches to deter the birds. His efforts are only partially successful: the pigeons are scared off by the flash of the tin in the sunlight and the finches are stymied by the net, but a number of wily sparrows have found their way in.

When in the garden, or gazing out of my window, I make an effort not to see the tree. Especially in spring, when the branches are heavy with clusters of blooms, I deliberately look the other way or close my eyes as my head turns in its direction. It is not that I do not appreciate the beauty of cherry blossom but that the sight brings to me a vision I care not to reconstruct.

It was not something I saw myself but of which I heard tell by someone who participated in it and subsequently joined the ranks of the screamers and dribblers.

In May 1915, there was growing on the outskirts of a small village in Artois a cherry tree such as this. It was magnificent. The trunk was tall and the branches spread as wide as the arms of a benevolent angel. It was laden with such a profusion of flowers that it promised a harvest beyond any in the memory of its owner. The bees were kept busy visiting it so long as there was light in the sky and men looked upon the tree, tasting in their imagination the sweetness of the juice to come. Yet this tree, like the apple tree in the Garden of Eden, was forbidden to all men, standing in the land between the British and the German trenches.

After a week or so, the petals fell and a young British officer, in the way of young men who enjoy a good prank at no one else's expense, crept out to it one night and, clambering into the branches, reached the top to hang a Union Jack from the highest bough. As he was descending, a German sentry heard a sound and, afraid for his safety in the darkness, fired off a flare. As it drifted to earth on its little parachute the magnesium glare illuminated the young officer. In a nearby salient, a German machine gunner saw him and opened fire. The bullets thumped into this gullible prankster, his body flung back against the trunk of the cherry tree, spinning round to become ensnared in the branches.

Back at the sector headquarters, the brigadier was annoyed. The sight of the officer hanging there was sapping morale. For two consecutive nights, British patrols were ordered to retrieve the corpse, but each time they were beaten back by the machine gun. In the face of this failure, the brigadier resorted to the artillery. The gunners were commanded to fire upon the tree and dislodge the cadaver. Round after round took away branches, splintered the trunk and cratered the surrounding earth, but still the body refused to fall. Finally, a direct hit on the tree brought it down. The body disappeared into one of the craters. In a few weeks, the young officer's unit withdrawn from the line and other soldiers posted to it, he was forgotten, reduced to just a name on a casualty list, a single-line entry in the obituary column of the *Times* and a standard letter of condolence from the king. As the summer rains fell, the crater filled up with water, the sides eroded and the body, in its shredded uniform with its tarnished buttons and its unravelling braid, was swallowed by the mud.

The human body is nothing but a castle waiting to be ruined, its moat bridged, its ramparts scaled and its chambers ransacked. We may think we are secure in our house of flesh, yet our walls are made of straw and our roof of tinder. Only the mansions of the mind cannot be breached.

In the silent hours of the night, I have often wondered if that stump threw up new shoots. Legend says it did, but legends are only lies touched by optimistic reality. Yet I cannot help hoping that it did, that it bore fruit, red as a brigadier's shoulder tabs or a junior officer's blood.

27

Although the previous evening's skies might have augured fair weather for the following day, every morning a damp fog drifted over the moors, enveloping the jagged summit of the tor to the north and wafting down the slopes of grass, rocks and stunted bracken like the wet smoke lifting from an autumnal bonfire of garden leaves. At the granite walls of the prison, it seemed to coagulate before spilling over into the yard, almost tangible in its solidity. Whatever it touched shone with its pervasive dampness. The scene through my barred window was almost monochromatic—the dun-coloured foliage, the grey stone and the leaden sky.

No doubt, it had been the intention of the prison's founder to situate it in a place that was not only isolated but also oppressive, the better to grind down the inmates into a sense of subservience and surrender. What the prison regime could not do to break the human spirit the austere surroundings might.

I was determined, from the moment I passed under the angled granite blocks of the prison's main entrance, not to submit to my circumstances. No matter how bleak my life might be, I was solid in my resolve to see it through, for I was guilty of nothing more than a sense of impolitic morality.

For the first few days of my incarceration, I assumed I had been put into a cell on my own for my protection. One of the gaolers, on leading me to it on my arrival, had commented, 'You ain't going to find this a walk in the park, sunshine. We've got men in 'ere—'ard men— as would tear yer 'ead off for a tanner, and eat yer tongue on toast for another bob.'

However, it soon became apparent to me that my solitary accommodation, far from protecting me, was intended to arouse the ire of my fellow inmates. I heard several mumble within my earshot that 'the dandy,' as they quickly nicknamed me, was getting preferential treatment. The animosity came to a head on the second Sunday when we were on exercise in the yard. I was standing against the perimeter wall when two prisoners sidled up to me, one of them keeping his eye on the nearest warder. I paid them no attention. Suddenly, with such a swift action I hardly saw it coming, one of them slashed out at me with a shard of glass mounted in a block of laundry soap. The glass slit through the sleeve of my prison-issue jacket and cut deep into my flesh. I felt the warm blood oozing over my skin and let out an involuntary yell. The two walked off, splitting up as they went, my attacker dropping his weapon surreptitiously at my feet.

The nearest warder, who I was certain had witnessed the attack, came slowly over to me, swinging his truncheon.

'Had a little accident?' he asked casually.

I held my arm out. The blood was visibly seeping into the material.

'Somebody's going to have to soak that jacket overnight in a bucket of cold water,' he remarked, and he turned away.

'I need a doctor,' I said.

'What?' he snapped back, facing me.

'I need a doctor,' I repeated.

'And I need a good fuck,' the warder replied curtly, 'but I'm not going to get it in here and if you want a doctor, you little cunt, you address me as "sir." '

I was beginning to feel faint from the shock of the cut and loss of blood. My assailant had known exactly where to slice in order to hit an artery.

'I need a doctor, sir,' I said.

'That's better,' the warder answered patronisingly. 'Now, you grip your biceps tight with your other hand and you come with me.'

All eyes were on me as I followed the warder across the exercise yard and into the prison sanatorium. There, a doctor gave me a shot of morphine and stitched the wound, bandaging it tightly. He did not speak throughout, save to issue orders to me to hold my arm out, grip my fist or relax my forearm. When he was done, I was led back to my cell and locked in.

Despite my injury, I was not excused hard labour and, the following day, was back breaking rocks at the railway sidings. The only allowance made was that I was given a clump hammer for the job in place of a sledgehammer.

Over the following week, convicts started to mutter to me under their breath, in the slopping-out line, at meals, in the railway yard. Despite the fact that a rule of silence applied during these periods, the warders took no steps to stop the muttering. In the exercise periods, when talking was permitted, the convicts were louder in their comments. I was accused of being a funk, a wheyface, a skulker. To every comment I made no response. There seemed no point. It was better to keep quiet and endure the insults than risk a confrontation.

Name-calling I could accept, but, worse, several more events occurred aimed at unsettling me. Seeing an attack by my fellow convicts, in which I am sure the warders had colluded, had not weakened my spirit in any way, they started to try to undermine my confidence. I returned to my cell on the Monday evening to find two books on my bunk, the first reading matter I had seen since my arrest. I eagerly picked up the first volume; all the pages had been pasted together. On Tuesday night, on going to clean my teeth, I discovered my flat tin of tooth powder had been emptied, then refilled with boot blacking. A drowned rat appeared in my fresh water bucket, weighted down with a stone so that I might not see it until the level had dropped; on another night, my slop bucket arrived filled to the brim with excrement, leaving me no room to relieve myself during the night and forcing me to piss into the fresh water container. These acts, I was sure, could only have been the work of the warders who had access to the keys of my cell, and, lying in my bunk after the lights went out, I wondered if they were being conducted by them on their own initiative or if the authorities or my stepfather had had a hand in them. That would not have surprised me. He had only to approach a judge or government minister in the smoking room of his London club.

Matters came to a head on Friday, a day of squally showers and periods of brilliant sunlight. My work party had been assigned to shovelling the week's broken hardcore into railway trucks standing at the edge of the sidings. As I was unable to wield a shovel, I was given the task of tallying the amount of stone shifted. To do this, I had to balance on the buffers of each truck, telling those below to stop shovelling when the load was sufficient. I was looking into one truck, measuring the depth of the stone with a yardstick, when someone below called my name. Turning, I was hit full in the face by a shovelful of stone. It knocked me off my balance, and I fell onto the trackside cinders on the far side of the truck, gashing a glancing blow on my skull against the corner of a wooden sleeper.

Dazed, I lay on the ground aware only of footsteps scrabbling under the stationary train. Opening my eyes and trying to focus on something to combat my dizziness, I saw indistinct figures looming over me, outlined against the grey sky. Rain was falling on my face, as hot as tears. I opened my mouth to drink, hoping it would revive me. It was curiously pungent and tasted tart and salty. It stung my eyes. Through it, I now saw a prisoner pissing onto my face, his grimy hand firmly holding his cock, moving it to and fro to spread his aim. Gagging and spitting, I screwed my eyes tight and tried to sit up. A boot, pressing hard on my shoulder, held me down.

'Scald the little shite!' someone above me said, adding to a second person, 'Jack 'ere's got a dose!'

There was a brief chortle followed by a curse, a dull metallic clang and a grunt. The stream of urine stopped abruptly. Something heavy thudded on the ground nearby. The boot disappeared and a sluice of icy water hit me in the face and chest, soaking me. It took my breath away.

'Get on with th' strap!' a new voice ordered, in a loud stage whisper. 'If one of th' screws gets wind of this, I'll have your fur for my collar.'

Boots scrabbled on the cinders. An arm helped me to sit up. A sopping cloth smelling of sweet tobacco was wiped over my face, then pressed to the gash on my head.

'Don't rat to th' screws,' the voice continued. 'If they ask, you lost your footing.'

I opened my eyes to find an unshaven, hard face close to my own. Its eyes were set close together and the lips thin and dry, spittle clinging to the corners of the mouth.

'Got it? You don't squawk.'

'I've got it,' I affirmed, and the face grinned, expansively. One of its teeth was crooked and chipped, the remainder coloured like old ivory by nicotine.

'You won't get no more bovver, but, if you do, you just say Mr. Rankin says to fuck off. That's me. I'm the con-boss 'ereabouts. And they'll fuck off. Just like magic!'

A whistle was blowing farther down the line of trucks.

'Time to scarper!' Rankin exclaimed.

He grabbed a long-handled shovel that lay nearby, the blade slick with fresh blood and a tuft of mousy-coloured hair, slithered under the railway truck and disappeared. No sooner had he gone than two warders ran up.

'Well, what 'ave we 'ere. If it ain't th' yeller belly! 'ad another little accident, 'ave we?'

'I slipped,' I said meekly, getting unsteadily to my feet. As I rose, I saw Rankin's face under the truck. He winked at me and grinned again.

One of the warders put a manacle on my legs and marched me back to the prison, where, once again, the prison doctor tended to my wound in silence before instructing that I be thoroughly cleaned. My clothes were taken away for laundering and, naked, I was stood against a wall in the yard, liberally dusted with delousing powder, handed a bar of carbolic soap and hosed down. These ablutions completed, I was led to my cell and locked in for the remainder of the day.

That night, about an hour after the lights were extinguished, when the only sounds to be heard in the cell block were the snores and grunts of sleeping convicts, there came a barely audible grating noise on my cell door. It was followed by a gentle rasping. I was instantly awake, my heart pounding. The lock snapped open and two figures let themselves into my cell, closing the door behind them.

Trying not to draw attention to my movement, I felt under my pillow for the only weapon I had—my spoon. One of the figures loomed nearer. I could barely make it out in the darkness. A hand suddenly clamped over my mouth, another pressing on my chest and forcing me down onto my palliasse.

'Shtum!' a voice whispered, close to my ear. 'Yer ain't in no 'arm.'

I lay still. The hands holding me down tentatively withdrew, ready to spring into action again if it looked as if I was going to holler. With a loud scratching noise, a match was struck. Its light briefly illuminated the cell. At the foot of my bunk stood Rankin. Behind him loomed a heavily built man with a large slice missing from his left ear.

'This 'ere's Mope,' Rankin said quietly, putting the match to the stub end of a candle which he placed on the floor beneath the spare bunk. ' 'e's me shtocker.' The other convict nodded his greeting to me. 'Now, you an' me's goin' to talk.' From inside his prison overalls Rankin produced a bottle, removing the cork with his teeth. 'Mope, get 'is mug, then drum th' rory an' th' landing. I don't want no screw creepin' up on us.' To me, he added, 'Get out of yer bunk and sit on the floor. If we talk low down, th' sound don't travel so good—but yer still whisper. Got it?'

I nodded. Mope did as he was ordered, passing over my enamel drinking mug, then positioning himself by the door, his nicked ear close to the metal panelling.

Rankin poured out a small measure of clear liquid from the bottle into my mug. He then bent over and sniffed at my fresh water bucket.

'This all right? No screws dumped in it?'

'I think it's clean,' I said.

Rankin, to be on the safe side, picked up the stub of candle and held it over the bucket. I noticed a stream of molten wax fall on his fingers. He seemed not to notice.

'It's clean,' he agreed, and he dipped my mug in it, drawing off an inch of water. 'If yer ain't used to Chat-O Dartmoor,' he said with a grin, 'it's best yer take it weak.'

Replacing the candle under the bunk, Rankin passed me my mug.

'What is it?' I enquired.

'Hooch. We make it. Out of taters and turnips. There's a deal of yeast in . . .'

Mope clicked his tongue. Rankin fell immediately silent, cupping his hands round the candle, plunging the cell into near darkness. After a few moments, Mope sighed. Rankin removed his hands from the candle.

'Bottoms up!' he said, taking a swig from the bottle and leaning back against the empty bunk.

I took a sip from my mug. Even though it had been well diluted, the liquor scoured my throat. I sucked in my breath.

'Another reason for waterin' it a bit,' Rankin remarked. 'Neat, you'd be coughin' like a cart horse by now.'

'How did you get in here?' I asked, now fully awake and in charge of my senses.

'Skellington keys. There ain't nowhere where I can't go in this nick,' he answered. ''ow do you think we get th' veges to make th' hooch? From th' stores.' He took another swig, his throat moving as he swallowed. 'Now, I got some questions and only you got th' answers. First off, what you been banged up for?'

'Nothing,' I replied.

Rankin gave me a look that immediately instilled fear into me. He might be my friend, and he had been my saviour in the railway yard, but he was not a man with whom to be trifled.

'No one's put in stir for nothin' an' I ain't got th' time to swaller crap,' he said pointedly.

'I have broken no law. All I have done is state that I will not fight in the war against Germany. At least,' I added by explanation, 'I will not take the life of another human being.'

'Why not?' Rankin asked. 'It's war, ain't it? They's th' enemy.'

'Because it is immoral. I stand in a field with a gun and I shoot a man at the other end of the field whom I do not know, against whom I have no grudge, with whom I have no argument and, probably, whose face I cannot even see. As for the Germans being our enemies,' I continued, 'they are not. The British government, the British monarchy, regard the German government and monarchy as enemies.

So be it. But does that mean my enemy is a German peasant wearing a *pickelhaub* and carrying a rifle?'

Rankin thought about this for a minute or two. The candlelight danced under the bunk, agitated by a draft coming in under the door. I took another sip of the potato-and-turnip liquor. It had a strange aftertaste, like that of burnt sugar.

'I've killed a man,' Rankin said at length. ''e was a lumber-cove, ran a tavern down by the docks. I used to go there to play cards. One night, I 'ad a repeater. That's the same card winning two 'an's, one after t'other. Only this was three 'an's. He told me I was cheatin', took me winnin's, pocketed the lot an' 'ad 'is bouncers chuck me out. Over twenty nicker, 'e took. I bided me time. Six months, so's not to arouse suspicion. Then, one night, I broke into 'is gaff. Coshed 'is old lady, dragged 'im from 'is bed, took 'im down the saloon bar and slit his fuckin' throat.'

'Is that why you're in here?' I enquired.

'No!' he exclaimed dismissively. 'If they knew that, I'd swing. I'm in fer larceny. Thievin'. Got eight. Done three. Five to go.'

Once again, Mope's tongue clicked. Rankin covered the candle. Along the metal floor of the landing outside, slow footsteps were advancing. Licking his thumb and forefinger, Rankin swiftly extinguished the candle. The footsteps drew closer, the sound accompanied now by the musical jingle of a bunch of keys hanging from a belt. Mope, in complete silence, stood up and positioned himself behind the door. The footsteps passed by. Mope waited, then, lying on the ground, opened the door sufficiently to poke his head out. After a moment, he drew it in and sighed. Rankin, after trimming the wick to make a small flame, relit the candle.

'What if,' Rankin expostulated, 'some German geezah was shaftin' yer tart? Layin' yer biddy. Wouldn't yer want to spike 'im?'

I laughed softly and said, 'That was what the magistrate asked.'

'So what did yer say?'

'I said I would attempt to stop him but that I would not kill him.'

'What if,' he suggested, ''e tried to top yer?'

'I would defend myself as best I could.'

'An' what if it was me what was poking yer piece?'

'I'd beat the shit out of you,' I said bluntly, 'but I'd not kill you.'

Rankin smiled. The candlelight shone on his stained, chipped teeth. 'Be quite a job, that.'

'I'd give it a go,' I replied.

'I bet yer would, an' all.' He paused, took another drink and sealed the bottle, slamming the cork home with the flat of his hand. 'Yer a puzzle, an' that's a fact. Yer get banged up in stir for speakin' yer mind. Yer get slashed and pissed on jus' to prove yer point. I'd not, I tell yer straight. An' one thing's fer sure. Whatever you is, yer ain't yeller like they say.'

'They?'

'The screws. Got their orders, ain't they?'

My suspicions had been well founded. The authorities had been behind the attacks and my stepfather must have been behind them.

'No,' I confirmed. 'I'm not yellow.'

Rankin picked up the candle. Once more, hot wax dribbled onto his fingers, but he ignored it. 'All clear, Mope?'

Mope sighed.

'No more bovver'll come yer way. Not in this hoosegow, anyways.'

He blew out the candle. The cell filled with the scent of the glowing wick and smouldering wax.

'We're tough buggers in 'ere,' Rankin concluded. 'Dartmoor ain't where they send th' friskers, ponces an' buffers. I doubt there's a cee in 'ere that 'asn't murdered. Or tried to. They shouldn't 'ave sent yer 'ere. That was wrong, that was. Out of order.'

Mope opened the door. From a few cells away came the sound of a loud fart.

'Mope,' Rankin said, 'tell 'im 'ow yer lost yer ear.'

Mope's voice was soft, almost feminine, and I realised this was the first time I had heard him speak.

'Some mucker bit it off,' he said.

28

The evangelist has been doing his rounds again. I heard him early in the morning, in the corridor outside my room, his voice competing with the sound of the rain that has been falling all day. He was preaching forgiveness to the staff, quoting all manner of biblical texts in support of his benediction. They humour him, allow him his fantasies and do not interfere with his proselytising so long as he does not alarm or disturb any of our more fragile fellow inmates.

This afternoon, as I was lying on my bed, my mind lost in a smoky dream of vague places I have not seen and indistinct people with whom I have not conversed for decades, there came a knock at my door followed by a twisting of the handle. I did not turn my head, assuming it to be Sister Cynthia or the doctor, looking in on me.

Gradually, into view over my feet materialised the preacher. He was wearing a tweed jacket with his shirt on back to front beneath it, giving him the appearance of wearing a somewhat ragged clerical collar. His face glowed with the joy of finding a would-be convert.

Raising my hand, I made as if to shoo him away, but he saw this as my reaching for salvation and swiftly moved to my side, taking hold of my hand between both his.

'What shall we say, then?' he asked, beaming down at me with the stare of the lunatic lingering somewhere behind his beatific smile. 'Shall we go on sinning so that grace may increase? By no means! We died to sin. How can we live in it any longer?'

I made no effort to respond to his rhetoric, nor did I make any attempt to remove my hand. He took this as a good sign that I was riding with him along the high road to the Lord.

' "All have sinned and fall short of the glory of God," ' he announced. 'Romans 3:23. 'The wages of sin is death.' Romans 6:23.'

At this juncture, he fell silent, waiting for me to respond or, at least, start to admit to my many sins. He wanted a sinner so badly, not only to forgive but to save. To encourage me, perhaps, he knelt by my bedside, his face level with mine on the pillow.

Yet he was to be disappointed. I have no true sins to confess. A man who has lived for decades in total silence, in one institution or another, can hardly have had the opportunity to commit any wrong against any god unless it be in his mind. Even in there, I have not filled my hours with desires for the many nurses who have tended me or the many do-good ladies of the parish who have from time to time visited me, departing saddened by my state or frustrated by my refusal to communicate with even so much as the squeeze of a hand or blink of an eye. There has been nothing I have wanted to covet, no wrong I would have wished upon another—even the pseudo-pope kneeling by my side—and no name I would have thought to take in vain. Save, possibly, my own.

There is, nevertheless, one wrong I have committed. It is not so much a cardinal sin as a cardinal omission. It lies in my silence, for I possess a fragment of knowledge of which the world should know. I should have passed it on; however, I have not. I have kept it to myself and it is too late now. I am old, the sun has shone, the moon has risen and set and the world has spun a thousand times upon its giddy axis.

The evangelist, taking my silence for a fear of the almighty and assuming that I harboured some sort of angst or hatred, started mumbling a prayer. I could not make out a single word. Perhaps he was praying in tongues. Perhaps he was praying in the vernacular of God, in Hebrew, in that paradisiacal idiom known only to angels and beautiful children on remote islands.

For a moment, I left him at the bedside, his knees getting stiff on the boards, his palms beginning to sweat against my hand and the rain pattering on the window, and I returned to that place where, usually only in the darkest and calmest hours of the night, I go.

It was not raining as I arrived there. The sun was warm upon the heather, the breeze balmy and the mountains stark against the blue sky of summer. Someone was calling me. I could hear it quite distinctly. Although it did not utter my name, I knew it was me the voice was addressing. I looked up. An eagle was riding a thermal high over my head, its thin piping whistle enunciating my name in the shrill language of raptors.

'If you forgive men when they sin against you, your heavenly Father will also forgive you. But if you do not forgive men their sins, your Father will not forgive your sins.'

In an instant, I was back in the room with Padre Paranoiac.

'Matthew 6:14–15,' he said.

Poor bastard! If only he could know. I have long since forgiven all those who have sinned against me and, if there is a god, I daresay I have been exonerated.

Slowly, I turned my head towards him. He had his eyes closed, the better to concentrate upon his celestial intercourse. After a few moments, he opened them to find himself in my gaze. He started, let go of my hand as if a current were running through it, leapt to his feet and, standing in the middle of my room, screamed. It was a high-pitched noise, like that of a rabbit caught in the noose of a snare.

Immediately there came the staccato rattle of running feet in the corridor. My door slammed back as Sister Cynthia and an orderly burst in.

'His eyes!' the evangelist stuttered. 'His eyes! I've seen Sheol. I've seen Diabolus.'

Another orderly entered and, with the first, restrained the evangelist and led him out. Sister Cynthia leaned over and touched my brow.

'Nothing to get fret up about, Alec,' she half-whispered.

No, Sister Cynthia, I thought, you do not understand. There is something terribly wrong about the world. I saw it long ago and the Very Reverend Father Loon saw it just a minute since in my eyes. And the only thing that could address it, put it to rights, died before the world learnt its lesson.

29

I had been imprisoned in Dartmoor for a little over five weeks when, one morning, a warder took me aside as I was queuing to slop out.

'You!' he ordered, pointing to me and signing for me to lower my buckets to the floor. 'With me.'

Not a little apprehensively, I followed him into a part of the prison I had not previously visited, where I was locked into a cell containing a table and four chairs, all of the furniture fixed to the floor with carriage bolts which had been rounded off to prevent their being extracted even with a spanner. I sat there for some time before the door was opened and a warder came in with a tin mug of milky tea and a sugared bun wrapped up in a square of greaseproof paper. He made absolutely no comment to me, simply placing the food before me.

'Why have I been brought here?' I asked, but he ignored me and left, closing the door hard and locking it.

About midday, the door was again opened and three men entered. The first was a prison warder, the second a priest and the third a dapper little fellow in a pin-striped suit and grey spats, carrying a polished but much scuffed briefcase embossed with faded initials in gold leaf. The prison warder stood by the door, the other two sitting across the table from me.

'Mr. Alec Marquand?' the trim man enquired.

I nodded and said, 'I have been waiting for at least five hours with only a mug of tea to drink. I require a glass of water and I wish to know why I am here.'

The priest glanced at the warder, who rapped on the door, passing on my request to a guard outside. I heard footsteps retreating.

'Mr. Marquand,' the priest started, 'my name is the Reverend Michael Bard. This'—he indicated his companion—'is Mr. Samuel Clements. He is a lawyer who has been employed to represent you and look into your case.'

'I have not requested an attorney,' I replied, 'nor do I have the means with which to pay for one. I therefore do not wish this meeting to continue and demand that I be returned to my cell.'

'A moment,' Clements interjected. 'I have been retained to look into the case of yourself and others, imprisoned elsewhere in the country, for expressing their conscientious objection. My fees will be met by the No-Conscription Fellowship.'

'I am not a member,' I said truculently, suspecting some trick.

'You are a member,' the priest remarked, 'simply by your being imprisoned for your belief.'

The cell door opened, the warder being handed a wooden tray upon which stood a jug of fresh water and three glasses. Putting these on the table, he resumed his post. The priest poured a glass and handed it to me. Clements took a manila folder out of his briefcase, snapped the brass catches shut and opened the file on the table.

'I have here,' he began, removing from the folder two sheets of paper held together with a treasury tag, 'a brief synopsis of your trial, the legality of which is, in my opinion and to be quite blunt, not a little dubious. However, since you have been in prison, others have been tried for a similar offence under somewhat more exacting legal circumstances and, were you to be freed, you would almost certainly soon be re-arrested and tried with somewhat greater validity in law and rigour.'

'So,' I said, 'whatever the case, I am a convicted felon for taking a moral stand.'

'In a manner of speaking, yes,' replied the Reverend Bard. 'Only a very small handful of people, all of them long-practising Quakers, have succeeded in convincing a court of their moral position. As you have not been a regular churchgoer, never mind a Quaker, the courts will come down heavily upon you. The precedent has been set that, and I quote a judge here, "Christianity and Christian values are not a haven of convenience for cowards."'

'I am not a Christian,' I declared, 'but this is not to say that I am without morality. I will not fight because of my moral, not my religious, opinion.'

'Quite, quite,' said Clements in the tone of an impatient schoolmaster dealing with a fractious pupil. 'I appreciate this and Reverend Bard appreciates this. On the other hand, the authorities do not and there is not likely to be a way by which they will be persuaded otherwise. There is, however, a means by which we can overcome the problem. To this end, I must ask you a series of simple questions by which, if your answers are acceptable, I feel fairly confident I can secure your release almost immediately.'

Such an optimistic statement immediately put me on my guard. It seemed to me as if I was about to be bribed or tricked by some legal chicanery into a worse position than I was already in, assuming such could have been possible. Yet, at the same time, I was exhilarated by the thought that I was being offered a way out of my captivity.

Removing another sheet of paper from the folder, Clements smoothed it out and, producing a gold fountain pen from his jacket pocket, unscrewed the cap and shook it once to get the ink flowing.

'Please answer with just a negative or an affirmative,' he instructed as he wrote my name at the head of the sheet. 'First question: do you consider patriotism to be important?'

'It depends on the circumstances,' I replied.

'Please, Mr. Marquand,' Clements said with a pained tone. 'Yes or no.'

'Then yes, under certain conditions.'

He sighed at my equivocation, ticked a box on the sheet and continued, 'Do you consider yourself to be a man of morals?' Before I could answer, he ticked the affirmatory box and went on, 'Would you be prepared to swear your allegiance to His Majesty the King?'

'Yes,' I repeated, 'under certain conditions.'

'Do you believe in a man's right to self-determination?'

'I do.'

His last question was longer.

'Would you be willing to serve your country in time of war, in a capacity which would aid the war effort but which would not compromise your beliefs, and would not involve you in a combatant role?'

For a while, I pondered the question. There had to be a catch in it somewhere.

'It would depend,' I answered. 'I would not accept a role in which I was aiding and abetting the killing of any other human.'

'Would you care to elucidate?'

'I would not, for example, drive an ammunition lorry,' I stated. 'I would not repair a gun limber, or guard prisoners, work as a telegraphist or messenger.'

'Would you be prepared to drive an ambulance?' the priest enquired.

'Yes, categorically,' I said.

Clements seemed suddenly relieved and, ticking the last box on the page, turned the paper round and pushed it over the table towards me.

'Would you please sign at the bottom?' he asked, and he handed me his fountain pen.

It was heavy, clearly a valuable item in solid gold, and I pondered on his wisdom in bringing it into an environment where everyone out of a warder's uniform was a felon. I signed.

'Excellent!' he exclaimed, dating the document and countersigning it, then blowing on it to dry the ink and slipping it into the dossier. 'I shall report to the relevant tribunal tomorrow morning. I suggest you ready yourself to leave this'—he looked around disparagingly—'penitential establishment and serve your country in the best way a man can, with humility and honour, your character unblemished and your morality uncompromised.'

'May the Lord go with you, my son,' said the priest, and he put his hand on my shoulder.

'Excuse me, sir,' the warder at the door said, just a little too loudly. 'You may not have any physical contact with the prisoner.'

'My dear man,' the Reverend Bard responded with a patronising smile, 'I am a cleric. Do you expect me to slip him a file? In forty-eight hours, he will have no need of it, nor, come to that, the passkey hanging from your belt.'

The priest and Clements shook my hand, assured me that they would immediately speak to the prison governor to ensure that I was removed from the hard labour detail and bade me be patient just a little while longer. With that, they and the warder were gone, the door locked behind them, and I was left with my thoughts.

Going over what I had done, I wondered if I had somehow capitulated, had betrayed myself by surrendering. I began to worry that I had, after all, somehow been duped.

30

I opened my eyes. Where the thin beam of sunlight cast through the door, the air was faintly blue with a haze of smoke. I blinked and rubbed my eyes, for they stung. Coughing to clear my throat, I looked about.

The croft was partitioned in two by a loose stone wall rising to the roof, the crannies of which had been stuffed with a mixture of mud and straw or seaweed. The roof itself consisted of couples, pairs of stout poles at each end of the building, lashed together and pinned at the top, supporting the roof tree, a thick trunk of pine stripped of its bark and blackened by the smoke of the fire. Running between this and the walls were tight ranks of thinner poles upon which had been placed a layer of seaweed, a layer of turf sods and then, on top of that, a thatch of heather and straw kept in place by plaited ropes weighted down by heavy stones which hung along the outer walls. A hole in the roof served as a chimney. To channel as much of the smoke as possible towards it, a *lum* of heavy planks smoothed with clay came down from the roof over the heath, an iron *slabhraidh* suspended beneath it and culminating in a hook for the kettle or cooking pot. Across the interior of the canopy and pierced by a stick, eight herring hung, gradually turning a dark tan as they cured. Every so often, fish oil dripped from them, sizzling in the fire or pockmarking the rim of dead ash around the hearth.

For furniture, the room contained three or four low stools, a much battered sea chest held together by tarnished brass studs, and some shelves made of flagstones protruding from the wall. On these were lined up the most basic of household utensils and tools—two iron pots, a stack of wooden bowls and drinking vessels, several knives with the blades thinned by honing, a beechwood basin containing wooden spoons and ladles, some wooden platters and crudely thrown pottery storage jars of oatmeal. A string bag hanging from a nail driven into one of the couples contained a dozen hens' or seabirds' eggs protected from breaking against one another by twists of straw. A small barrel beneath one of the shelves contained potatoes kept fresh by being covered in dry sand.

Behind the partition was a smaller bedchamber, most of the space taken up by a low oblong box filled with compacted heather overlaid with straw and covered by a coarse blanket. Upon a wooden shelf fixed to the gable end rested a small metal dish containing two combs and a wooden clasp for pinning back long hair.

My back was sore. I had dozed off whilst sitting on one of the stools, my spine coming to rest against the hard stone of the wall behind me. I stretched to ease my muscles and pressed my fingers into my sides to get the blood flowing.

The curtain that hung over the door parted and she entered, carrying a deep wooden bowl half-filled with milk. Sitting on a stool across the fire from me, she started to whisk it vigorously with a *loineid beag,* a curious implement consisting of a short wooden handle with a stiff circle of cow's tail hairs fixed to the end. When the milk was frothy, she scattered some oatmeal upon it and poured it into a wooden cup which she put on one of the hearthstones. I reached forwards, took it up and drank it. My mouth was dry from breathing in the smoke and I was glad to ease my throat with it.

Soon, it was night, the roof lost in the shifting ballet of shadows thrown out by the fire. Along the wall hung several cruisie lamps, their guttering reed wicks casting a faint yellow light upon the floor, the smell of the fat burning in them pungent and cloying.

In this snug twilight, she was seated by the fire, washing a bundle of dulse she had collected along the shore in a wooden bucket, shaking it dry into the fire, the little explosions of steam rising up with the smoke into the broad canopy of the lum. When she was done, she slung a pot of milk over the fire, raising the hook on the *slabhraidh* up a few links in the chain to prevent it boiling too harshly. When the milk was simmering, she pressed the dulse into it, stirring it gently with a spoon.

Later, the fire dying down and a thin sliver of moon edging over the island's ridge, she moved into the bedchamber and, taking off her outer garments, slipped under a blanket, wrapping it around her, her head resting on a calico bolster stuffed with gulls' and eider ducks' feathers. I did not join her but watched as her breathing slowed and her limbs relaxed. Only when she was asleep did I start to sketch her, the soft angles of her arm, the tumble of her hair about her face, the turn of her ankle where, on warm summer nights, it protruded from the blanket.

Just before dawn, I took my leave, stepping out through the curtain and stealing away into the darkest hour of the night like a thief.

I've been to her croft on many occasions over the span of my life. From time to time, I have sat at the fire, warming my hands as heavy flakes of lazy snow settled upon the beaten earth outside, adding a split log and watching the resin bubble and sizzle as the flames took hold. A gale howling outside, I have eaten a stew of charlock and braxy mutton that has simmered in the pot for hours, the meat flavoured with thyme and silverweed and flaking from the bone like the flesh of a boiled cod. The curtain tied back, I have leaned against the doorpost and watched the sun set over the boulders, listened to the sea lapping on the beach, whispering over the pebbles.

And, on every occasion, she has been there. Just her, not the man or woman—not even the cautious dog. I have touched her dress as she has brushed past me, felt her hair against my cheek, watched her as she has gone about her chores, walked with her upon the slopes of the island, listening on the shoreline as she has summoned a seal to her side with a sharp yelping cough.

She has never seen me. I have only ever been a ghost lingering in her presence. Yet, at times, I am sure she has felt my being there with her, for she has looked at me and she has smiled and I have felt the despair lift from my soul, dissolve like mist in a summer glen.

31

The hillside was steep and cut into narrow terraces retained by low stone walls and faced banks. Through the scattered ranks of gnarled olive trees, the waters of Moúdhros Sound lay like a sheet of dull steel between the arid hills, watched over by the bald summit of Prophitis Ilias. I could not help thinking how appropriate the colour was, for Greek mythology had it that the island of Lemnos, upon which I was walking, had been the home of Hephaestus, the god of metalworkers, who was exiled here by Zeus. To compound the image, riding at anchor upon the sound was a mottled armada of grey-painted warships.

Leaning against one of the olive trees, I paused to catch my breath. It was hard going. Although the sky was overcast, it was still hot, and the path, more suitable for the cloven hooves of goats than human feet, was so rocky, I had all the while to watch my feet. That I was wearing heavy military boots did not help. The hobnails in the soles occasionally caused me to slip and, in one place, I fell at least ten feet onto one of the terraces, cracking my shin on a tree root and reminding me of my tumble from the slick steps on the path to Dùn an Làmh Thoisgeal. Unscrewing the cap to my water bottle, I took a swig, swilling the water round my mouth before swallowing it, tasting the grit of the dust that had accumulated in my mouth.

Rested, I took the folded map out of the breast pocket of my tunic jacket and spread it open on a smooth boulder, aligning it to the landmarks of the distant hills and a peninsula that projected into the sound to the south of the settlement of Kallithéa, the white-washed houses of which I could make out clearly across the sea.

According to my reckoning, my destination was about half a mile farther on and slightly higher up the hillside than the path. Taking a compass reading confirmed it.

Walking on, I became increasingly excited. The map, which I had copied from an outdated Baedeker guidebook of Greece I had come across in a small shop in Moúdhros town, displayed the whereabouts of a small eighth-century B.C. necropolis close to a site of contemporary occupation, although whether this consisted of secular buildings or a religious structure was as yet unknown.

Finally, after quitting the path and scrambling up a number of terraces, all of them in varying states of decrepitude and abandonment, I reached a piece of flat ground of about six acres in extent, rising slightly at the southern end. The ground was haphazardly strewn about with large sections of cut stone between which grew little except sparse tufts of grass upon which goats had been grazing. Some were nibbled down to the roots whilst, all about, small pellets of goat dung littered the earth.

Leaving my water bottle hanging from a broken bough on an old olive tree at the edge of the site, I set about looking for signs of structures. The outlines of ancient buildings were not difficult to trace. Contours of foundations stood in places a foot high whilst, at the edge of the southern rise, a number of sections of columns lay half-buried where they had rolled, one still attached to its echinus. It did not take me long to work out that there were ten distinct buildings on the site, varying in size from a small square structure to a large domestic house including a peristylium with an exedra leading off from it, divided from the former by a row of four low columns, the plinths for which were clearly visible.

My initial survey complete, I sat under the olive tree, leaning against its trunk and fitting my back into a groove in the knotty wood. Somewhere amongst the stones, a bird was calling with a single consistent, strident note. I closed my eyes. It was good to return to be amongst ancient stones and in the company of the past. For a while, I dozed fitfully, dreaming of nothing in particular but twice seeing, in the misty realm of my subconscious, the girl from Eilean Tosdach. The first time, she was sitting at the water's edge of the tiny shingle strand by her croft, the water lapping at her feet and her hair damp from the spray being thrown up by a gusty wind. On her second appearance, she materialised in front of me, walking through the ruins by which I was surrounded, wearing a Dorian chiton, her arms bare, one hand balancing an empty hydria upon her head. On both occasions, I could see her face, pacific and happy.

After an hour or so, I got to my feet, rolling up my sleeves and unclipping from my webbing belt the entrenching tool I had brought with me, opening out the pointed blade. Walking to the remains of the large house, I set about excavating a few shallow trenches in places where I thought I might be lucky in finding something of interest. Although it had rained fitfully for three days, the soil was dry, every blow of the tool sending up a spatter of gravel and a fine mist of dust, which soon began to cake my forearms. In less than thirty minutes, I had dug up over two dozen fragments of pottery, including the shapely handle of an *oinochoë*, the rim and base of a *krater* and a piece of a black-figure *kylix* the size of my palm. When I spat upon it, smearing my saliva across the surface, an illustration of three cavorting dolphins clearly materialised into view. Against the footings of a wall, I came across a piece of a marble frieze upon which a hand had been carved, apparently gripping an udder. It took me several minutes to realise the figure had not been depicted milking a cow but holding onto one of the lower extensions of a wine skin.

Gathering my finds together on a rock by the olive, I sat down and scribbled quick notes on them. I had no idea of what use they might be, but I felt I had to record them if only to give purpose to my outing. Yet my expedition into the hills had not been just an exercise in academic curiosity or achievement, no matter how slight, but an escape from the world in which I now dwelt.

I had, by the time I arrived in Lemnos, been in the army for just under four months, during which time I had received the basic training of every recruit save that I was excluded from weapons instruction.

After a fortnight's induction process, in which I was marched up and down a parade ground until my feet were too blistered to continue, taught to read a map, blanco my equipment and polish my buttons and cap badge with Brasso so that no residue remained in the detail, I was posted to the Royal Army Medical Corps as a private. Much to my satisfaction, my stepfather's desire to have another officer in the family was thwarted. Had he even wished to mention it, he could not say his stepson was serving, for then the truth would out: I was a squaddie, a common Tommy.

Some days later, attached to a brigade, I was sent to a barracks near Winchester and embarked upon a course leading to my becoming a battlefield casualty orderly. The routine followed the same course day in and day out. I rose at six, prepared my bed and locker for inspection, then underwent half an hour's physical exercises on the parade ground. These were conducted regardless of the weather: for several consecutive days, we ran on the spot and did fifty press-ups in two inches of snow. After a quick visit to the ablutions, we were fed a breakfast of fried eggs, bacon and bread, washed down with tea, and given fifteen minutes to disperse to our allotted tasks or lectures for the day. All my instruction centred upon first aid and the treatment of injuries sustained in active fighting.

Major Endicott, an elderly military surgeon recalled from retirement, was forthright in his approach. At our first lecture, he addressed us quite straightforwardly.

'It is not your responsibility to save the lives of your comrades,' he declared. 'No indeed. It is your task to keep them alive until they might be treated in the casualty station. You are not doctors. You are medical orderlies. This does not diminish your status. Indeed no. If doctors were gods, then you would be angels, bringing the lost to them that they might find salvation.'

Every lecture or demonstration I attended was concerned with medical matters, and I was soon proficient in applying triangular bandages and tourniquets, stanching the flow of blood, dressing wounds, bathing eyes, giving morphine injections—we practised on apples with syringes full of diluted ink—and temporarily immobilising broken limbs with splints. For our own protection, we were taught how to lift a stretcher, bending the knees and pushing upwards rather than using our backs, and carry a heavy pack.

One demonstration concerned gunshot wounds. Under the command of a sergeant major, my squad was marched to a rifle range near a village called Chilcomb where, on the butts, there had been erected a gallows from which were suspended two dead pigs. Both were Tamworths, their bristly hair ginger and their ears still alert in death.

As soon as we were standing easy in a line facing the pigs from a distance of about twenty yards, the sergeant major picked up a Lee-Enfield .303 rifle, thumbing a cartridge into the breech and slamming the bolt forward and down in one quick motion. At a nod from Major Endicott, he raised the rifle to his shoulder and, taking the correct stance, released the safety catch and fired at the pig on the left. The bullet struck it in the shoulder, the heavy body knocked slightly back by the impact.

'As you will see,' the major stated, 'the bullet has made a small hole on entry. You will also have noticed that it caused the pig to sway slightly. Now, the flesh of a pig is similar to that of a man, in density and so forth. Yes indeed. However, one of these creatures weighs twice as much as any one of you.' He cast his eye along the line. 'If this bullet caused a twenty-five-stone pig to sway, you can imagine what the impact would be like on even a strongly built man. A thigh shot will knock him off his legs. Indeed it will. A hit in the shoulder will spin him round. If you will now follow me . . . '

He led us down the rifle range and, on reaching the pig, stuck his index finger in the bullet wound.

'Quite a neat little hole,' he said. 'Of course, if the creature were alive, it would be bleeding quite heavily, but not as badly'—he swung the pig round—'as here.'

Where the bullet had left the pig's body there was a raw hole the size of a saucer.

'This, gentlemen, is the exit wound. It has been caused by the bullet striking a bone, deforming into a lump of red-hot copper and lead and continuing on through the body. This is where you should pay most attention.' He let the pig swing back. 'Marquand! How would you deal with this?'

'I do not know, sir,' I admitted.

'The answer is quite simple,' Major Endicott said. 'You would not. This pig—this man—was shot at close range. This wound is considerable. You will not treat it at all. If necessary, you will give the injured man a dose of morphine, to ease his pain, but then you will move on. There is nothing you nor the surgeon at the casualty station, when and if he finally arrives there on a litter or stretcher, will be able to do for him. It is your job to move on to help those who have a chance of surviving their injury.'

The two pigs were shot several more times, from different distances, the major and a corporal taking us in groups to show us how to pack a wound, remove splinters of bone or, if the bullet was near the surface, remove it without causing too much haemorrhaging. I paid attention to every procedure, noting down salient points in my notebook for further attention, yet my mind was numbed. I had just been instructed, by a doctor, to sacrifice one man for another.

So much, I thought, for our regimental motto of '*In Arduis Fidelius*,' or the Hippocratic Oath or the sanctity of human life. Here was I, who had refused to take another man's life, being ordered to arbitrarily decide upon the life or death of a comrade.

I made no friends in my unit. Soon after my arrival, it became common knowledge that I was a conscientious objector—the word *conchie* was scratched on the door of my foot locker—and I was in effect sent to Coventry. Despite this, no one sought to harass or confront me. I was for all intents and purposes in a state of military purdah, a non-person in the ranks. Where my superiors were concerned, this had its advantages, for it was deemed unwise to give me cause for complaint in case I went running to the No-Conscription Fellowship and kicked up a fuss. Consequently, I was treated with a certain degree of laxity. Nevertheless, I determined to teach them that I was as good as the next man, all the time striving to ensure that my uniform was as unblemished as the other soldiers' and that I was never out of step during parades.

It was getting late. The few hours' leave I and the others of my unit had been granted was coming to an end and I had to be back at the camp on the outskirts of Moúdhros by 17.30 hours. With some reluctance, I decided to abandon my finds. I had nowhere to keep them safe. Had I put them in my pack, they would only have been further broken, and I considered they had been damaged enough by earthquake or weather: it would have been a travesty to have them pulverised by war.

As I prepared to leave, I pondered on those who had lived here, worshipped their gods and made love to their women, drunk their wine and pressed their olives into cloudy oil. And what, I thought, of the other visitors who had followed in my footsteps up the hill—farmers and merchants, pilgrims and priests, sailors and warriors . . . For a moment, I wondered if I should do as Byron had done at the Temple of Poseidon on Cape Sounion, carving my name into one of the rocks with the entrenching tool, but it seemed blasphemous to deface this place. Better it should be left unscarred for those whose spirits inhabited the wind.

It was at that moment, as if one of the *lares* was nudging me on the arm, that I recalled the story of Philoctetes. It was here, on Lemnos, that he had been marooned by his fellow seafarers who could no longer stand the stench of the suppurating, gangrenous wound upon his leg, caused by a snake bite. No one missed him until war broke out. Then, as the possessor of Herakles' bow and arrows, he was visited by Odysseus and a doctor, the one to persuade him to fight, the other to cure his leg. Yet his leg was healed. The soil of Lemnos had cured him. Thereafter, Lemnian earth became a valuable salve, dug up annually on a propitious day by a priestess near the village of Kotsinos, which I could see from where I was standing beneath the olive. It was compressed into tablets, stamped with a relief of the head of Artemis and sold throughout the Mediter-ranean.

Leaning down, I lifted a stone and scooped up a handful of soil. It was as dry as talcum, thin drifts of it falling through my fingers like the sands in hour-glasses. Watching until half of it had leaked away, I spread my army-issue khaki handkerchief out on the rock beside the pottery fragments, putting the rest into it, tying the corners tightly and placing the little package in my pocket. I was, however, certain that the efficacy of Lemnian earth was hardly likely to be valid. Considering the quantity of goat dung on the hillside, the earth was more likely to give one tetanus than alleviate an asp strike. Yet I was, that day, on my way to battle and prepared to consider any possible miracle.

As I set off from the ruins, a depression in the slope down to the first terrace caught my eye. It was clearly not a natural feature, as there was, over the top of it, part of an archway of dressed stone, the remainder having fully collapsed, the cavity behind it fallen in. This, I assumed, might have been an entrance to a tomb. Having no time to investigate it, I marked it on my map and was about to turn away when something polished caught my eye. Bending down, I brushed the earth aside to uncover the shell of a tortoise. For a moment, I gave it no further thought: tortoises are commonplace through Asia Minor and this one might have died whilst in hibernation in the hollow, per-haps caught by the cave-in. I was about to turn away when I noticed that there were four holes neatly drilled in the carapace, in such a position as must have been made after the animal's death. Using a sharp stone, I scratched around the shell and lifted it clear from the soil, shaking it to dislodge its contents and flipping it over. On the flat plastron of its underside were two more holes and, where the tail plate curled inwards to protect the tortoise from a rearguard attack, there were seven other holes, of which one was lined with a little ring of bone.

Unconsciously, I tapped on the flat surface of the shell with my knuckle. It resonated, much as the body of a violin might. Now I knew what I had found. It was the sound box for a lyre. Holding it,

I wondered what the music it had produced had sounded like and heard, again, in my head the strange song of the girl as she washed her hair at the pool on Eilean Tosdach, which accompanied me all the way back to the outskirts of the encampment in which I was billeted.

32

I have become convinced of late that Dr. Belasco no longer regards
me as merely a clinical dilemma but as an enigma which he is determined to solve. He has taken to bringing with him on his visits to me
a dossier upon the front of which are written my particulars—full
name, approximate age, file number and, obtusely, my military identi-
fication number.

Last evening, as I was lying on my bed after having eaten my supper, he came and sat with me, talking to me as always in soliloquy.

'Steak-and-kidney pie,' he remarked, looking at the remains of suet
pudding on my plate. 'The food of the working man. And how have
we been today?' He briefly studied the chart hanging in its metal
folder at the foot of my bed. 'Nothing to be unduly concerned
about.' He replaced it and sat on the chair at my writing desk, putting
the dossier next to his elbow.

All this I watched at the periphery of my field of vision.

'Tell me, Alec,' he went on, 'do you never wonder what the world
must be like now, outside this room, or the garden? Beyond the gates
of St. Justin's? It has been many, many years since you last saw it.'

True, I thought, and the last time I was moved, it was in a cream-
painted Daimler ambulance with a chromium-plated bell on the front
bumper and blacked-out windows.

'Are you not the least bit inquisitive?' he enquired, continuing, 'If I
were in your shoes, I should be. I would not be able to contain my
curiosity. Just to see how buildings have changed. I'd not necessarily
want to revisit places I had known. It would be enough just to get
out, if only for an hour, and see for myself.'

I made no response, gave him not the least indication that I was listening to him. He prattled on about how the world changed so rapidly these days, but he was not going to tempt me.

After about a quarter of an hour, there was a firm knock on the door and one of the orderlies, a young man sporting a fresh scar under his ear, entered. Paying me not the slightest heed, he quickly bent to the doctor's ear and tersely whispered something to him. I tried to catch the gist of the message but could not. Immediately the doctor stood up and left the room. I could hear the two of them hurrying down the corridor, their voices louder now that they had left me, but still incomprehensible.

I waited for a minute or two, then, swinging my legs onto the floor, went to the chest of drawers upon which he had left the file. Taking great pains not to move it, for his departure could easily have been a subterfuge and, at this moment, he could have been standing out on the lawn, in the gathering darkness, watching me, I untied the bow of faded red twine that held it shut and opened it.

On top of the papers within was a medical record sheet detailing my general health, height and weight, distinguishing marks, current regime of medication, blood pressure and so forth. Beneath this was a single piece of paper giving my medical history, outlining every ailment from which I had suffered since entering St. Justin's—a chipped tooth, a mild bout of influenza, a bad bruising from a stumble in the garden and a stye below my left eye which had proved resistant to repeated applications of Golden Eye Ointment and had necessitated the use of antibiotic cream and eyedrops. Attached to this by a white paper clip were three portrait photographs of me from the front, left side and behind. Next was a much dog-eared carbon copy, in faded blue ink, of the first page of another medical report that must have been written soon after my demobilisation from the army. This I picked up and held under the light the better to read it.

It was letterheaded 'Craiglockhart War Hospital for Neurasthenic Officers.' The typing was faint, but I was able to make out most of it:

Although not an officer, Private A. S. Marquand was referred to this establishment as a case worthy of our attention. He has been thoroughly examined and informed that his present condition and symptoms are the result of a disordered emotional state due to experiences he has received in the theatre of battle and not a disruption of his nervous system caused by the near explosion of grenades, bombs and shells. Although his hearing seems not to be defective, this information appears not to have registered with him in the least and he remains mute. His current state, in which he is completely uncommunicative, seems not to be physically but in fact psychosomatically induced. He responds by reflex to external stimuli, such as the application of a hot glass rod or a piece of ice, but does not react with any indication of pain. For all intents and purposes, he seems to have shut himself off from the world around him and has chosen to keep his own counsel. This form of psychotic behaviour, particularly to this degree, is not common and we suggest he is not simulating his condition in order to avoid further military service but is . . .

I turned the page over. The reverse was blank and the remainder of the report missing.

Although it was so very long ago, I remember that place, the austere house set on the southern edge of Edinburgh, the stonework always damp from the rain that blew incessantly from the Firth of Forth. It was full of men in far worse condition than those with whom I now reside. Here, they are mostly simple men whose minds have turned, for whom age or disease has distorted reality or created fantasies to keep their souls from fading. There, every one of us was young, some of us handsome, well educated, well brought up. A few were disfigured by wounds. One or two were amputees. Not a few were of the aristocracy, the sons of wealthy landowners who could call themselves Lord or the Honourable. Money and titles meant nothing, however. We were all reduced to the same level, blathering dolts trying to make sense of what we had seen, where we had been, how much we had had to suffer.

The next page in the dossier was the first of over twenty written in diarial form, each one outlining in detail what Dr. Belasco had said to me and what reaction, if any, I had made to his comments. Mostly, he remarked that I had made no response whatsoever, but every now and then he had noted that my eyes had blinked, my fingers had twitched or my lips had slightly parted.

Following this section in my file was the beginning of an introduction to a scientific paper concerning my psychological condition. I was inclined to read it but was soon lost in the medical terminology as arcane as an alchemist's textbook.

It was flattering to have this young doctor take such an interest in me. It did occur to me that his attention might be more a matter of furthering his career prospects with an original piece of research, but I did not begrudge him this and was prepared to indulge him. Indeed, considering his possible motivation, I felt sympathy for him. There was no way in which he was going to break my barriers down, storm my barricades and loot the fortress of my soul.

For all his searching for a way through my armadillo scales, he has yet to discover the one place to which he could have access if only he were sufficiently cunning. He has not even looked for it.

When I first arrived in St. Justin's, I was accompanied from my previous institution, as I had been throughout most of my adult life, by two wooden-framed canvas-covered suitcases. They were older than I was, the canvas originally green but now faded and blotched with small rusty spots of mould. The hinges were made of stoutly sewn leather straps that had suffered from mildew, the locks metal but no longer provided with a key. The lids were scattered with torn or peeling travel labels—'Wanted on Voyage' 'Peninsular & Oriental Steam Navigation Co.,' 'Thomas Cook' and 'GWR First Class.' In better days, these suitcases had belonged to my parents and, had they possessed voices, could have told of luxury cabins on white-painted liners bound for Port Said and walnut-veneered Pullman carriages, of dhows in Aden and gondolas in Venice, of the darkness in the Simplon Tunnel and seats at the captain's table.

One case contained my clothes, the other my few pairs of shoes, toiletries and odds and ends. Or so my minders thought. What they did not realise was that the second suitcase had a craftily disguised false bottom. This was no deceit on my part but my father's—or that of his luggage maker. When travelling my father had used the compartment to hide his foreign currency, circular notes of exchange, passport and tickets, cuff links and gold half hunter and my mother's linen jewellery wrap. I utilised the space to transport those items that were dear to me, which I did not want to be found, scrutinised, studied and possibly used against me.

On arrival in St. Justin's, I was shown to my room, that which I still inhabit, and left to unpack or not, as the case might be. Waiting until I was certain I was alone, I removed the bottom drawer from the chest of drawers. It is a heavy, ancient piece, crafted from solid wood in the days before the advent of cheap, flimsy chipboard and plywood furniture. Just as I had hoped, for I had come from a room with similarly old-fashioned fittings, beneath the lowest drawer was a space about three inches deep, the bottom of it the base of the whole structure. I quickly emptied the contents of the hidden compartment into it, replaced the drawer, closed the compartment and let the nurse on duty do the rest of my unpacking for me.

Since that day, my secret possessions have been secure. Even when the room is given a thorough cleaning and the chest of drawers moved, my secret remains safe. My only safeguard against discovery is a pencil I have nailed to the rear of the bottom of the drawer with five hypodermic needles: this acts as a back-stop and prevents the drawer from being pulled right out without being lifted for the last inch or so.

Sometimes, in dead of night, I remove the drawer and survey the contents. Not needing to check them, I rarely touch them, but I look at them much as a parent might gaze upon a book of family photographs of the children when they were young, playing with a dog or digging sand castles on a beach with a yacht sailing by in the distance.

Nothing in my cache of dreams is of financial value. There is a broken, tarnished military cap badge consisting of a tiger arching over a rose: from somewhere in my memory I seem to recall the emblem was referred to as the cat and the cabbage. The fragment of pallid glass from the broch, that might have been a piece of a *lachrymonum,* is next to it. I should have surrendered it to Mr. McGillivray, along with the arrowhead and the broken comb, yet I did not, for it reminded me—

it reminds me still—of her skin. And there are other bits and pieces, flotsam washed up on the shore of my early life.

The real treasures lie in a cracked leather, quarto-sized writing compendium, the sort of item ladies carried their headed notepaper in whilst travelling abroad, with a gold Waterman's pen, gauche-looking foreign stamps in indecipherable currencies and envelopes embossed with their initials. The compendium, scratched and battered with the zip broken, contains drawings I do not want to lose yet which I never look at for fear of what they, or the memory of them, might do to me.

Instead of opening the leather, the hinge crackling and leaving a thin trace of hide dust on the base of my secret closet, I merely stroke it, as if it were a creature I have loved which has long been preserved, mummified like those beasts buried with Egyptian noblemen and long since preserved not so much by the embalmer as by the hot sands of the desert.

I listened carefully. There were no footsteps in the corridor. Some-where far off in the building, an inmate was yelling at the top of his voice. I could only catch the occasional word. It was obscene. Several of the inmates suffer from Tourette's Syndrome. As an undertone I could just make out the subdued voices of the staff, cajoling, tempt-ing, trying to calm down their antagonist.

Quickly I slipped off my bed and pulled the bottom drawer out, resting it on the floorboards. Were I to put it down on the rug, it might leave a suspicious indentation. Reaching into the space, I removed the compendium, opening it carefully. A shimmer of dust fell off it. I blew upon it to disperse the telltale sign. I did not rifle through the contents but, opening a manila envelope, felt inside and withdrew a sheet of paper at random.

For a moment, I wondered if I dared look at it. My life now, like that of any old buffer who's nearing the end of his trespass upon earth, is constructed of memories. It is all the elderly possess. There is nothing else. The present follows a predetermined routine, whilst the future is creeping ever closer and predictable, even if the schedule is unclear. There is only the past in which to dwell. Yet what if, for whatever reason, the past must be denied? That is my dilemma.

I looked. It was just a fleeting glimpse, the sort a man might make at the sun or a bright light suddenly switched on in the darkness of his room. Or his life.

She was there, a head-and-shoulders portrait, the cartridge paper yellowed with age but still crisp to the touch, not yet fragile. Her eyes bore a faintly quizzical look. The wind was playing with her hair. Behind was the mountain beyond the summit of which, I suddenly remembered, was the plateau of Bealach na Clachan and the ruins of Saint Maelrubha's little community.

Without further consideration, I slipped the sketch into the doctor's file, beneath the third page of his treatise, closed and replaced the compendium, slid the drawer back into place and, checking there were no signs of my activity, returned to my bed.

Closing my eyes, I left the room and caught the paddle steamer from Glasgow.

The stern rope was let go and the steam capstan hauled it in. At a snail's pace, like a reluctant child leaving its mother at the schoolyard gate, the vessel drifted away from the shore, the water starting to thresh between the hull and the stone quay hung with wicker painters. Within minutes, the steady rhythmic thump of the paddles commenced, the bow swinging tightly round to head west towards the sea.

For a while, I leaned on the rail of the passenger deck, watching the docks and ship-building yards slide by. Here and there, a brilliant pinpoint of light or scatter of sparks drifting to the water indicated where an arc welder was working. Small craft busied themselves close in to the shore, ferrying men or materials to the yards whilst, on the opposite shore, cargo ships lay alongside off-loading coal, pig iron, lengths of steel girder. The stiff onshore breeze carried the tang of coal smoke and the distant tattoo of riveters' hammers.

Gradually, the sides of the firth parted, the dry docks and shipyards giving way to fields and woodland before becoming industrial again at Greenock. At Gourock, the vessel moved onto a southerly heading down the Firth of Clyde, the paddles accelerating and slapping into the water creating twin wakes. Over to starboard, behind Dunoon, the mountains of Scotland began.

I left the deck and entered my cabin, closing the door and flicking the venetian blinds down so the wooden vanes shut out the view. My luggage was piled in a corner, just where the porter had placed it.

Switching on a reading light on the bulkhead, I lay down on the bunk. The varnished wooden sides were high, to hold one in during rough weather, and the brass catches highly polished. It was bizarrely like a lidless coffin. The paddles lost their steady tempo. I sensed the vessel turning, keeling over slightly to starboard. It must, I thought, have reached the southern tip of the Isle of Arran and was veering south-southwest into the rougher waters of the Irish Sea.

In the darkness, I heard a latch open. A man in a white coat entered my cabin. I assumed he was the steward bringing the order of beer and sandwiches I had placed in the smoking room on embarking. Yet he carried no tray. Instead, he picked up a dossier and left. I felt a sudden urge to sit up and demand what the hell he thought he was doing. My father had told me of the risks of sailing to foreign climes. Robbers, he would recount, are as common east of Marseilles as ticks on a terrier. And east of Suez, he warned me, they have pole-fishers who, whilst a vessel is alongside in port, inveigle long bamboo canes culminating in a steel hook through portholes carelessly left open; if you tried to grab the pole, you would sever every one of your fingers, for the thieves lined the poles with razor blades.

I let him go.

In the early hours, I was made aware that the paddle steamer was slowing. Leaving my cabin, I went out on the deck, standing beside a derrick holding one of the lifeboats. On either side was land: the vessel was making its way north up the narrow Sound of Kerrera towards Oban. Along the deck aft of the paddles, two deckhands were busy preparing to lower a gangway over the side. On a low hillside off to port, a dim light shone where there was a village. A harbour surrounded by a small fishing town hove into view. The buildings showed few lights, but a number of lanterns were swinging to and fro on the quayside.

I returned to my cabin and sat at the table, listening to the sound of voices and footsteps on the deck outside. The paddles stopped, the vessel ceasing to vibrate. The plate of beef sandwiches, which had after all been delivered, was stale. The beer tasted flat. I took a sip, then poured the remainder away into the tiny porcelain hand basin in the lavatory leading off the cabin.

After a short while, the vessel cast off once more and the vibrations of the engines recommenced. I removed my shirt and shoes and, lying down on the bunk once more, pulled the blankets up to my chin and rolled onto my side.

I wanted so much to sleep, a deep sleep within a deeper slumber, a place in which to escape from what had passed and what had yet to be.

33

For six days, my unit was occupied setting up a field hospital on a hillside overlooking the town of Moúdhros. The site chosen, which sloped gently downwards from a citrus orchard towards the road to Hephaistia in the north of Lemnos, had to be cleared of grass and goat droppings, graded into platforms, bisected by drainage and sewage ditches and laid out with a series of wide pathways which, when they ascended the hillside, had to be cut into steps faced with planks of timber. It was heavy going, our problems exacerbated by bad weather and the delivery, on the third day, of the actual paraphernalia for the hospital—crates of dressings, surgical implements, operating theatre equipment and two hundred folding military cots—ahead of the tents into which they were to have been placed.

'That's the bloody Barmy Army for you,' Sergeant Philips exclaimed in a world-weary voice. 'Bullets but no bloody *boondookees.*'

Private Cody, another medical orderly who shared my tent in the encampment nearer Moúdhros, asked, 'What's a *boondookee*, Sergeant?'

The sergeant was a career soldier. In his forties, he had served in the Sudan and British East Africa, suppressing—or so he would have us believe; there was always a mischievous glint in his eye when he mentioned it—'tribes of kaffirs what you've never heard of and what you don't want to, neither,' whose arrows were tipped with a poison that could fell a rhinoceros in twenty paces and kill it in as many seconds, who could melt into the bush like a morning zephyr and track an ant over a rooftop in a rainstorm.

'A *boondookee*,' he informed us, 'is what the Bantu folk of Buganda call your common or garden Short Magazine Lee-Enfield .303 service rifle. The word's from their language, Ki-Swahili, but they borrowed it from the Persian. *Bunduq*'s Persian for a musket, see.' We never knew when he was spinning us a yarn or displaying a genuine erudition.

This banter was all a part of his plan, however. He had fought alongside three generations of privates and foot soldiers, inexperienced innocents who had signed on with a smirk, in a desperate hunt for excitement or glory, an escape from the drudgery of labouring, the poisonous fumes of the blast furnace or the lung-destroying dust of the mill and the mine. He knew their ways, accepted their foibles, forged their weaknesses into strengths and understood their fears. By talking of campaigns long forgotten, in unmapped countries, he kept our minds occupied and stopped us brooding on the future; we all of us knew that even the army did not erect a hospital if it did not anticipate casualties to put in it.

On the fourth day, we were kept for half an hour after morning parade, standing in ranks. A high wind and intermittent driving rain did not help to keep our spirits up. The sergeant had given us the order to stand easy, but those with rifles were kept busy ensuring they remained as dry as possible. The rest, like myself, who did not carry arms, just stood around, shifting from foot to foot to relieve both the ache in our calves and our boredom, turning our backs to the wind. Finally, a Rolls-Royce staff car swung into view down the track between the tents, its suspension creaking as it rocked over the ruts in the road, splashing through puddles. As it approached, we were called to attention. When the vehicle stopped, those soldiers who were carrying weapons presented arms, their hands slapping against the wooden stocks of their rifles.

A colonel in a cavalry officer's uniform stepped out of the vehicle and balanced upon the wide running board.

'Gather the men around,' he ordered.

On the command from the parade sergeant major, we broke ranks and ran to crowd before him.

'Gentlemen,' the officer began, his arms akimbo and his legs apart, his voice loud over the sound of the wind and rain, 'many of you have not yet seen action, but, over the coming days, you will have the opportunity to serve your king and country. You will no doubt have deduced that we are here to give the Turks a bloody nose. This is what we shall do. Be assured of it. It will not be easy. There will be trials and tribulations a-plenty for all of us. Yet we will succeed.'

With that, he opened the car door, got inside and was driven away. We fell in, were dismissed and headed for our billets.

'Well, that was a load of cobblers,' Private Cody remarked as he untied the flap to our tent. 'Trials an' tribulations! Bullets an' blood, more like.' He sat down on his cot, the frame creaking under his weight, and started to unwind his puttees. 'Let me tell you something. It's a little game. If you give letter A the mark of one, letter B the mark of two an' so on down to Z with twenty-six, what score does bravery get?'

'I don't know,' I replied, more concerned with wondering how to dry out my boots, and not wanting to struggle with the mathematics of his puzzle.

'Bravery gets eighty-nine. Courage gets sixty-eight. Honour gets ninety-one. But you any idea what scores the 'ighest of the lot?' He did not wait for my response. 'Bullshit. One hundred and three.'

The rest of the day was spent in preparation for the coming action, wrapping bandages, packing medical kits, sterilising syringes and hypodermic needles, checking the seals on tins of petroleum jelly and vials of morphine. At 17:30 hours, we were dismissed to our tents to make our personal kit ready.

As dusk fell, a runner came round the lines with the order that all troops were to assemble in our units to be addressed by our officers. Cody and I joined the forty or so other field medical staff in one of the newly erected hospital tents. Waiting for us was a captain, his waterproof cape dripping where he had draped it over a chair.

'I've just come from a meeting of the top brass,' he announced as we stood before him, 'and it has fallen upon me to explain to you what is to come. I'll be as brief as possible, as you have much to do by way of preparation and precious little time in which to do it.

Today is Thursday and it is anticipated that this foul weather will blow over tomorrow. On Sunday, at 06:30 hours, we shall make a landing on the peninsula of Gallipoli, on the western side of the approaches to the Dardanelles. Those of you with a modicum of geographical knowledge will know that he who holds the Dardanelles controls access to the Black Sea. This, in turn, will blockade the port of Constantinople.'

Just then, a strong gust blew through the tent, ruffling the canvas and stretching the guy ropes.

'The landing will take place at five locations, designated S, V, W, X and Y beaches. We shall be going in on V beach. For many, the landing will be made from piquet boats or lighters towed in groups of four by launches. However, we are to take a somewhat more luxurious means of transport. Those of you who have been bringing supplies ashore may have seen a particularly un-naval-looking craft in the bay. She is the *SS River Clyde,* a ten-year-old collier which has been adapted as a massive landing vessel. Sally ports—that is, large steel doors—have been cut into the sides of her hull to allow rapid egress.

'The plan is to put two thousand troops into the vessel, then run it aground on the beach, driving it as far up as its momentum will allow. However, should she not reach the actual beach, a steam hopper will bring three lighters in and lash them between the bow and the beach, forming a pontoon bridge. To reach the pontoon, troops will run along gangways, lashed to each side of the ship's hull, reach a platform at the bow and, from that, drop to the lighters. Covering fire, if needed, will be provided by machine guns mounted in *River Clyde*'s bows and protected by sandbags. Other units, mainly a company of the First Battalion of the Royal Dublin Fusiliers, will be landed in a series of piquet boats.'

He paused, to let the information sink in.

'The beach itself is in a bay called Ertugrul Cove, gravel, not sand, and about three hundred yards wide. It is not very expansive, perhaps only thirty feet from the water's edge to a bank varying in height between five and eight feet. Beyond this, the land is generally flat, rising gradually at the right-hand end of the beach towards a village called Sedd el Bahr. Protecting this settlement and standing between it and the sea is a ruined medieval fortress which has the appearance of a crusader castle; despite its dilapidation, it could provide more than adequate sniper positions. There is also a crescent of rocks sticking out into the sea below the castle. Halfway between the beach and the first of the village houses are a series of barbed wire entanglements and spiked metal stanchions. The Turks have, we believe, two companies of troops dug into a trench system along the top of the bay, where there are some low cliffs, and on the slope behind the barbed wire. These will, however, have been softened up by an hour-long naval bombardment prior to the landing, provided by the battleship HMS *Albion*. Any questions?'

We looked one to another, but no one spoke.

'Finally, it is anticipated that casualty numbers during the initial landing will be light. Fire upon us will, at best, be sporadic. That is all. Platoon sergeants to see me for specific briefings at 09:00 hours tomorrow. May God be with you all on Sunday.'

Cody and I returned to our tent and pumped up our primus stove. Like all soldiers, our first consideration after being given our battle orders was to brew up a dixie of tea. As the tent filled with the homely smell of burning paraffin and the water boiled, we sat without speaking, each immersed in his own thoughts. It was not until he was pouring the tea into my mug that Cody broke the silence.

'Funny, ain't it,' he said. 'Seventy-two hours from now we could 'ave kicked it. Lying facedown in the dirt. You want sugar?'

I shook my head. It was a joke amongst the medics that wherever Cody went he had sugar somewhere about his person. He unbuttoned one of the breast pockets on his tunic to produce a twist of paper containing half an ounce of sugar.

'I don't fancy lyin' face down,' he continued after testing his tea with his lip to ensure it was at drinking temperature. 'If I'm face down, and I ain't snuffed it, I'll choke on the dirt. I'd rather lie on me back. See the sky. Know what I mean?'

'Yes,' I said, 'I know what you mean.'

'Still, one bright side to it,' he remarked. 'At least we're medics. All we got to cart around is a field casualty kit and a canteen. The poor bastards as do the fighting've got to carry the bloody kitchen sink— ration pack, water bottle, ammo pouches, entrenching tool and their *boondookee*.'

When we had finished our tea, we visited the ablutions and turned in. There was a three-quarter moon that evening which sporadically showed through the clouds as it set, casting faint shadows against our tent, which was pitched near a tree. Occasional rain squalls rattled upon the canvas.

'You awake?' Cody enquired, fifteen minutes after we had extinguished our lantern.

'Yes,' I replied.

'I got to say, I'm shit scared,' he admitted.

I admired him for his confession. It took courage for him to acknowledge his fear and his awareness of his mortality.

'You'll probably find we all are,' I said. 'Every tent's got someone in it who's afraid.'

It was some minutes before he spoke again.

'You're a conchie, aren't you?'

We had never discussed our pasts and I had assumed that, on reaching Lemnos, either nobody knew or they did not care. We were all stuck in it together and that was an end to the matter.

'Yes,' I answered, 'I am a conchie.'

'Why?'

'Does it matter?'

'No,' he said, 'I don't mean why're you a conchie. I know 'bout that. Read it in the paper. You're a Baptist or a Quaker or one of them funny religious lot. What I mean is, why're you 'ere? You didn't 'ave to be.'

'I'm an atheist,' I declared, 'but, no, I suppose I didn't have to be here.'

'So why is you? 'ere.'

I thought back over the recent months and came to no conclusion. I was not there because I had a calling to tend the dying, nor was I there to get out of the vicissitudes of a convict existence or a sense of patriotic duty: nor were my hatred for—and desire to prove wrong—my stepfather and my love for the girl on Eilean Tosdach reasons. I was, I realised then, there because circumstance had brought me to this place, a sequence of events over which I had no real control. It was as if I had drifted there upon some vague tide in a sea I had had no intention of sailing, in a craft I could not steer.

'I'm here,' I said at last, 'because I am nowhere else.'

'At least you got ordered in. I volunteered,' Cody replied. 'Bloody stupid, if you ask me. In the first month. All me mates were signin' up. I went along with the crowd. Like a bloody sheep, I was.'

'What did you do before you joined up?' I asked.

'Milkman. 'ad a good round. South Kensington. Delivered milk to all the toffs. Lord an' Lady Muck. The Earl of This an' the Duke of That. When some of them found out I'd taken the King's Shilling, they gave me another. See me on my way. Brave lad, they called me. Stupid fucker, more like. Soon to be a stupid dead fucker.'

'The captain said they expected only light casualties,' I reminded him.

'Yeah! An' elephants play pianahs!' he exclaimed obtusely. 'Anyway, what the fuck! Time for a bit of shut-eye.'

He turned over to face the tent wall. An hour later, I heard him sobbing quietly to himself.

The following morning, the order was given to move out. At 10:00 hours we were fallen in and, carrying our kit, were marched to a compulsory church parade, mustering in the open air just up the hill from the encampment where a small valley formed a natural amphitheatre. The weather was fine; the wind had dropped and there were patches of blue sky showing to the east.

The chaplain stood on the top of a loose stone terrace, a table at his side serving as an altar. The service began in the usual way, with a prayer and a hymn or two. I positioned myself near the back of the congregation, paying little heed to the proceedings until they reached the chaplain's address.

'The Almighty is with us,' he declared with the surety of an unshakeable faith. 'He marches at our side, His banners unfurled with ours, His sword drawn in the name of our cause. We are fighting not just for our king and our nation but also for the Lord God, our Father in heaven, Who has made us in His image and Who stands by us in our time of need.'

I looked about and wondered, if there truly were a god, how he could have been so spectacularly remiss as to make us in his image. My comrades-in-arms were, seen as an army, a motley bunch of shop-keepers' assistants, insurance office clerks, farmhands, street traders, stevedores and tram conductors dressed in a common khaki uniform with the 1908 pattern webbing equipment, and each was kneeling in the dirt of a Greek island, the name of which at least half of them were ignorant, praying like never before that, no matter what happened on the morrow, he would survive. The individual's thoughts were with himself, not his fellows. The fate of the man kneeling next to him was as inconsequential as that of a falling star.

'Remember,' the chaplain concluded, 'no matter what happens on the field of battle, your place in the everlasting kingdom is assured and you will rise up to sit on the right hand of Jesus Christ, Our Lord in heaven.'

It was, I thought, the old lame justification laced with the same timeworn bribe. I remembered my homily delivered to the magis-trates in that panelled room closed to the public eye. There could, I considered then, kneeling in weak sunlight on an island in the cradle of what we have chosen to term our civilisation, be no greater hypocrisy than the proclamation of divine right.

Had I been courageous, I would have got to my feet and said my piece. 'For fuck's sake,' I would have shouted, 'don't treat us like bloody fools. Tell us the truth. We're not fighting for God or right. The world is not run by monarchs but money lenders.' Yet I kept my peace. We were too far down oblivion's highway by then and passed the last turning off to sanity.

The Lord's Prayer was chanted and the hymn 'Onward, Christian Soldiers' sung with gusto. I could not help recalling with irony that the hymn had been originally written for children to sing on a Whit-suntide walk and wondered if, somewhere on the Turkish peninsula, there was a mullah addressing the Turkish troops, promising them a place in paradise with Allah should they fall in battle.

As soon as the service was over, we formed ranks and marched down to the town where lighters lay alongside to ferry us out to the *River Clyde*. She was riding at anchor in Moúdhros Sound, a sturdy-looking vessel with one tall funnel, two masts, one fore and the other aft, her fo'c's'le heavily fortified, as we had been told, with sandbags. In places, her superstructure had been strengthened with extra plates in an attempt to armour her.

Once aboard, we discovered the medical units were virtually the only troops present. It fell to us to ready the accommodation for the rest, who would join us the following day.

I found myself a top bunk in one of the holds and deposited my kit there, going on deck as the engines began to turn and the ship swung round for the open sea. On the dock, a cheering throng of those units remaining on Moúdhros saw us off. A band on shore played 'Tipperary,' yet none of a unit of the Royal Munster Fusiliers who were with us on board showed any sign of emotion. They, like us, knew they were heading into the unknown.

It was choppy once we were out of the protection of the Sound, and Cody was seasick, spending an hour leaning over the side, vomiting. That night, as I lay on my bunk, the last thing I did before turning over was check in the top left-hand pocket of my tunic, feeling for the thin metal thermometer case I had placed there, containing the curlew's bone.

34

Only those who are old, who have seen it all, find comfort in darkness. For those who are young, it holds grotesque imagined fears or cloaks the uncertainties of life. It is a threat, whereas, to me, it is something to which I look forward every day.

It could be that this acceptance of darkness is an unconscious preparation for death. Our minds, knowing the inevitable is just that, start to acclimatise. In this way, the fear of the unknown is alleviated, replaced by an acknowledgement verging upon the welcoming.

For me, it is nothing of the sort. I accepted the reality of death when most men gave it no more thought than a pestering fly, to be brushed away with a single flick of the hand. Where I am concerned, darkness affords me the opportunity to travel, not into my past with a nostalgic pining, and certainly not into my indubitably brief and hesitant future, but to places where I am happy, where there are no tears unless they be of joy and no screams that are not those of laughter.

Last night, after the orderly who sits by my bed had departed, I went on a veritable journey, my destination Mervyn Stanwood's print that hangs upon my wall. I closed my eyes, seemed to drift ethereally across the room and then entered the picture. Upon my going into it, what had previously been a two-dimensional interpretation of an English village street became four-dimensional.

I arrived by way of the footbridge, my boots heavy on the wooden boards and echoing under the arch. Beside me was the ford, the water running over the smooth flags, with small fish darting here and there, only obvious when they changed direction, showing their silver flanks to the sky. Ahead of me rose the main village street, ascending towards a church built in the Perpendicular style behind a massive yew tree, its canopy at least forty feet in diameter and its trunk thicker than a monolithic pillar. On either side of the street were whitewashed houses, some of them thatched, a blacksmith's and a dairy, outside of which were lined up a number of churns. The scene was populated by villagers. The blacksmith shoed a nag tethered to a brass ring mounted in the wall of the forge. Two girls in skirts down to their ankles played with a hoop. A woman sat in a window at a spinning wheel. The vicar, a portly cleric with a cross of pinchbeck hanging round his neck by a chain, walked down the street with the purposeful stride of a man either with a calling or on an urgent errand. A postman, burdened by his sack, handed a letter to the dairyman, who was grasping the halter on a Jersey cow of which only the forequarters could be seen through the gate into the dairy yard. On a cottage roof, a thatcher was repairing the ridge, a supply of hazel wood spars and liggers suspended from his belt by a length of coarse twine.

On the riverbank, just downstream from the ford, a small boy was squatting on an up-ended half-barrel, surrounded by tall stands of rosebay willow-herb in full, glorious flower, the flaxen seeds drifting on the breeze and catching in his hair. His attention was held by a worm he was transfixing upon a hook, piercing it in several places and winding it round to secure it, leaving a length to dangle enticingly free. His fishing rod, a mere green sapling with a length of thin string attached to it, leaned against the wall of a house abutting the water's edge.

Stepping off the bridge, I started up the street. It was high summer, the air filled with the warm promise of a lazy evening, bees fumbling at hollyhocks growing against a wall, their furry thighs powdered with pollen, swallows dipping under the eaves to their nests and a dog, stretched out on a step, twitching its paws in a dream of rabbits or rats.

As I made my way through the village, I spoke to no one. They seemed not to see me, as if I was not so much a stranger of whom to be suspicious but an invisible ghost. I was, I thought, nothing more than the tingle that ran up their spines and tickled the napes of their necks when the candle flame danced and the shadows did a little unexpected jig.

Halfway up the street, by a set of solid oak stocks and the cast-iron village pump, I turned into an alleyway running between two cottages, one thatch-roofed and the other slated. It was cool in the shade, the cobbles moist underfoot. The wall of the thatched cottage was dappled with moss and stonecrop growing from chinks in the mortar. My footsteps echoed.

After some little way, the passage opened into a carefully tended garden. Mauve spires of lupins reached up to my shoulder, the scent of sweet peas assailed me and a dense climbing rose scrambled over the wall of a third cottage, casting the deep-set windows in semi-darkness and spilling pink-tinged petals upon the wide sills. Passing through a small wicket gate, I walked down a path and, without knocking to announce myself, entered the cottage.

It was a small, two-up, two-down property, the front door giving directly into a room in which there was a table, some chairs, a stove with a small range to one side and a dresser upon which stood a row of willow-patterned plates and some cups. To the left, a narrow wooden staircase rose to the upper storey whilst, through a second door, I could see a scullery containing a heavy porcelain sink, a galvanised metal pail and an iron mangle for wringing out clothes. The floor was flagged and gently sloped towards a drain covered by a metal grill.

I sat at the table, upon which was laid out a simple meal of sliced pig's brawn, thickly cut bread, a pat of newly churned butter on a brown dish and a mug of ale. The froth having settled on the top told me it had been poured for some minutes in readiness for my arrival. I broke a slice of the bread and, smearing butter on it with a pointed knife, added a piece of the brawn and began to eat. On a shelf by the fire was a huge cheese, the grey net of cheesecloth embedded in the rind and stippled with brown mould. The ale slaked a thirst which, until then, I had not realised I felt.

The late afternoon sun sloping through the window and the ale made me drowsy. I nodded off, resting my head upon my arms on the table. It was night when I woke to find the girl in the room with me. She was seated across the table from me, a cat purring loudly in her lap, a linnet perched upon her shoulder, trilling. I raised my head and sat up. She smiled and spoke to the cat in its own language.

'My sweet witch,' I said, taking her hand and kissing her fingertips.

She smiled. The candle behind her glimmered, casting her hair into a halo of golden filaments.

'Tell me of your day.'

When she spoke, it was in the language of seraphs, a musical dialect that fell and rose like the sound of a mandolin being played in a vast subterranean cavern, the melody fading into the distance only to echo back as a faint cadence from the metallic-tinted stalactites and blackly mirrored pools of immobile water.

Later, carrying the candle in a pewter stick, I followed her up the stairs, and we lay close in a huge bed, the mattress soft and the cover filled with down. With my hand on her breast, I fell asleep again.

Sometime just before dawn, when the night was at its most still, I felt her moving next to me, her hand upon my shoulder, her hair tickling my cheek and her breath cold upon my neck. I opened my eyes. It was not her face close to mine but that of Sister Cynthia.

For a moment, I was startled and had to fight the urge to cry out. Yet my bewilderment soon passed. I was in control once more.

'There, Alec,' she murmured.

The first fragments of the new day were coming through a gap in the curtains. By its faint light, I could see now it was her hand upon my shoulder.

'It was just a nightmare.'

I must, I realised, have been making a noise in my sleep and wondered if perhaps I had been talking. There was a pencil and a shorthand notebook lying on the chest of drawers. It came to me that she must have been at my bedside for much of the night, listening in the hope that I would give something away.

My making to sit up, she took her hand away. I looked in the direction of the sink.

'I'll get you a glass of water,' she said.

While she busied herself at the tap, I took a quick glance at the notepad. It was blank.

35

'That'll've stuffed the buggers!' Cody exclaimed as the dull distant thumping of heavy naval gunfire subsided, then ceased. 'There ain't goin' to be one Johnny Turk standing upright after that little lot. Know what I mean?'

The *River Clyde* began a sharp turn. I rested my hand on the bulkhead. It was vibrating and clammy from the condensed breath of two thousand men. Down in the bowels of the ship, the engines were churning at full speed. The clean light of a fine spring day coming through the open sally port was the only source of illumination.

All around me in the port forward main deck hold, the men of X Company of the Royal Munster Fusiliers were hunkered down, holding onto their rifles or absentmindedly checking their equipment for the umpteenth time, each lost in his own thoughts. A few smoked Woodbines. One clamped a small home-made briar pipe between his teeth, the tobacco in it extinguished by the spume that drifted in upon us whenever the vessel struck a wave full on. The stiff breeze created by the ship's speed blew across us, tugging at our tunic collars and the loose webbing straps of those nearest the outer hull.

'Can you tell me what time you have?'

I looked to my left. Squatting next to me was a private in the Munsters, his hands clasped before him as if in prayer, his rifle resting against his shoulder, the butt prevented from slipping by a rivet standing proud of the deck plating.

Glancing at my watch, I said, 'A quarter past six.'

He made no reply and seemed to withdraw back into himself, his eyes filled with a faraway stare. I wondered where he was, what he was seeing in the quiet recesses of his mind, behind the fear—a pretty girl lying in the grass on the banks of the Shannon on a warm afternoon or a small fishing boat making its way up Lough Corrib with a storm building over Galway and the Atlantic.

From beyond the sally port, we heard a sudden outbreak of gunfire. It was concentrated and prolonged.

'If that's sp'radic fire,' Cody remarked laconically, 'I'm Mr. Punch, Judy and the fuckin' crocodile.'

Suddenly the ship's engines stopped. With hardly a sound and no sense of jarring, the *River Clyde* had run aground.

We stood up and moved towards the sally port. Across the heads and shoulders of those in front of me, I could see a number of piquet boats heading across the bay for the beach. The surface of the sea around each little craft was boiling, the men in them being hit repeatedly by volleys of machine-gun fire. Some jumped into the sea. Others merely slumped forwards or were knocked overboard by the impact of the bullets striking them. Those who jumped sank under the weight of their kit. Few resurfaced.

'Christ! That's the Dublins,' someone said.

Over this, my first, surreal experience of the tumult of war, I could think only of one thing, that the First Royal Dublin Fusiliers had been at the Battle of Colenso, and I could hear my abhorrent stepfather's voice as clearly as if he were standing at my side: 'In every fold and behind every anthill the Irishmen lay thick and waited for better times.'

We waited for the order to go, but it was some minutes before it came. The lighters forming our pontoon bridge to the shore were not yet in place; then the block and tackle lowering the gangplank momentarily jammed. At last, Captain Geddes gave the order and those by the sally port started to charge out, screaming and cheering at the tops of their voices, for all the world like bit-part actors dashing out into the footlights of some grim stage upon which they have only a minor role to play, but are determined to make the most of it.

Not ten men had disappeared outside before the hull plates of the *River Clyde* rattled as spray after spray of bullets struck them. Yet still they ran out, bellowing defiance, and I, moving forwards with my rank, came nearer and nearer to the sally port.

When my turn came, I found my mind a blank. I just leapt over the raised step of the sally port, swung to my right and headed down the gangway.

For the first thirty feet it was level, but then it sloped downwards. All along its length lay the men with whom I had been standing but thirty seconds before. Now, they were dead, or crawling forwards or trying to head back. One hung by his foot from a rope, his body swaying as the bullets struck him, just as the pig's had done.

I kept going, my fist gripped tightly around the shoulder strap of my medical kit bag, and I, too, was shouting now. 'Fuck! Shit! Cunt!' The obscenities made no sense but seemed to give me the strength to carry on.

Halfway along, a young lieutenant lay before me, raised up on his elbow. He was also yelling, a fine spittle of blood spraying from his mouth.

'Follow the captain! Follow the captain!'

And I did, not because I was courageous, or disciplined, or angry at the carnage, but simply because no other alternative offered itself to me.

Descending the sloping section of the gangway towards the lighters was hard going. I kept stumbling over those who had fallen, stepping on faces and hands, feeling my weight sink into the soft flesh of bellies. Few of those upon whom I trod complained.

As long as I was running down the gangplank, I was peppered with the shrapnel of bullets hitting the hull, their heat whipping past my face. A fragment grazed the angle of my jaw below my right ear, one scorched a line in the fabric of my uniform and another struck my belt buckle, deforming the clasp. Otherwise, I was unscathed.

I reached the first of the lighters. It was a flat-decked barge, the gunwales not more than a foot or two high but removed at the bow. Strewn across it were discarded equipment and the bodies of those who had gone ahead of me and also made it down the gangway. Another volley of gunfire raked the deck. I threw myself down between a length of ribbed planking and a man lying with his face towards me. He was immobile, blood seeping from his ear and a wound in his chest. A bullet struck him, his body twitching, then settling under the impact. As I stared into his face, only inches from my own, one of his eyes winked at me, yet I could tell from his glazed look that he was dead and the wink a mere reflex.

When I thought the strafing had ceased momentarily, I scrabbled on my hands and knees over the bodies and threw myself across the space onto the second lighter, once again hurling myself to the deck. Here, there were fewer dead, but of those still alive no one was in a fit state to carry on to the shore.

Ahead of me, at the bow of the lighter, a man quickly stood up and disappeared over the side into the sea. Another followed him. Then another. Beyond them, the shore was covered with a heavy mist of dust caused by the naval bombardment, the sun shining weakly through it. It might, I thought vaguely, turn out to be quite a warm day.

There was a thump. Someone landed heavily next to me and grunted. At the same time, a pack hit me in the small of my back.

'Fuck this for a barrel o' monkeys!'

It was Cody.

'Fuckin' light casualties, my arse!' he exclaimed contemptuously; then he hawked and spat out of the side of his mouth. 'Haven't those bloody tars hit anything on shore? They've been hammerin' the fuckin' coast for over an hour. With a fuckin' battleship!' A bullet struck the deck a few inches from his shoulder, leaving a shiny scar in the metal and whining off into the sky. 'Know what I mean?'

Not waiting for an answer, he commenced dragging himself forwards on his elbows. I followed.

At the bow, we stopped and chanced a quick look round the end of the gunwale. The lighters had not been moored and were drifting away from the beach on a fast current, coming broadside on to the shore. On the beach, a few dozen soldiers were hunkered down beneath the low bank. They were not forty yards from us, but they might just as well have been forty miles.

'Nothin' for it.' Cody started to shrug his pack off his shoulders. 'We're swimmin'. An' I ain't cartin' all this crap.'

'That's your ration pack,' I said.

'You hungry?' he rejoined. 'This ain't no picnic. Just keep the medical bag. Besides,' he added, 'that'll float.'

I undid the buckles on my own back-pack and let it fall free.

There seemed to be a lull in the flow of men coming out of the *River Clyde*. Above and behind us on her prow, the machine-guns had stopped giving covering fire. The enemy were concentrating their fire on the Dublins, fifty yards to our left. Those who had made it to the shore from the piquet boats were also crouched under the bank, bullets hitting the rim and spitting up little puffs of grey soil.

'Now or never,' I said.

As one, Cody and I got to our feet, took two quick strides and launched ourselves into mid-air.

I hit the water and immediately sank to the bottom, which consisted of loose sandy gravel and rocks. My uniform was suddenly very heavy, my boots leaden. The cut on my jaw stung from the salt water whilst the medical pack, the strap still over my shoulder, began to rise to the surface. Opening my eyes, I peered around to get my bearings and to see where Cody was. To my left was the long dark shadow and bulk of the hull of the lighter. To my right was the beach. The water was clear but pinkly tinged. I wondered if the sun had at last risen over the crusader castle.

Towards the beach, the sea bed began to shelve. Kicking against a rock on the bottom, I started to rise, my buoyancy aided, as Cody had predicted, by the medical kit. Just ahead of me was a figure, moving past between me and the shore. It seemed to be walking on the sea floor. I thrashed my arms and headed towards it. If it was Cody, he was going the wrong way.

My lungs were bursting, but I had to set him straight. With a few strokes of my arms, I managed to break the surface, gulp air and submerge again. Cody had stopped, no doubt, I thought, because he realised he was going in the wrong direction. Two more strokes brought me up to him, the current pressing me along.

Yet it was not Cody. It was the Irishman who had asked me the time. His mouth and eyes were open, filled with water and despair. Small bubbles were escaping from his tunic. One of his boots had caught in a crevice, anchoring him. His right arm floated freely at shoulder height. The thumb and index finger of his left hand were caught in a buckle on his webbing. As he died, his mind dense with panic, he must have been frantically trying to rid himself of his pack. His rifle lay on the gravel beside him.

As I looked at him, the current snatched at him, slowly spinning him round. His boot came loose and he drifted swiftly away, still in a vertical position as if taking a stroll.

I struck out for the shore. When my feet touched the bottom again, I stopped swimming, keeping only my head above the surface; as it became shallower, I pulled myself along by my hands, digging my fingers into the gravel and cracks in the rocks, the medical kit floating behind me.

The water's edge was strewn with bodies. Bits of equipment and personal possessions—caps, letters, a boot, cigarettes—floated by. Here, the sea was red and I realised the pink tint farther out had been not weak sunlight but diluted blood. Through it flicked shoals of small fish.

Edging cautiously forwards, I used the body of an officer as cover. He lay on his left side, facing the land, his right arm half-severed at the elbow and lolling about as the wavelets lapped at him. Looking over the corpse, I could see a group of men crouching under the bank about ten yards in from the water. Between them and the sea lay other men, some dead, some dying. One, ahead of me, was moaning and talking incomprehensibly to himself. There was an urgency to his muttering. He might have been praying or cursing.

Cody was amongst those sheltering beneath the bank. He still had his medical kit with him and was attending to a soldier with a badly gashed thigh.

I waited. The machine-gun fire strafing the beach was coming from a trench under the walls of the old castle, about sixty yards off.

The machine gunners were so close, they hardly needed to aim. The puffs of smoke from the barrel were clearly visible and I watched as the line of bullets struck the top of the bank. Those fired high hit the sea behind me, hissing into the water.

After a minute or two, I assessed how long it was taking the machine-gun to complete a single arc of fire and reckoned that if I was to get up and run for the cover of the bank a moment after it had passed by, I might just make it.

Plucking up my courage and steeling my nerves, I was about to make a dash for it when the officer's body quivered. Contrary to Major Endicott's instruction, I slipped my hand over the officer's neck and pressed my finger to his jugular to feel for a pulse. Should he still be alive I could at least ease his passage into eternity with an ampoule of morphine. There was no pulse, only a warm, damp hole into which the first joint of my finger slid. His body quivered again. It could have been some postmortal spasm, but this time it was accompanied by a dull knock from somewhere deep in his rib cage. A single bullet hit the water not twelve inches from his head.

I instinctively ducked down. The body quivered a third time, the vibration of the copper and lead slug tickling my cheek. Now, I knew. A sniper, probably on the battlements of the old fortress, must have spotted me. Very slowly, I let my body swing round in the water until it was parallel to the officer's corpse; for a few minutes, he and I lay, side by side, like grotesque lovers.

Yet no other shot struck him and I was beginning to wonder if the sniper had given up, assuming me dead, when the moaning soldier let out a shriek. It was piercing and inhuman, a noise like tearing metal straight from the gates of hell.

Risking it, I squirmed forwards to look round the top of the officer's head. Ten feet away, the wounded man was kneeling up. From his uniform I knew he was a private in the Munsters. His hair was matted with blood and gravel. A jagged triangle of his scalp hung over it. He raised his arms up as if in supplication and I could see he was about nineteen years old, barely a man but no longer a boy.

'Mary!' he shouted, his voice high-pitched with fear.

'Get down!' I shouted.

He heard me and turned my way. His face was tunnelled with blood, the white of his skin showing through only where his fingers had clawed at his cheeks. One of his eye sockets was raw and empty; his other eye was closed by congealing blood.

'Mary?' His voice was quieter, calmer.

'Yes,' I replied, for what else could I do or say? I could not soothe the pain of his body with the contents of the medical pack, yet I might have been able to soothe that in his soul.

'I'm sorry, Mary,' he said, in the soft accent of the west of Ireland that he would never see again. 'I do so love you.'

The sniper's bullet hit him in the chest. He pitched forward onto his face, the fingers on the ends of his supplicating arms scrabbling in the gravel like obscene crabs digging a hole in which to hide. Another bullet hit his thigh. A third struck him in the shoulder.

It was then I surrendered, not to the Turks but to circumstance. I rose to my feet, still clutching the medical pack, and stepped over the officer's body. The wet gravel slipped under my boots. I stumbled but kept on going, my eyes narrowed as if against a bright light. In three steps, I was beyond the water's edge. The drier gravel was loose. It was as if it were clawing at my feet, deliberately trying to slow me down. My only thought was that this was not surprising, for it was a Turkish beach and Turkish gravel and would, therefore, do all it could to slow or bring me down.

In twelve steps, I was in the cover of the bank, throwing myself down and pressing myself against the earth between Cody and a corporal in the Munsters with a bandage wrapped untidily around his wrist.

'Brought a bucket an' spade?' Cody asked.

'No,' I stammered.

My heart was beating fast. I was gasping for breath and amazed I was still alive.

'Just as well. This fuckin' beach ain't got a fuckin' grain of fuckin' sand on it. So much for the fuckin' Turkish seaside.'

A fusillade of machine-gun fire struck the top of the bank. Small pebbles, tufts of grass and clods of earth rained down on us. A few bullets droned off into the air.

'Do you see what you've done now?' the corporal said. He grinned, removed his cap, shook the dust off it and put it back on his head, bending the peak down as far as he could over his eyes. 'Would you know it,' he went on, 'but six months ago we were in Rangoon. Paddies in the paddyfields. Gold pagodas and pretty girls. Waists like wasps, they had.'

I glanced out to sea. The machine guns on the bows of the *River Clyde* were returning fire, but they were ineffectual. One of the protective sandbags was leaking a fine spray of sand onto the lighter below. In the water bobbed corpses whilst along the edge of the beach lay strewn a flotsam of men, dead and dying, for whom there was nothing left.

'What a fuckin' cock-up!' Cody remarked angrily. 'From fuckin' start to fuckin' finish. An' we ain't fuckin' finished yet.' He felt in his tunic pocket and took out three soggy twists of cloth. 'An' me fuckin' sugar's dissolved.'

I wanted to laugh, yet there was something in me that prevented it. Perhaps that was my first moment of silence.

'Still,' Cody continued, rummaging again in his tunic, 'I ain't bereft.'

He produced two pieces of Callard & Bowser butterscotch, flicking one of them over to me with his thumb. The wrapping had come off and the sweet was stippled with the flocculent detritus from the seams of his pocket.

'Reckon I'm better fuckin' organised than th' fuckin' wankers what set up this fuckin' massacre. Couldn't sell fuckin' candles to fuckin' convents.' He grinned expansively. 'Know what I mean?'

I said nothing but nodded, put the sweet in my mouth and sucked hard upon it.

36

In the middle of the afternoon, as I was dozing in the armchair by my french windows, with the sun warm upon my legs, Dr. Belasco came to my room accompanied by an orderly pushing a wheelchair. I assumed, for this has happened on occasion in the past, that I was to be taken to be examined, perhaps to be X-rayed. Neither of them spoke, which surprised me. Dr. Belasco is usually voluble.

Once in the wheelchair, however, I was steered along a series of corridors down which I could not remember having ever gone, arriving eventually in the front lobby of St. Justin's. On the right was a window of sliding glass panels behind which a receptionist sat. Opposite this was a settle and several chairs arranged around a low table scattered with colourful magazines of a variety I had never before seen. A notice board mounted on the wall carried a series of sheets of paper, some of them coloured and all of them pinned up neatly. A very large colour photograph in a black wooden frame on the wall depicted a high volcanic mountain with snow fringing its summit, a flat tree in the foreground beneath which was standing an elephant, its trunk upraised to pluck at the foliage overhead.

The doctor held the main door open and the orderly pushed me through, turning left down a ramp onto an expanse of tarmacadam marked out with oblongs in white paint. A number of quite extraordinary vehicles were parked about the place. Their bodywork gleamed, some of them with a metallic sheen, as if microscopic flecks of silver had been added to the paint. All were streamlined, their headlights incorporated into their shape, their spokeless wheels made of solid silvered metal or protected by circular silver discs.

'You are wondering, aren't you, Alec?' Dr. Belasco said at last. 'I doubt you have ever seen the likes of such—how would you have called them—automobiles?'

I did not respond, did not even move my head. I had no need to: the orderly was slowing spinning the wheelchair round so that I could not help but take in my surroundings.

'The world has changed a great deal since you last visited it,' Dr. Belasco continued, at the same time nodding to the orderly, who directed the wheelchair towards a small dark blue vehicle of a sort well beyond even my imagination. It contained only two seats and was open, lacking a roof; every other vehicle I could see was enclosed.

'This is not my car,' Dr. Belasco admitted. 'It belongs to one of the consultants, but he has agreed to lend it to me—to us—for an hour.' He opened the door. The base of the vehicle's chassis cleared the road by only a few inches.

The orderly helped me out of the wheelchair and into the passenger seat. Once I was settled, he placed a blanket over me up to my neck, tucking it in behind my back. A restraining strap was then put over my shoulder and midriff and attached to a buckle, presumably to ensure that I did not attempt to abscond. These preparations complete, Dr. Belasco joined me in the driver's seat.

'We shall not go far,' he said, 'just around the town and maybe a short way into the countryside.'

He turned a key and the engine burst into immediate life with a soft thrumming sound. Releasing what I took to be the brake and pushing a short stick forwards, which I realised was a means of altering the gearing, he increased the engine speed and we moved gracefully away, without so much as a judder, down the drive to a pillared gate, out of St. Justin's and onto a tree-lined residential road of substantial houses set back behind privet, box and beech hedges.

After several hundred yards, we reached a junction. A large number of vehicles was passing in either direction and it was several minutes before Dr. Belasco could edge out into the main stream.

'There are now over thirty-five million vehicles in Britain,' he declared. 'This equates not quite to one vehicle of some sort or another for every two people. The figure does not include bicycles and the like, only powered vehicles. Quite a number more, I would imagine, than when you last travelled in such a fashion.'

We came to a small area of shops and were obliged to drive slowly behind a double-decker omnibus painted in blue and cream. Upon its rear end was pasted a poster advertising holidays with Thomas Cook. So, I thought, recalling my battered suitcases, some tiny things were still the same.

'I'm sure you recognise the greengrocer's shop, Alec,' Dr. Belasco said.

I allowed my head to move just sufficiently to see a shop, a red-and-white striped canvas awning projecting out over the pavement to keep the weather off a variety of fruits and vegetables.

'However, some of the produce may be new to you,' he said. 'Avocado pears, passion fruit, lemongrass.'

We moved slowly on.

'There's a chemist's shop. Nothing much changed there, I'd say. Still a purveyor of potions and poisons. Yet what of next door? The dry cleaner's. Are you not curious how one can launder clothing without getting any of it wet? And look, at the end of the precinct—a Chinese restaurant. It does good business. Cantonese-style sweet-and-sour pork, cashew nuts and king prawns, beef in oyster sauce. Does that not make you wonder, Alec? Does it not make you want to know? Perhaps even try the cuisine?'

We left the shops, passing a church and a police station, which I noticed had a blue lamp hanging from an iron bracket to one side of the entrance, as it would have had when I was a small boy. In a short distance, we were in a rural landscape of low, rolling hills. The fields were mostly pasture in which sheep and cattle were grazing. Here and there, copses of deciduous trees broke the line of the hedges. One hillside was thickly covered with ranks of dark pine planted in rows, the ground beneath devoid of undergrowth. For a while, the road followed a river, the water slow or, in places, tumbling quickly across stones or smoothly over a weir. Finally, Dr. Belasco drove up a hill and pulled in to one side, switching off the engine.

Before us lay the river valley, a small village in the centre of which was an ancient and narrow stone bridge, some scattered farms with white farmhouses and green-painted corrugated iron barns. The scattered fields interspersed with trees were a collage of green and, where a bright yellow tractor was ploughing, ochre.

'So much has changed,' Dr. Belasco remarked, 'and yet so much is just the same.' He turned to look at me, his hand upon the steering wheel, the sun bright upon his face. ' "What man that sees the ever-whirling wheel / Of Change, the which all mortal things doth sway, / But that thereby doth find, and plainly feel / How Mutability in them doth play / Her cruel sports, to many men's decay?" '

I did not shift my gaze from the panorama before the car, yet I thought, the doctor knows his Spenser. I remembered, on the turn of a second, *The Fairie Queen* and how the girl on Eileen Tosdach had so reminded me of Duessa the changeling.

He looked at his watch and started the engine once more.

Reaching the outskirts of the town, we came upon a garage. In a workshop, I could make out men in stained working clothes repairing vehicles raised above their heads on ramps. At the roadside was a tall sign bearing a golden scallop shell upon a red background, and I realised it was the same insignia as I had seen on the overalls of the mechanic in the village in which Rupert had halted to buy petrol, shortly before we hit the cart horse.

For just a fleeting moment, I was back in that spring Saturday a lifetime away, feeling the wind on my face and smelling, once more, the sour scent of the hawthorn blossoms in the hedgerows of a world long since lost. I could not quite hear Rupert's voice calling me from my seat on the milestone and tried to remember the names of the towns and the distances carved upon it. If, I thought, I could recall these details and then get hold of a map and a pair of protractors, I might be able to triangulate our position and discover the identity of the village. There was a book of road maps of Great Britain in a compartment in the door panel of the car, and I was almost tempted to try to sneak it out under the blanket at the end of my ride. Yet no sooner had the idea occurred to me than I dismissed it. For me there is only the now and the next.

Although driving, the doctor must have been simultaneously studying me, for he suddenly said, 'The Shell petrol sign means something to you, doesn't it?'

Yes, I thought, it does, but you will never know what.

It was then I understood the motive behind this excursion. He wanted to shock me, to jar my memory, to force me into a need to communicate with him. If, he anticipated, he showed me the wonders of the world from which I had withdrawn myself, aroused my curiosity or was somehow able to bring to me a cue that might trigger off some memory, he might be able to get me to start to talk.

How mistaken he was. He thought I had excluded myself from the world but did not realise that those pieces of the world I wish to retain have stayed with me, as vivid as the day I lived them. What he also could not comprehend is that whilst there are some things I have striven never to forget, there are others I have tried to disregard yet cannot.

37

I lay quite still, my head resting against a bale of bracken brought from the hillside to line her bed. The sun was bright and I shielded my eyes with my arm across my forehead. From somewhere nearby came the subtle music of a light wind rustling tall grass, or it may have been heather. A seabird riding an invisible stratum in the sky cried, its cracked song like a brief lament. The girl returned its complaint, her mouth open and briefly twisted as she squawked in reply. The dog, which until then had been asleep on its side, woke and raised its head. When it saw me, its tail wagged against the ground, beating a cloud of dust from the dry earth. The fire in the hearth was smouldering, a thin wisp of smoke rising from it, dissolving in the air before the wind could take it.

Under her arm, she carried a wooden bowl and, bending, displayed the contents to me—three tern's eggs, the shells the pale blue of an evening sky after rain and patterned in dark brown like the craters of an undiscovered moon. I touched one. It was still warm from the breast feathers of the hen.

Dropping a few strands of stiff, dry seaweed onto the fire, the girl knelt and blew gently until they caught, piling kindling of driftwood and heather twigs onto the new flames. When the fire was burning brightly, she put the eggs into an earthenware pot of water, placing it on the hearthstones. It would be an hour before the eggs were hard-boiled.

Suddenly the air was split by a strident screech. She looked up. The terns, indignant at the robbery of their nest, hovered above her on the wind, their forked tails spread and their wings raised. Then, one after the other, they dived. She ducked, laughing, as they levelled out. The birds swept upwards, banked and dived again. This time, I was their target. I raised my arms to defend myself, but there was no need. Lifting a broom of twigs, she struck the first bird in mid-flight. It fell, was dashed against one of the rocks beside the stream, its neck snapped. In its black-tipped scarlet beak, I could see its pronged tongue quivering. Its mate soared away into the sun. The girl put the broom down and touched my shoulder.

'Eyes right, chum.'

It was Cody.

Beyond him, Captain Geddes was crouching with the rest of us, leaning his shoulder against the bank, his revolver hanging from a lanyard around his neck.

'I need volunteers,' he said. 'We can't stay here all day, like rabbits in a warren waiting for the ferret. I want to see if we can get a toe-hold in the castle. If that can be achieved, we'll be able to find a point overlooking the machine-gun position and maybe put paid to that damned sniper at the same time.'

As if to lend weight to his stratagem, a single shot rang out, striking a stone on the bank above and ricocheting off with an insectile whine.

A sergeant came forwards, working his way through us on his hands and knees, keeping close in to those of us hugging the bank and choosing men to join him as he reached them. As he came up to me, I felt as I had at school when being picked by the team captain to play in the inter-house soccer match. The nearer he came, the more apprehensive I became: but the sergeant passed me by. He wanted fighters.

Eventually, there were eight of them, including the captain. He glanced around the end of the bank where it tapered off, eroded into a shallow depression by rainwater coming down the hill from the village. The Sedd el Bahr fortress had been a target of the naval bombardment, the round bastion facing the sea being severely damaged with three gaping holes in it about twenty feet up, approachable by a ramp of fresh rubble. Below this were a number of small dunes covered in low scrub and rocks.

'We make for the dunes,' Captain Geddes said. 'Once there, we recce the ruin and, if we can, make for the central hole and get a lodgement in the castle. At worst, at least we shall secure the eastern end of this infernal beach.'

Never a truer word spoken than in jest or fear, I thought. Looking down the camber, the spit of land curving out towards the *River Clyde,* I counted twenty-seven corpses, those who had died of their wounds curled up or hunched, the rest lying as they had fallen, like marionettes dropped on the nursery floor by a bored and fractious child, their limbs awry and their heads askew. Around them was scattered the detritus of war—rifles, packs, entrenching tools, canteens, caps and ammunition belts. Although it was over an hour since we had landed, the sea was still reddened at the water's edge. Runnels of blood, now congealing in the sunlight, scarred the rocks or drew dark brown lines in the gravel. The gunfire had lessened considerably, but if anyone of us moved into sight, we drew a concentrated burst. It was, indeed, a Mephistophelian landscape.

In the way of soldiers, some of the Munsters off to our left, sheltering under another section of bank, took to taunting the Turkish machine gunners by hoisting a cap on a bayonet and moving it along the rim above them, their plan to force the Turks into wasting ammunition. They stopped when a bullet struck the bayonet, shearing off its point and driving it into a corporal's shin, smashing his femur.

Captain Geddes went first, followed by the six men, the sergeant taking up the rear. They had, I estimated, about thirty yards to go without any cover before they were safely in the dunes. Making no pretence at hiding themselves, they sprinted for it. It took the Turks a few seconds to react. Then the machine gun opened up on them. Three of the men were hit, knocked out of line towards the water, one of them who caught the full impact of the burst seeming to lift through the air under the impact. The captain and another were struck but kept going.

'T'at's t'ree more gone to a better place,' said a soft Irish voice.

No one else spoke.

In the diabolic clamber ashore, there had been no time to think, only to act. The camaraderie of the regiment or the platoon had been set aside in the mad dash for the lea of the bank. From the moment we left the lighter to the second we reached cover, we were not soldiers in a disciplined fighting force but individuals chancing the odds.

Now, after being together for an hour, the men around me had reformed their bonds and affiliations, made new friends to replace those lost. They knew one another once again, remembered who came from the same town, had queued up with them in the same recruiting line, had sustained the same rigours of basic training, and seeing Liam from Moy, or Sean from Belclare, fall forty feet away brought home to them the precariousness of their own predicament.

When one of those brought down started to crawl towards the sea, no one called out to him to guide him back. He was already lost to them and they, in their own minds, were already moving on towards the destinations their own fate had in store for them. When the sniper in the castle put an end to his misery, no one was looking at him.

Except me.

After that, we were all of us subdued, each of us given to his own thoughts. I allowed my mind to wander, but no matter how I tried, I could never get far from the beach. The fate of Captain Geddes and his little band preyed upon me. If they were still alive, I pictured them edging in through one of the blast holes in the fort, treading carefully over the detritus of those who had lived there: sheikhs with black turbans, curved *djambias* with jewel-encrusted hilts fashioned from rhino horn tucked in their belts, pet cheetahs curled on cushions, the hookah bubbling in the corner, tended by veiled slave girls.

At about eight o'clock, another attempt was made to get men ashore from the *River Clyde*. Instead of them streaming out of the sally ports as we had done, they were released in groups of three or four. Yet, whilst this may have seemed a sound ploy, it was flawed. The men still had to cross the pontoon of lighters and a lifeboat, coming together in one small place where the enemy fire could be concentrated upon them. We watched as they were scythed down like hay in August.

For a while thereafter, we came under intermittent but persistent fire. The Turks must have sent up reinforcements, for now we were not only strafed by the machine guns and sniped at from the fortress battlements but also potted at by riflemen in trenches fifty yards beyond the barbed-wire entanglements halfway between the beach and what was left of the houses of Sedd el Bahr. Every now and then, men took sips of water from their canteens, not because they were thirsty but because any activity passed the time. Three men played whist, their pack of cards soggy. No one smoked, for amongst all of us there was not an ounce of dry tobacco. Lookouts kept watch up the slope in case the Turks decided to rush us, but they were no fools. There was no need for them to attack. They had us well and truly pinned down

When I had jumped into the sea, my wristwatch had filled with water and stopped. The hands read 6:25. Through the morning, I tried to judge the passage of time, but it was hopeless. There was nothing against which to count off except the sun.

At irregular intervals, the machine guns on the *River Clyde* stuttered ineffectually at the shore. We wondered why the gunners were bothering, but there was a reason. So long as they kept firing, the Turks not only had to keep their heads down but also could not tell when the next exodus from the ship might happen; had the gunners fallen silent for a while, then suddenly opened up, they might just as well have flown a signal pennant.

Sometime in the middle of the morning, a third effort was made to bolster our numbers on shore. With no hint of a warning, a platoon of soldiers burst from the ship and ran at full tilt down the gangway onto the lighters. Only a few made it to the beach, but it seemed to us that they were, in any case, being considered expendable, a distraction to draw enemy fire away from a number of piquet boats that had approached the stern of the *River Clyde*. Once there, the small craft divided into two groups, advancing down either side of the vessel. Those on the port side came under heavy fire, but those to starboard fared better. They got in close to shore before the Turks found their range.

There was nothing we could do to assist the soldiers. All the covering fire they got came from the *River Clyde*'s machine gunners and riflemen on her bridge and superstructure. We just watched, almost dispassionately, as they came towards us, wading through the sea or stumbling up the gravel beach. I found myself choosing one and following his fortunes. It was like being a child watching raindrops river down a windowpane, betting against myself which one would reach the sill first. In my mind, I heard Rupert's voice saying, 'To toy with another's life, rather than one's own, is, perhaps, the greatest immorality of all,' and I felt ashamed of what I was doing, yet it did not prevent me from playing my macabre little game.

The last man I picked was a lieutenant in the Hampshires. I watched him jump from the piquet boat and wade towards the spit of rocks. He could not have been more than twenty, for his movements were firm, determined, those of a young man who believed he could not die. A private next to him fell and he stumbled. I thought for a moment that the same bullet had done for both of them and was about to choose another, but I was mistaken. The officer got up and, unscathed, came on, crouching low, looking back, waving his revolver and shouting encouragement to those following behind him.

The rocks were slick. He stumbled a second time. I could not take my eyes off him, consciously willing him to succeed, to win the race to take another step, another breath. Reaching the gravel beach, he paused to glance back at his men. Stationary only for a second, it was sufficient for the sniper who must have been following him in his sights, and he took a bullet in the left shoulder, which spun him round and knocked him over.

I felt tears welling up. Not one of the scores of men I had seen die since dawn, not even the private in the Munsters whom I had deceived, had touched me. They were merely casualties, the statistics of defeat.

Yet this lieutenant, in a different regiment from that to which I was attached, whose name I did not know and who, two minutes before, I had never set eyes upon, filled me with an intense amalgam of sorrow and anger. My jaw was set, my teeth ground together. I wanted, at that moment, to avenge his death, not at a distance, with a vague silhouette of a man hovering in front of the v-sight of my rifle, but close up. I needed to have the Turk lying on the earth before me, his eyes pleading, his voice muttering, *'Af! Af!'* as my bayonet slid easily into his belly, his taut skin popping or farting like a damp balloon as the blade released the pressure in his body, not stopping until it struck his spine. My rage was irrational, inhuman; even as I fumed, I knew it was wrong, that it was the baseness of my kind in me coming to the fore which I had to suppress. To give it its head would be to denigrate myself, to admit I was little better than an animal, governed solely by instinct, not reason.

The machine-gun fire moved off to the left where another piquet boat was coming within range. After waiting to be sure the enemy gunners had shifted their attention, the lieutenant rose clumsily to his feet, pushing himself up with his right arm. His tunic was torn where the bullet had exited through his back. He had dropped his revolver, which was now being lapped by the waves, the barrel clogging with gravel.

Immediately my rage and sorrow evaporated, to be replaced with an acute urgency.

'Lieutenant!' I yelled. 'Over here!'

The chaos, the newly dead and the injured ceased to exist for me. I did not hear the gunfire, the screaming, the cursing. I was focussing my mind upon the lieutenant as if, like the power of prayer, my concentration might bring him safely into the bank.

Those around me, seeing why I was shouting, joined in. The lieutenant looked up, saw us and lurched in our direction, but after three faltering steps he collapsed and lay down exhausted on his side.

The machine gun strafed us again. Bullets struck the top of the bank, then cut a swath along the water's edge, picking off two or three stragglers and rolling a corpse back into the sea.

'Did you see that?' Cody asked, tugging at my sleeve.

'What?'

'Th' fuckin' machine gun,' he replied. 'The fuckers can't see 'im. Or else 'e's below their trajectory. Watch.'

There was another burst. Bullets splattered into the gravel on the far side of the lieutenant but did not hit him.

'If th' fuckin' Turks could see 'im,' Cody went on, 'they'd fuckin' kill 'im. Know what I mean?'

The lieutenant tried to sit up.

'No!' I hollered. 'Lie down!'

He was dazed and continued to struggle to get up.

With no further thought, I started crawling towards him as fast as I could on my hands and knees. A few feet out from the bank, the sound of the Turkish gunfire was much louder. Coming up to him, I grabbed him by his collar and pulled him hard towards me. He toppled over, falling heavily next to me and grunting with pain.

'You're safe,' I said, my lips close to his ear. 'Just lie down. We'll get you into cover.'

His face was set, his jaw clamped in pain, but he made an attempt to nod and I could tell, from his eyes, he understood what I was saying.

There was a scrabbling sound on the gravel. Cody came up beside me, dragging a medical kit behind him.

'Give me the morphine,' I said.

Cody ripped the webbing straps out of the brass buckles and, fumbling in the contents of the pack, handed me a syringe and a small glass ampoule. I tried to snap it open at the neck, but the glass was too thick.

'Give me the glass file.'

He fumbled some more.

'I can't find the fuckin' thing,' he answered.

I put the top of the ampoule under my collar, biting on it through the material, salty with my sweat, and snapping it open with my teeth. In a few seconds, I had the syringe filled and the needle inserted in a vein on the back of the lieutenant's hand. His breathing was shallow and gasping. He was in shock. As the drug took effect, however, his breathing became more regular, his face relaxed and he went limp.

'Give him a minute to get really groggy, then we'll drag him,' I said.

'Better look at his fuckin' shoulder first,' Cody remarked.

Lying beside the lieutenant, we turned him over onto his front, Cody making sure his head was turned to one side. The exit wound was ragged. The bullet seemed to have entered just under his coracoid process, been deflected by the head of the humerus and shattered his shoulder blade on the way out. Several sharp splinters of his scapula were adhering to his torn tunic. Blood was not so much flowing from the wound as seeping from it.

Another burst of machine-gun fire came over our heads. The bullets fizzed through the air. It was at least a second before we heard the muzzle reports.

'Reckon that's a fuckin' Maxim,' Cody remarked, dispassionately.

'The wound'll need packing,' I said.

Cody reached for the medical pack.

The lieutenant groaned. I removed his cap, to place it under his head as a makeshift pillow. The leather liner to the brim was stained dark with sweat, the regimental badge hanging by just one end of the cotter pin that held it in place. In the centre of his brow, behind where the badge would have been, was a small, livid bruise. He must have banged his head, the metal loops on the back of the badge digging into him. I pulled the pin out and put the badge in my pocket.

I could have tossed it away, yet I did not and have often wondered at my motivation. Perhaps I hoped to return it to him one day, a memento for him to pass down to his grandchildren. Perhaps it was I who wanted a keepsake of him, the young man upon whom I had wagered with myself and won or lost, depending on how you viewed the race.

'Gentian violet,' Cody said.

A small packet landed on the gravel. I tore it open and scattered the powder around the edge of the wound, working it into the torn flesh with my finger. It would not only prevent infection but also help slow the bleeding. As the lieutenant's skin and my own turned a brilliant dark purple and my fingers grew sticky with his blood, I remembered the horse, how its blood had clung to my shirt and hand.

'Found th' fuckin' alky.'

I looked up. Cody was sitting up, the medical pack between his legs, the flap open. In one hand he held a brown bottle of medicinal alcohol; with the other, he was rummaging in the kit.

'What're you doing?' I shouted, although he was not three feet from me.

'Lookin' for th' fuckin' lint!'

'Fuck the lint!' I screamed.

I could hear my own voice. It was detached from me, like hearing an actor speaking lines I had written.

'Get down!'

The bullet struck Cody in the temple. The side of his head exploded.

My eyes were bathed in a tepid fluid, my sight blurred as if I were looking through a veil of muslin. Into my mouth, still open from my last words, came pieces of a spongy substance, the consistency of soft cod's roe. I bit into it. It was warm and tasted metallic. I choked and tried to spit it out, but it clung to the lining of my cheeks, to my teeth and tongue.

Eventually, I swallowed.

38

There was a time, long since past, when men believed in evil, truly had an unshakeable faith in it and feared it as they did no other thing. As plain to them as the hairs on the backs of their hands, it was what held sway over their lives, tempting and tormenting them, trying their mettle every hour they were awake and some of those when they were not.

No matter what they did during the week—fornicated with their best friend's wife whilst he was tending to his fields or livestock, stole from a stall in the market when the merchant's back was turned or cheated their master—come the Sabbath, they would creep out of their crowded pews and into the confessional, where, with their heads bowed, they would admit their wrongdoings in hushed tones to the invisible priest behind the latticework screen, seek absolution for their weaknesses and accept their penance. Those who did not subscribe to this weekly cathartic ritual were risking their very souls, for they would go to their death without forgiveness and be cast without succour into the fiery pit where they would work out their damnation for eternity.

However, there was an alternative for the clumsy sinner, forgetful malefactor, he who died without a member of the clergy in the near vicinity or the dedicated profligate who, at the final count, had not the courage of his dissolute convictions. Commonplace in ancient times, there lived upon the earth men who earned their daily crust consuming the sins of the newly departed, scoffing them up before they reached the ferryman on the banks of the river of everlasting dreams.

It was such a simple process. The sin eater, usually a recluse or a wandering tinker, would arrive at the place of death to find the still-warm corpse lying on the slab or in the comfort of its own bed, naked save perhaps for a cloth to preserve its modesty. Upon the cadaver's chest would be laid out a little pile of coarse salt and a piece of bread, broken from the end of the loaf, whilst upon its eyes would rest two coins. Kneeling by the corpse, the sin eater would mutter a few prayers; then, without using his hands, he would lick the salt and bite the bread from the cooling and stiffening flesh, collecting the coins as his rightful fee. The sins of the dead were thought to have been soaked up by the food, the salt being deliquescent and the bread capable of mopping up whatever evil the former had not absorbed. Once the dearly departed's assorted wickednesses had been transferred to the living, he would depart, set off upon the high road and disappear.

It is said that as a sin eater's career evolved, he became increasingly disfigured by the nature of the sins he had consumed. His face would twist and his body contort with the evil it contained. He might acquire the never-healing wounds of the murderer's victims, the diseases of the venereal rapist, the active fingers of the pickpocket which could never be still. Towards the end of his life, the burden would be so great that the sin eater would no longer be capable of holding it in, metamorphosing into one of the Furies, a diabolical creature of incarnate wickedness. His knowledge of evil would surpass that of all others. Not a secret of history would be unknown to him, for in him reposed the very essence of evil, distilled into one vessel from which no living being could remove the bung. He would be beyond forgiveness, redemption and sympathy, for he had taken the money and sealed the contract.

Only one person, the hag called Baba Yaga, could release the sin eater from his interminable torment. A hideous cannibal who lived in a house erected on stilts made of the legs of giant chickens, with a picket fence around it the poles of which were decorated by lanterns fashioned out of human skulls, she was the guardian of the well of the water of life, the sole substance that could wash the sins away. And once she had cleansed the sin eater, she would let him die, his task accomplished and his spirit at rest.

Sometimes, I think I am one of those benighted souls, condemned to walk the earth until the moment of their last wheeze and stutter, carrying the burden of a million sins in the marrow of my bones and the corpuscles of my blood. For I have seen the iniquity of men and have partaken of it, have consumed the flesh and transgressions of another, drawing them into my body, and am, therefore, damned.

Or, perhaps, I am being pessimistic, for the world is no longer a place of good and evil, of right and wrong or black and white, but one of getting away with it. The borderlines have become diffuse and confused, so that what is evil to one is justified in the eyes of the god of another. For every cardinal sin, there is a cardinal excuse. For every grenade thrown and bomb dropped, there is a validation. It is all just a matter of perspective.

What I should like to think is that when my heart makes its final flutter and the electricity in my brain closes down, those sins I have kept so close for so long, acknowledged yet unspoken, will die with me. Yet in my soul I know that they will not. I am mortal, but they are perpetual and will endure to the end of time.

39

Reaching Bealach na Clachan, I allowed the horse to drink its fill as I sat on the wall of one of the ruined cells and gazed down upon Breakish. Far out to sea and little more than a speck at the apex of its spreading wake, the paddle steamer was making its way towards the Outer Hebrides. It was a fine day, the shadow of the clouds moving over the sea, the faraway islands seeming nearer than they really were. Saint Maelrubha's disciples would have recognised the panorama and, I thought, would probably have understood the world as well, and marvelled at how slightly their preaching or teachings had affected it. Little would have seemed to have changed since the days of the pagan King Niall of the Nine Hostages, who kidnapped one royal nobleman from every kingdom he conquered, to ensure the people remained subjugated. Only the technology of warfare would have puzzled or intrigued the saint's followers.

When the horse was done, I topped up my canteen and set off once more, allowing the animal to set its own pace. I lacked confidence as a rider and did not wish to risk an accident during my descent down the steep track that ran along the bleak mountainside. Consequently, it was dusk by the time I arrived in the village, just as it had been on my first coming to the place. Ogilvy met me at the door of the inn.

'Alec, it's so very good to see you safe and sound.'

I smiled, dismounted and undid the strap that held my small bag to the saddle.

'I received the letter,' he went on, tethering the horse. 'Your doctor explained how things are with you.'

He took the bag and I followed him in. The parlour looked exactly as it had when last I left it in the company of my arresting party.

'Here,' Ogilvy offered, 'will you not sit down? Take the weight off your legs. I'll bet you feel shaped to the back of that nag out there.'

He pulled a chair out from the table and set it down by the hearth. Peat blocks were stacked to one side of the grate. The fire burned strongly, the air heavy with its warmth.

'It'll have been a tiring day. You'll have a wee nip of barley-bree? Your doctor advised that I shouldn't give you whisky, but'—he grinned and put his hand on my shoulder—'how can you sit by a fire of peat with an old friend in the Highlands and not have a dram of malt in your fist?'

He poured out two glasses, handing me one. I noticed his measure was larger than mine.

'*Slàinte!*'

I drank. It was smooth and mellow.

'That's a real whisky,' Ogilvy declared, looking approvingly at his glass, now half-empty. 'Twenty years in the cask, sweet as the song of little birds. When I knew you were coming, I ordered a bottle in from Kyle. And to hell with the medical men. Whisky's been healing souls longer than doctors. And now, food!'

He stood up and went into the pantry. I followed him.

'You'll want to know what's been happening hereabouts,' he began as he removed a joint of lamb from a meat safe. 'Mr. McGillivray's gone. He left in the spring of 1915, to serve with the Cameron High-landers. They made him a Major. He was killed in the September, during the battle for Hill Seventy near Loos. In all, thirteen men from Breakish went off to the war. Three returned.'

He stopped talking for a minute as he sharpened a carving knife, the two remaining fingers of his right hand gripping the whetstone.

'Breakish is now a place of old men, sad women and a few young lads grown to age before their time,' he continued as he sliced the cold lamb. 'You'll remember Jamie? He's a strapping young man, a fisherman like his father before him. Handsome, too. His mother's moved away. I've heard she's living with her sister in Invergarry and gone into service. The sister's a maid in a grand house there. Since she left, I've run the inn on my own. It's not so much of a problem. Since the war, there've been few folk coming to stay.'

Putting the sliced meat on a plate and placing beside it several cold boiled potatoes and a pickled onion, he carried my meal into the parlour and set me a place at the table.

'I finished my life story,' he said, 'and sent it off to a publisher in Edinburgh. To my utter surprise, they've taken it on and sent me an advance for a hundred pounds. It's to appear in the bookshops next year. Who knows?' He laughed at the thought. 'I might become a famous author. I could do with it. The advance is what's keeping me going now that the inn isn't so busy. Not,' he added, with a grin, 'that it ever was!'

I smiled again and turned my attention to the meal. Ogilvy poured himself another whisky and added a drop to my own glass.

'I've prepared the same room for you as you had before. Your doctor said it would be good if matters here were as similar now as to how they were then. He was of the opinion this might help you. Mind you, Alec, I'd've put you in there anyway.'

For as long as it took me to eat, he leaned back in a chair by the fire and did not speak. Only when I put the knife and fork down did he move, taking the empty plate away.

'Will you take a walk with me?' he asked.

I nodded and we set off in the early evening light along the quay before the houses. The tide was out, just one boat lying on the mud and shingle, her mast tilted over. There was no one about, but candle-light glimmered in a few of the windows.

'Breakish is to be sold,' he said. 'Mr. McGillivray had a son, but he's not interested in being the new laird. Some of the houses are empty already. Folk are moving away, especially the youngsters. Going to Australia, Canada. There's no future for them here. Another five years and Breakish will be occupied only by ghosts.'

We walked on, saying nothing, looking out to the sea and listening to the hush of the waves outside the little harbour.

'Your doctor seems a kindly soul,' Ogilvy remarked at length. 'He's told me all about Gallipoli, let me know because he said I wasn't to mention it.' He put his hand on my arm. 'By all accounts, you were a brave man, Alec. He told me you got a medal.'

I looked at him but made no reply and we continued on our way, passing the little church and graveyard of simple headstones until we reached the end of the harbour inlet. From there, out to sea, we could just discern the outline of Eilean Tosdach.

'There was a mighty storm,' he began. 'Three months ago. A real typhoon, the likes of which I never saw in my days at sea. The waves broke over the houses in Breakish. It smashed six of the boats to smithereens on the quay. Only three, run aground behind the headland for caulking, were left undamaged. A steamer making for Skye ran onto the rocks six miles to the north. No one survived. We had bodies floating into the bay for a week, as the tides brought them round.' He turned to face me. 'The croft, you remember, faced out to sea and was right there on that tiny beach. The storm struck at night. They'd not have stood a chance.'

Even had I so wanted, there was nothing for me to say, yet Ogilvy knew what was in my mind.

'No sooner had the wind abated and the sea gone down a bit, I went along to the broch. If they had endured, I was sure the girl would come ashore as she had in the past. I waited all that day, and the next. She never came and I saw no sign of life on the island.'

He and I set off back to Breakish. He did not speak again until we arrived at the inn.

'You must rest tonight, Alec. Have a good night's sleep. I've spoken to Jamie for you. He'll take you out there in the morrow.'

Despite Ogilvy's exhortation, I did not sleep and, at dawn, rose to sit on the bench by the inn door. The air was chilly, an onshore breeze giving it an edge. At seven o'clock, Jamie came up to me. He was, as Ogilvy had told me, now a strongly built young man in his late teens. Regarding him standing before me, I was glad he had escaped conscription.

After Ogilvy had given us each a plate of hot porridge and a mug of tea, we set off in Jamie's fishing boat, the one I had seen in the harbour the evening before. It was not the same craft as I had previously sailed in to Eilean Tosdach but bigger and obviously newer. He must, I thought, have been making good money from the sea.

We did not talk and I presumed he had been informed I was now mute, and why.

In less than twenty minutes, we reached the tip of the island where the causewayed broch stood. At this point, I had expected Jamie to make down the strait, but instead he steered along the seawards shore, lowering the sail and letting the craft drift in to a place where there was a low projecting shelf of rock about three feet above sea level.

'I'll wait for you here, sir,' he said, tossing a rope with a grappling hook into the scrub and securing it to the bow. 'The homestead is just along a way. Don't be more than an hour.'

The combe was less than a hundred yards off. I approached it quite openly and entered it on a pathway running through the rocks by where the chicken coop had been. The wicker hurdles were still there but askew; nearby, the vegetable beds were covered with newly emerging weeds. The croft itself was semi-derelict, a section of the roof caved in. The hide curtain still hanging in the doorway, I pushed aside and entered. The simplest of domestic utensils lay strewn about—some wooden bowls, spoons and ladles, an iron pot, several wooden plates and a heavy pottery jar made not on a wheel but by coiling. From a nail driven into a beam hung a string bag. Tipped on its side between the hearthstones were the charred remains of a three-legged stool, whilst where there would have been a bed there was now a pile of the turves that had formed the roof.

As I stepped out of the ruin, I heard a dog bark. It was up towards the ridge. I waited, to be sure I was not just imagining it. It barked again.

Setting off as quickly as I could, I headed up the slope. Just below the top of the ridge, an oblong of ground had been cleared of bracken and heather. In the centre of the clearing were two low, untidy cairns, little more than clumsily erected piles of stones. By the nearest, a number of crows were scattered about the ground, being harassed by the dog, which was running at them, then, finding the birds emboldened, retreating from their sharp beaks when they came at it. On my approach, however, they rose and veered off on the wind, cawing peevishly and settling on the scrub a short distance away, from where they observed me.

No sooner had the crows flown off than the dog darted forward, picked something white up off the ground and ran with it to the far edge of the clearing.

A number of the cairn stones had fallen, or been loosened by the dog, to lay bare the head, right shoulder and arm of the old woman; I could tell it was her from the tangle of long grey hair still tied in a now disintegrating bun. Her corpse had rotted badly, the flesh in tatters where the birds had been feeding upon it. The hand was missing, the arm ending in a blackened stump from which hung fibrous strips of tendon.

Beyond the cairn, the dog sat on the ground, its paw holding down the missing hand as it gnawed at one of the fingers, breaking it off and chewing upon it.

It was then I knew there was nothing left for me to experience. I had seen whatever wickedness there was to see. Never again would I be shocked, be aghast at what lay before me, be perplexed or confounded, or afraid.

Facing the mountains and the crumbling tower of the broch of Dùn an Làmh Thoisgeal across the strait, I raised my head and screamed. It was not so much a piercing screech as a caterwauling howl that echoed in my head, born neither of pain nor sorrow, nor anger nor surrender, but of catharsis. The wind took my soul away, scattering it over the heather as it might thistledown. And when I had no more breath, I just stood, silent and empty, my hands by my side and my eyes closed, only the wind holding me up.

How long I remained immobile by the cairns I do not know, but it must have been a good few minutes, for the dog, in the meantime, had finished off the hand and, plucking up its courage, had crept back to gnaw on the old woman's arm.

Gaining my senses, I gave the dog as hard a kick as I could in its midriff. Intent on feeding, it did not see the blow coming and yelped as my boot struck it, lifting it clear of the ground. It limped away as fast as it could into the scrub.

The second cairn was undisturbed, but I knew I would have to dismantle a part of it. I had to discover who lay beneath its stones. And so, one by one, I lifted them aside until, through a crevice, I saw a naked foot. It was badly decomposed, but I knew instantly it was that of the old man.

I rebuilt the cairns, adding more stones I found in the undergrowth and fitting them firmly together in the style of the broch builders so that the dog would be unable to dislodge them. Finally, I arranged several flat slabs against the base to act as a deterrent to scrabbling, digging paws and inquisitive, stabbing beaks.

As I was placing the last stone, I saw Jamie approaching me up the ridge. He was striding through the bracken, young and confident, unafraid of *briosags*, trolls or any other casters of spells.

'We've to go, Mr. Marquand,' he said. 'We've to take the tide when we can.'

I followed him down towards the combe. As we arrived at the croft, I hung back. Jamie walked on a few paces, stopped and turned.

'Just a wee moment, Mr. Marquand,' he said and he carried on.

When he was gone, I pulled the medal out of my pocket. It was cast in silver, the king's head on one side, the other embossed with the words 'For Distinguished Conduct in the Field.' The ribbon attached to it was dark red with a single royal blue stripe down the centre. Carefully, I slid it into a crack in the wall of the hovel, working it well in so that no one might see it.

As we sailed back to Breakish, I wondered what might have become of her. That she had survived the storm was obvious: who else but her would have buried the dead? Yet it was just as evident from the derelict croft that she no longer lived on Eilean Tosdach. Like me, she was lost.

In the afternoon, I walked along the shore to the broch. It was just as I had left it, only my excavation trenches were now shallow pools surrounded by clumps of sedge. Sitting on the boulder upon which I had eaten my lunch that first day, I gazed across to the island. No longer a place of mystery and danger to me, it was now just an expanse of rock and wind-shaped scrub rising out from the sea, of no value to anyone save a fisherman caught, as Jamie's father had been, unawares by the fickleness of the malicious sea.

'You'll be off on the morrow,' Ogilvy remarked as I returned to the inn. 'Jamie's told me of what you found. I'm sorry.'

That evening, I ate little. Ogilvy sat at the table with his gold-nibbed fountain pen, correcting the galley proofs of his autobiography, which had arrived that day. At nine, I left him and, mounting the stairs to my room, washed myself in the basin, undressed and got into bed. It began to rain, the first spots pattering on the windowpane.

It was already daylight when I woke, but still raining. Down on the quay a dog was barking with a steady, insistent yap and I realised, as I gained my wits, that it had been this which had roused me from my sleep.

Tugging on my trousers and going to the window, I opened the pane. The dog stopped its racket. Below, standing in the rain a little way off, was a figure looking up at me.

It was her, her hair wet and clinging to her face, her clothing soaked through. Brushing her hair from her cheek, she held up her hand, opening and closing her fingers in a childish wave.

For a moment I was transfixed, then, spinning round, ran from my room and sped headlong down the stairs, tripping over the steps and almost falling in my haste. Slamming open the inn door, I rushed out onto the quay. There was no one there. Both she and the dog had vanished.

Ignoring the chilling rain, I sprinted to the first house. The door was shut. I rattled the latch. It was locked. So was that of the second house. I gave a quick glance over the quay into the harbour in the hope that I might see her coracle moored by the steps. Only Jamie's fishing vessel lay alongside.

Doubling back, I headed up the path that left the village for the mountains and Bealach na Clachan. For the first three hundred yards the track went across open pasture. There was no one upon it.

Footsteps came hurrying up behind me. It was Ogilvy.

'Alec! Are you all right? You'd best come back or you'll catch your death.'

He took me by the arm and we returned to the inn.

'I heard you tumbling like an avalanche down the stairs,' he said. 'It must have just been a bad dream.'

Perhaps, I thought, but if she had truly been standing there in the rain, and had been more than just a dream or the answer to a prayer, she was gone now. Yet I knew I would see her again, often, over the rest of my life, for whenever I was in need of love or comfort she would come on my command and we would sit together in the croft in the combe and listen to the gulls crying, the waves shifting the shingle and the driftwood spitting in the fire.

40

At about eleven o'clock every morning, an elderly lady with blue-rinsed hair comes round with a trolley upon which is an urn of boiling water and a number of large insulated jugs containing tea, hot milk, coffee for those who will not react adversely to the caffeine and thin beef broth. I accept whatever is given to me; usually, this is the latter, which is intended to give me iron. As if I need it! My body is long past requiring anything to pump up my red blood cell count, and my will has iron enough.

As a general rule, she enters my room with the beverage, places it on my bedside table, whether or not I am in the bed, and leaves, sometimes with a smile and sometimes not. Today, however, was different.

The door opened on time, but instead of the tinted lady serving me it was Dr. Belasco.

'Morning, Alec,' he said cheerily. In one hand he had my broth; in the other he held a cup of coffee. 'Do you mind if I join you?'

As I was sitting in the armchair at the french windows, he put my drink on the desk within my reach, pulled over the chair and sat next to me, looking out.

'It won't be long now before the leaves start changing,' he observed, and he sipped at his coffee. ' "In those vernal seasons of the year, when the air is calm and pleasant, it were an injury and sullenness against Nature not to go out, and see her riches, and partake in her rejoicing with heaven and earth." It was John Milton who wrote that, and yet I cannot say I necessarily agree. Autumn has a drama, a magnificence that spring lacks. The greening of bushes and the first flowers are not as thrilling, not as life-enriching somehow, as autumn. Autumn signals fulfilment, the success of the year. Spring is merely a time of promise.'

Slowly, I reached for my cup and brought it to my lips. The broth was saline and rich, reminding me of my childhood, of hot drinks served in a cold nursery. Just the smell of the redolent fat and beef juices brought back a picture of my mother standing in the door, a fur wrap about her shoulders, the diamonds on her wrist glistening in the creamy light of the gas mantle.

'Now, Alec,' Dr. Belasco resumed, 'I think you know what I am going to ask you about. And you know as well as I do that it will be a one-way conversation, for you will not reply, and yet, regardless, I must still ask you. A few days ago, you placed in my folder a drawing of a young girl.'

I kept looking out of the window. Were I to have spoken, I would have parried his Miltonic quotation with Matthew Arnold's 'Coldly, sadly descends / The autumn evening. The Field / Strewn with its dank yellow drifts / Of wither'd leaves, and the elms / Fade into dimness apace, / Silent . . . ' Or alternatively, and more appropriately, Thomas Hood's 'I saw old Autumn in the misty morn / Stand shadowless like Silence, listening / To silence.'

'Who is she?'

I knew exactly what was going through his mind. If only he could discover the identity of the girl from Eilean Tosdach he would, he believed, have the key to my vault. One turn, one click of the tumblers, and he would be in.

Out of the corner of my eye, I could see him watching me. His face was calm, but I could tell, within, he was hoping for a breakthrough.

And I thought, he is a good man, I am an old one whose clock is running out of minutes and, perhaps, now is as good a time as any to break just one rule of a lifetime of self-imposed regulation. What was more, by breaking it, I would not be really helping him solve his mystery but considerably compounding it and confounding him. It occurred to me that I could set him off on a quest that would last to his final day and that he would go to his grave none the wiser than he was now. Unless, of course, he turned amateur archaeologist–cum–sleuth and rooted through some dusty basement archive in a provincial museum, or a box in the loft of a modest house in Scotland—or Canada, or the Antipodes or wherever else the Scottish diaspora had spread—and he found a little bag containing a broken bone comb, a spindle weight, a notched seal's rib and a piece of unrecognisable iron and accompanying notes by Alec Marquand, BA; and he read them, got in his car and headed north, hiked over Bealach na Clachan; and he reached the end of the track and got out, going into the inn, if it was still there, and, if he was smart, he would start talking to the locals and win their trust and someone would tell him of the story of the *briosag* of Eilean Tosdach, which they would call Eilean Donas, for old habits die hard on the wild west coast, whom they called Meigead, the Bleating One, and how her beauty sucked the souls from men.

Then, he would know and she and I should have the last laugh.

I began to lift myself out of my chair. This did not startle him. He had seen me move under my own locomotion many times before. It was only as I knelt in front of the chest of drawers that he stood up and came to my side, kneeling next to me. He might have been a son leading his father to confession if my room had been a chapel and the chest of drawers draped with a lace doily and mounted with a crucifix.

Gradually, I started to ease the drawer out. He reached out to help. I put my hand on his, gently pushing it away, and glanced into his face. He was startled. This was the first time I had shown any sign of being truly aware of his presence.

At last, the drawer reached the pencil stop. I paused. He was looking at my neatly folded clothes, wondering what the hell there was in them that could be of interest to him. He must have been fully aware of the contents of the drawers. I was sure he must have gone through them whilst I was being bathed, walking in the garden or having a shit.

Now, I thought, I'll teach you something, and I lifted the drawer out. It fell heavily onto the floorboards.

One by one, I removed the contents of my treasury, lining them up next to the drawer: the lieutenant's tarnished cat-and-cabbage cap badge, the piece of Roman glass, a square of faded khaki cotton tied like a tiny pudding cloth and containing an ounce or two of Lemnian earth, a silver Victorian crown dated 1890 with the old queen on one side and Saint George slaying a dragon on the other. The last item I produced was the now-dented, once-chromed thermometer case. I unscrewed the end and tipped it up. Onto my hand slid the curlew's bone.

I had not seen it for years. Placing the case on the floor, I touched the bone as gently as I could, moving it with my index finger until it fitted into the life line on my palm. Just doing that brought her back to me so powerfully, I felt she could have been with us in the room and involuntarily looked over my shoulder. The door was shut. We were alone, the doctor and me.

Slipping it back into the case for safety, I removed the compendium and opened it. One by one, I removed the drawings, carefully fanning them over the floor. There were many more of them than I had remembered.

'Well, I'm damned!' Dr. Belasco exclaimed. 'I would never have guessed. . . . ' He laughed quietly and put his hand on my shoulder. 'You are a wily old codger.'

One by one, he picked the drawings up, handling them gently, as if they were fragile.

'She's extraordinarily beautiful. And, from the paper, I'd say you drew these a long time ago. From life?'

From life, I thought, from life.

'There's something about her,' he went on. 'Something utterly out of this world.'

Out of your world, I said to myself, but in mine.

And it was then I knew that he was a man like me and I wished he could have known her, too.

41

I am unsure of when it was—it must have been about five or six years after the war ended—yet there is a day indelibly embroidered into the tapestry of my mind.

It was September 6, a Wednesday. A military ambulance, painted grey with a white circle on the side containing a stark red cross, pulled up before the portico of the Craiglockhart home for members of the officers' mess who had lost their marbles.

I had been waiting in the entrance hall for the better part of the morning, seated in a wheelchair with the brakes locked on and a blanket over my knees. My hair had been combed, I had been shaved by one of the orderlies and my fingernails had been trimmed close. This latter aspect of my toilet was not just a matter of appearance, nor even of hygiene: all the inmates' nails were kept short to stop them scratching themselves or others. As a further, though in my case unnecessary, precaution, I was held into my seat by a wide leather belt kept tight around my waist and buckled at the back of the wheelchair, out of my reach.

Every so often, a nurse would come to see that I was all right, carrying one of those little drinking cups like a child's dolls' party teapot, with a spout on it. She would hold it to my lips and allow me short sips of tepid water.

It was whilst sitting there that I came to know what day it was. Over the porter's desk was a calendar and a clock that ticked monotonously, one cog to the second. Whoever had been on duty earlier in the morning had forgotten to change the date, and it was whilst I was waiting that an officer, seeing it unaltered, ordered the correction be made. I watched as the clerk behind the desk stood on a chair and turned the knobs on the side.

At noon, a male orderly approached me carrying my two suitcases. I had packed them the previous evening, successfully preventing anyone from assisting me. I might have been mute, but I was not incapable and the medical staff knew it. The doctor was all in favour of my seeing to myself as much as possible. I had heard him inform the nurses that the more I could be treated with 'routines of normality', the better it would be. Then, as now, I was not a dribbling imbecile who needed to be fed like a baby with a spoon and pusher and have its arse wiped when the digestive process was complete. I was just a silent, enigmatic man they could not quite fathom out.

'Right, sir,' the orderly said. 'Are we ready for the off?'

The ambulance driver, the single stripe of a corporal upon his sleeve, entered and wheeled me out, down the wooden ramp covering part of the steps and over to his vehicle. A second attendant opened the rear doors. I was helped out of the chair and onto one of the stretchers in the ambulance. As I lay down, a blanket was placed over me, straps were buckled to hold me into the stretcher and my cases were deposited against the rear of the cab. The wheelchair was collapsed and wedged into the foot well of the seat next to the driver.

It was, I recall, one of those days of that incessant dismal drizzle so ubiquitous to Edinburgh, the clouds low and the granite buildings and cobbled streets sheened with a miserably damp patina.

The ambulance windows were open, but as these consisted of little more than slits covered by hinged metal plates, I was afforded very little view. I caught glimpses of austere terraced houses, a church with a spire, the castle and the façade of the Royal Caledonian Hotel, the tops of the trees lining Princes Street Gardens, on which the leaves were turning to autumn and beginning to drift free. Every now and then, a sound came to me over the grinding din of the ambulance engine: the clip of hooves upon the road, a hawker's cry, muffled by the steel sides of the vehicle, incomprehensible, like the distant call of a muezzin biding the faithful to prayer over the rooftops of an alien city.

At last, the ambulance halted, the doors flung wide and pinned open. I was unbuckled from the stretcher and assisted into the wheelchair by the corporal driver. Once again, the belt was secured around my waist. The air was tainted by the tart perfume of soot and iron and I knew, without looking, that we had stopped in the fore-court of Waverley station. An officer in a smart uniform was waiting for me.

'Hello, Alec,' he greeted me. 'How are you?'

His voice carried no Scots burr. I looked up. It was a moment before I recognised him.

Receiving no return greeting and being unsure of my recognition, he said, 'It's Rupert, Alec. It's been a long time.'

I looked at him, then away, at the railway porters leaning on their barrows, newspaper vendors and an assortment of passengers alighting from taxis, hansom cabs or trams. He took this signal of my awareness as an indication that I was in some kind of communication with him.

'I've been given the assignment of accompanying you to a hospital in Aldershot. In truth,' he added, 'I requested it.' He picked up my hand and shook it. I let him. 'It's a military establishment,' he contin-ued, 'that specialises in'—he paused, searching for the most judicious words—'the treatment of your kind of ailment. I'm afraid it's going to be a long journey, but I understand the train has a restaurant car and we've a private compartment.'

The corporal took my suitcases whilst Rupert pushed my wheel-chair. We entered the great canopy of the station roof, the glass criss-crossed by a spider's work of blackened steel girders inhabited by urban pigeons, the droppings of which pockmarked the floor beneath their favourite roosts. Wisps of steam rose from the locomotives standing at the platforms. A departing train whistle echoed, the sound fading as the engine commenced to gout black smoke towards the roof, dense clouds rising as if from explosions.

At the ticket barrier, we were obliged to join a queue to gain entry to the platform. A board over the barred gate announced the depar-ture of the half-past-two express to London.

The station was bustling: trains to other distant parts of Scotland—

Oban, Fort William, Aberdeen, Inverness—tended to leave in the mid-afternoon, to reach their destinations by nightfall. I sat back in my wheelchair, looking around but, at first, only half-registering the activity going on about me. After months, perhaps years, of being contained in a solitary hospital room, visited by not more than a dozen different people, I felt slightly ill at ease, confused by the crowds churning about me with an almost Brownian motion, yet no one particle ever colliding with another. In those days, I was just beginning to slip deeper into my shell, drawing the scalloped and chamfered edges more tightly together to block out reality's ugly glare.

Opposite the entrance to the platform, not far from the ticket office door, was a news vendor's stall. I watched the passengers who made purchases from him. The men almost entirely bought newspapers, some of them studying the headlines on the billboards propped in front of the stall before deciding which to read. The women predominantly availed themselves of journals. Both sexes sought to buy the *Strand Magazine* or *John Bull*. Close by, a confectionery stand displayed bars of Bourneville chocolate in crimson and gold wrappers, tall glass jars of boiled sweets and sticks of pink puffball candy floss spun by a tubby man wearing a grimy apron and a dented straw boater. This stall attracted only those passengers accompanied by children. Not a single unaccompanied adult bought confectionery all the while I observed it.

Yet whilst I was disconcerted, I was also taken by and gradually drawn into this cavalcade of milling humanity and, just as I had on that cacodemonic beach, I commenced picking out one person and following them with my eyes as they proceeded through the station: a man dressed in a kilt of black-and-white Menzies tartan with a large sporran set with a silver clasp and a dirk in his sock; a nanny in a blue hat leading a fractious boy of about five wearing a sailor suit; a businessman with a wing collar; a pretty woman with a bunch of flowers nestling in the crook of her arm like a baby. It was after some minutes of engaging myself in this innocent pastime that my wandering attention fixed upon a beggar slowly working its way through the throng.

A stooped figure wearing a sort of monkish cowl over its head and too many dirty clothes, giving it a dumpy appearance, it kept close to the walls as if hoping it might, at any sign of alarm, step backwards and disappear into a fissure in the stonework or, by changing its shape or colour in some chameleonesque way, camouflage itself and become invisible. If a passenger happened to come within a predetermined distance of it, it would hold out its hand, palm up. Few gave it alms— a woman with a fox fur–collared coat gave something almost without breaking her step, whilst a plumber in a cloth cap and carrying a bag of tools from which a length of lead pipe projected paused, put his load down, rummaged in a jacket pocket and placed a coin in the upturned hand. The beggar seemed not to acknowledge the gift. The hand merely closed upon the coin and withdrew into the rank clothing.

'Irish,' the ambulance driver said, following my gaze. 'Things're bad in Ireland. Always are.'

We edged nearer the platform barrier where a ticket inspector stood. Beyond him, at the far end of the train, the locomotive hooted once, a jet of steam thrusting out from the pistons as the building pressure was released. By the guard's van, two porters were engaged in manhandling a heavy trunk onto the train. At the next door, two postal workers heaved canvas sacks of mail aboard.

At the far end of the station concourse, a police constable appeared. He stood with his legs astride and his arms behind his back, a little colossus of authority dressed in black serge and silver buttons. At his arrival, the beggar slid—it is the only appropriate verb to use, for one could not see its feet moving beneath the agglomeration of ragged clothes—into the shadowy space between the news vendor and the confectioner. Here it hid, looking out every few seconds with animal-istic cunning from the cover of the stalls. It was at least a minute before the constable turned and walked away out of the concourse, satisfied that all was well within his domain.

'Mind your backs, please!'

A porter was approaching the ticket barrier, propelling a heavy handcart before him laden with portmanteaux, hatboxes and leather-bound suitcases. Behind him were two other porters pushing trolleys.

Taking up the rear of this procession was a portly woman dressed in a sable coat accompanied by a diminutive husband, two children, a governess and an emaciated young man who could have been either the woman's secretary or the children's tutor.

Rupert pushed my wheelchair to one side, out of the way.

'Wait here, Alec,' he said, as if I were likely to move off of my own volition. 'I'll see to the tickets.'

The corporal carried my cases near to the ticket barrier as I continued my perusal of the crowds as if observing a carnival.

With the policeman departed, the beggar quit its hiding place and began to work the queue, touching a sleeve here, holding a hand out there, all the while keeping a feral lookout for danger. To a man, the waiting passengers ignored it.

Gradually, it came nearer to me. I came to be assailed by the rank odour of sweat, stale urine and poverty. For a moment, I thought it was going to omit me from its alms seeking, but just as it was about to pass me it turned to face me. It did not thrust its hand out to me, nor did it pluck at my sleeve where my arm lay resting on the side of the wheelchair. Instead, it looked hard at me as if studying me from the deep shadow of the cowl: then, slowly, it tilted its head to one side. The grainy light casting down through the grime of the station roof momentarily shone under the cowl. I saw its bright eyes and they seemed to be laughing.

'We're on our way,' Rupert said, walking over to me, replacing our travel warrants in his uniform pocket as he went. 'The train's leaving on time.'

At his approach, the beggar shuffled quickly away. Rupert took hold of the wheelchair and began to propel me towards the ticket barrier. The corporal went ahead of us down the platform, carrying one of my cases in each hand.

Glancing back, I suddenly saw, as if dematerialising from mid-air, the constable appear at the end of the confectioner's stall. The beggar spied him and started. It was quick, but not quick enough. The constable took four rapid steps and snatched at the beggar's shoulder. It twisted away from him, but his fingers closed upon the cowl, ripping it off the beggar's head to reveal a matted mass of filthy tangled hair. A dozen or so coins fell out of the beggar's clothing to chime and bounce upon the tiles of the concourse floor before rolling away. Save one, a silver sixpence, they were all farthings and ha'pennies, low-denomination coppers.

The wheelchair was turning. I was moving on.

I craned my neck. The constable had shifted his grip, getting a better hold and pulling the hunched figure upright. One of its grimy hands came up and brushed the hair away, the head again tilting slightly. Its face was besmirched with dirt and the red blotches of rosacea, yet its eyes were defiant in the way a cornered cat's might be, and, over the sound of hurrying footsteps, the train whistle that blew again, the ticket inspector's urbane voice and the metallic orchestration of sounds that is every railway terminus in every city of the world, I swear I heard the beggar plaintively mew.

Placing my hands on the arms of the wheelchair, I made to lift myself out of it, but the leather restraint had been rebuckled at the back. I pushed harder, grunting at the exertion, in the hope that it might give, but it held firm.

Rupert, oblivious to the little drama being enacted on the other side of the ticket barrier and assuming my moving in my seat was just a matter of my getting comfortable, set off down the platform, pushing me ahead of him. He had to steer the wheelchair to one side to negotiate the trolleys of mail sacks. I took the opportunity to look back again. The police constable was standing by the news vendor's stall holding a ragged jacket, a bemused look on his face. Its recent occupant was nowhere in sight.

Five minutes later, the carriage couplings chinking together as they took the strain, the train began to move, at first infinitesimally but soon at a walking pace, then faster, and faster still, as if dragging me, the reluctant traveller, away from the past to project me into the silent years that have been forever since.

For the next hour, as the southbound express swung round the bulging coastline of Lammermuir, always keeping close to the sea and swinging through the towns of Dunbar and Berwick-upon-Tweed, I sat ensconced in a first-class compartment and wondered if it had been her. There was no way of telling for sure, yet I felt somehow it had been. It was the way in which she had brushed her hair aside, tossing her head slightly in the action, and the look of rebellion in her eyes, the spark of the fire of the spirit that smouldered in her, never to be diminished.

And what, I thought, if the buckle had been weak and I had risen from my wheelchair and walked across to her. We would not have spoken, for we would have had no need of words. Yet, perhaps, I might have at last broken my silence and told the constable that it was all right, I would take charge of her, would see to it that she ceased begging in the station. With Rupert's help, I would have taken her to a nearby boarding house, paid for her to be washed, purchased clothing for her, taken her with me on the journey ahead: and, just as I would have saved her from destitution, so would she have rescued me from silence.

South of Durham, Rupert accompanied me to the dining car, helping me to keep my footing whenever the train lurched over a set of points or a level crossing. I was unsteady on my feet after so long either recumbent in my bed or in a chair at a window in Craiglockhart. We sat opposite each other across a table for two, the silver cutlery and glassware shining in the light of a small table lamp mounted by the window.

'This is very luxurious,' he remarked as we took our seats. 'Quite like the old days. . . . '

He ordered for me what he had himself—French onion soup, Dover sole, lamb cutlets and a summer pudding, followed by the cheese board and a small bunch of sweet Muscat grapes served with a pair of silver shears.

I picked at my food, consuming half the soup and fish and just one of the cutlets. Rupert also requested a bottle of claret.

'It says in your file,' he told me conspiratorially, 'you're not to be allowed alcohol, but I can't see any harm in a small glass of claret.' He nodded to the waiter to pour me a measure. 'It would be pretty churlish of me to drink without sharing, don't you think?'

I put down my knife and fork. The wine was dark red, almost black, the colour of midnight roses. He raised his glass to me.

Slowly, I placed my fingers around the stem of the glass and lifted it from the table. The train swayed at that moment and the wine slopped in the glass but did not spill. Cautiously, I held the glass up.

'What shall we drink to?' he asked.

He leaned over and touched my glass with his own.

'Absent friends?' He paused. 'Fallen comrades?'

I made no suggestion. There was so much we could have toasted: human frailty or stupidity, the Irishman I saw walking under the sea, Captain Geddes, who survived, or poor Cody, who did not.

'I was at Passchendaele,' Rupert said meditatively. 'I don't think you knew that, did you, Alec? August through to November 1917. Bloody fiasco. Like Gallipoli, really. The inane sending of brave lads up the line to death.'

He stared out of the window, but there was only the deepening darkness there and he did not see it, anyway.

'How does the poem go? "What passing-bells for those who die as cattle? Only the monstrous anger of the guns. Only the stuttering rifles' rapid rattle Can patter out their hasty orisons."'

A garish orange glow, perhaps from a bonfire of stable straw across the fields of passing night, glinted briefly like a tiny, far-off explosion in the last of the evening twilight.

'It changed us, of course. Yet I've often wondered, you know, Alec, since the war . . . Did it make men of us or did it break us?'

He knew I would not answer and I am sure that quandary was to haunt him for the rest of his days. As for me, I have never given the enigma a second thought.

The train entered a cutting, the light from the dining car window flickering on rocks, retreating to scatter itself on track-side foliage.

'Remember the horse?' he asked.

I could see it then, lying on the road, the bright yellow Model T Roadster a little way off with the engine stalled and the mudguard wrenched, the cart horse biting at each breath as if at fresh, green grass and the curds of blood on my cricket whites.

Rupert held his glass out and said portentously, 'I give you the horse. Our first instruction, unheeded in the rush of blind youth, of the certain improbability of mortality.'

Carefully, I sipped the wine. It was full-bodied, warm and rich with an aftertaste of tannin, oak casks and late sunlight.

The train rolled on southwards into the gathering night of England. We returned to our compartment. Rupert took out a book to read from his valise. It was bound in dark blue morocco with gold tooling, a crest impressed upon the front cover. He saw me watching him and held it up so that I might see the spine.

'A biography of James Hannington,' Rupert said, 'the first bishop of East Africa. He was martyred by the natives.'

The train rattled over a set of points, passing a good train in a siding, the wagons being loaded with coal from a series of chutes. In the distance, I could make out the wheel of the coal mine pit-head, lit by a string of bare bulbs like an obscene skeletal Christmas tree.

'It seems,' he added, 'that his congregation took the principle of the holy communion a stage further and ate not just the host but also the choicest parts of he who was administering it.'

He spoke in such a matter-of-fact way, almost whimsically. This was not a terrible thing to him, nor was it a blasphemy. It was merely an historical fact, as plain as the arrowhead I had found at Dùn an Làmh Thoisgeal. I wondered how he might feel if he had been forced to eat another's flesh, but then he would never be in such a position, for he had gone through a cleansing war and the world was civilised now. And I considered how the world had not changed one jot, when such gratuitous violence could be taken as read, mentioned dispassionately in conversation in a railway carriage travelling through the night across the East Riding of Yorkshire.

At length, Rupert turned off the compartment lights, leaving on only the reading lamp over his seat. I dozed fitfully. Every so often, I opened my eyes to gaze out of the window. The night was black, only interrupted if the train passed through a station, the gaslight dim upon the name board, a wooden bench, a bed of geraniums robbed of their colour.

And I thought of her.

42

Dr. Belasco stayed with me for over an hour this morning. He took my pulse and temperature, measured my blood pressure, examined my eyes and, with a glass pipette, siphoned off a sample of my urine from the glass overnight bottle under my bed.

The figures entered in my dossier, which he placed upon the writing desk, he set up a small methylated spirits lamp and a test-tube rack on my chest of drawers. Next to this, he placed a pair of test-tube tongs and a bottle of blue reagent.

'This is called Fehling's solution,' he announced to me. 'It is an alkaline liquid which I have just prepared. It consists of equal volumes of two other liquids, one containing cupric sulphate pentahydrate and the other potassium sodium tartrate tetrahydrate, known as Rochelle salt and sodium hydroxide. It is used to detect the presence of simple sugars such as glucose.'

He lit the methylated spirits lamp, put a small amount of the reagent into a test tube, added several drops of my urine and, holding the test tube with the tongs, gently heated it in the flame.

'If a simple sugar is present,' he explained, 'it will cause a red precipitate of cuprous oxide.'

As he gently agitated the test tube over the burner, the liquid began to change colour. I could see a red haze forming in it. He studied this for a moment, then stood the test tube in the rack, pulled the chair over to my bedside and sat down.

'I must tell you, Alec,' he said quietly, 'that your kidneys are beginning to fail. Their function is not just to rid the body of unwanted fluids but also to produce chemicals that regulate your blood pressure and make red blood cells.' He put his hand on mine. It was warm and dry, the skin firm but soft. 'Your blood pressure is high and has been rising consistently over the last few weeks. Furthermore, you are anæmic and there is sugar in your urine. These are certain symptoms of renal failure. There is nothing I can do, nothing anyone can do.'

He might have been hoping for some reaction from me, yet I made none. There was nothing to say.

Letting go of my hand, he rose to his feet and started to clear away his minimal laboratory, placing the items in an enamel tray and pouring the contents of the test tube and reagent bottle down the sink, flushing them away with a running tap.

'You'll not ask me, so I shall tell you,' he continued. 'It will be only days now. I'll call in later.'

With that, he stepped towards the door, where, pausing, he turned.

'Will you tell me who she is?' he asked.

I waited for a moment before turning my head in his direction, yet I did not speak. To have done so would have been somehow to betray her. Instead, I eased myself up onto my elbow and swung my legs over the edge of the bed. He made no move to help me but remained by the door.

Going to the writing desk, upon which my dossier still lay, I picked up the pencil he had used. The point was blunt, but there was sufficient lead showing for my purpose. Holding it between index finger and thumb, I started tentatively to write upon a blank temperature chart.

I could not remember how long it had been since I last shaped a word. My hand moved at a snail's pace. The letters seemed alien, hieroglyphs from some undeciphered cuneiform text.

When I was done, I picked up the sheet of chart paper and walked unsteadily across the room towards him. My hand shook, not just with the trembling of age but also with the enormity of my action. For the first time in a lifetime of self-imposed solitude, I was deliberately communicating with another.

Upon the paper, in a childish unpractised script of which I could have been ashamed yet was not, I had written simply: 'She is yours.'

He accepted the sheet and looked into my face. A single tear ran down his cheek.

'I'll treasure them,' he whispered. Then, wiping away the tear with his index finger, he smiled. 'I knew you were there, all along.'

I did not allow a single facial muscle to move, but, inside, how I was laughing! He must have seen this in my eyes, for he put his hand on my shoulder.

'You've never been alone,' he said. 'I know that now.'

He left and closed the door. I made my way to the chair at the french windows and sat down. The sun was bright upon the lawn, the oak tree casting a deep shadow. One of the garden's resident squirrels was searching beneath it for acorns buried the previous autumn. Its tail twitched nervously.

Of course, Dr. Belasco was right. I have never been alone. Wherever I have gone, she has always been with me. Even then. Out there in the garden, I could see her. She was walking across the lawn, her bare feet sinking into the cool turf. It was the motion of her passing that caused the leaves of the bushes to shimmer. It was at her approach that the squirrel was uneasy.

Now, still sitting in the chair with the sound of the midday meal trolley clattering in the corridor outside my door, I wonder if what we had, she and I, was love or something more.

I cannot say, for I have never consciously known of love. Certainly I have never made love. Think of it! I am as old as Methuselah's grandmother and still a virgin.

Yet perhaps that's been my problem. I have loved too much, without even knowing it, and am now silent to keep that love pure, unsullied by the evils of my fellow creatures.

It's time to get ready to go. I have not needed Dr. Belasco and his bottle of Fehling's solution to tell me as much. For the last two days, I've found breathing intermittently difficult. No doubt, the hour of the morphine injection, of the sweet dreams that have no end, is drawing inevitably nearer.

I wonder, as the last door handle rattles and the last hinge squeaks and I step through into the anteroom between this second and the next, and the next, if she will be waiting for me in those castles of stone in the air, those fantasy towers standing on the bleak shore of a mountainous land somewhere in the northern hemisphere, her finger running down the life line on my palm, drawn not this time in Indian ink but in the diluted blood of an ancient man who has seen it all, kept his counsel and come through.